Reckless

By Maya Banks

He can run, but he can't hide

Sheriff J.T. Summers promised to keep an eye on his best friend's little sister. What could possibly go wrong? A lot. "Little" Nikki Durant isn't so little anymore. She's sex on a stick, and she's pointed right at him.

Nikki has always loved J.T., and she's through waiting for him to come around. The soaring summer temperature is nothing compared to the heat generated when she sets fire to his senses. With a take-no-prisoners attitude, she's out to get her man. But no matter how many ways she offers it, J.T.'s not buying.

What's it going to take to get him to realize her love for him isn't a passing fling? Get herself arrested? Hmm...

Warning: This title contains one very frustrated hunky sheriff, one very determined heroine, sex by the pool, sex in the office, and yes, they do make it to the bed. Eventually.

Color My Heart
By Red Garnier

Sometimes love won't come. Other times it just won't go.

Hannah Myers has had disastrous relationships in the past, but catching her now-ex-boyfriend cheating on her was the worst. As she picks up the pieces of her shattered heart, the last thing she expects to find in the hall outside her apartment is a young *god* asking if he can help. Yeah, he can help! He can take her clothes off, for starters...

Billy Hendricks has dated in the past, but he's never met anyone like Hannah. Their sudden affair is supposed to be just a casual summer fling. But to Billy it is anything but casual. He's seen the passion in her artwork, and he wants more from her than sex.

Hannah tells herself she will not fall in love with Billy. A smart girl needs to safeguard her heart. But how can a smart girl get hunky, wonderful Billy out of her system? Why, with another man!

With Hannah flinging her summer love right and left, things are bound to get colorful.

Warning: This book contains creative sex and a sinfully hot ménage a trois. It may cause heart palpitations, S.O.S. calls to your better half, and all kinds of 911 emergencies. Keeping the A/C on at all times is highly recommended while reading!

Heat of the Moment

By Elle Kennedy

In this heat wave, anything and everything goes.

Shelby Harper has lusted over Navy SEAL John Garrett for over a year, but no matter how many sexy signals she sends out, the man shows a complete lack of interest in getting naked. Then she overhears Garrett talking to his SEAL teammate—a discussion in which they conclude she's vanilla. Stung, Shelby sets out to show them exactly how un-vanilla she is.

Garrett can't believe it when sweet, sexy Shelby suggests a wild and sweaty ménage. He's been trying to figure out how to ask her out without coming off as a guy who only wants to get in her pants—her friendship is too valuable to him to risk it. But if a crazy, heat-wave three-way is what Shelby wants, then he's ready and willing to give it to her.

Once she gets it out of her system, however...well, then he'll let her know he wants her all to himself.

Warning: This title contains two dangerously hot Navy SEALS and a heroine determined to get it on with both of them. Be prepared to take a cold shower (or maybe two) after reading this heat-wave ménage.

Lady Sings the Blues
By Mallery Malone

Summertime...and the living is steamy in Hotlanta.

Alina Gabriel has hit on the perfect formula to make her club, The Scarlet Lady, the hot spot in Atlanta's night life. Men flock to see her alter ego, retired exotic dancer Miss Scarlet; and women line up to see Joshua Hanover and his blues band steam up the stage.

Alina herself isn't immune to the blind guitarist's sensual songs and musical dexterity, but she refuses to be just another notch in his groupie belt.

That is, until Joshua debuts a new song, "Red-Letter Woman", to entice Miss Scarlet to dance. The song and dance leave them both hot and bothered, and when Alina retreats to her office for personal relief, Joshua joins her and offers to strum her desire.

But Joshua wants more than a one-night stand. He's pushing for an encore, and Alina wonders if it's her he's after—or her exotic persona.

Warning: This title contains sensuous solos, decadent duets, dirty dancing, and a man who's really good with his hands.

Red-Hot Summer

A SAMHAIN PUBLISHING, LTD. publication.

Samhain Publishing, Ltd.
577 Mulberry Street, Suite 1520
Macon, GA 31201
www.samhainpublishing.com

Red-Hot Summer
Print ISBN: 978-1-60504-171-1
Reckless Copyright © 2009 by Maya Banks
Color My Heart Copyright © 2009 by Red Garnier
Heat of the Moment Copyright © 2009 by Elle Kennedy
Lady Sings the Blues Copyright © 2009 by Mallery Malone

Editing by Jennifer Miller
Cover by Scott Carpenter

Reckless, ISBN 978-1-60504-034-9
First Samhain Publishing, Ltd. electronic publication: June 2008
Color My Heart, ISBN 978-1-60504-041-7
First Samhain Publishing, Ltd. electronic publication: June 2008
Heat of the Moment, ISBN 978-1-60504-045-5
First Samhain Publishing, Ltd. electronic publication: June 2008
Lady Sings the Blues, ISBN 978-1-60504-051-6
First Samhain Publishing, Ltd. electronic publication: June 2008
First Samhain Publishing, Ltd. print publication: April 2009

Contents

Reckless

Maya Banks

gladder that no one was around to see him cower like a goddamn sissy behind his desk. Mr. Bad-Ass Sheriff. Protector of the citizens of Barley. Hiding from a woman.

Yep, all that was left was for someone to cut off his balls and tie a ribbon in his hair.

"J.T.?"

J.T. looked up to see Toby March standing in the door with a slightly queasy look on his face.

"What is it?" he asked his deputy.

"Uhm, you need to come out here and see this."

J.T.'s eyes narrowed. "Just tell me what's wrong."

Toby glanced over his shoulder then back at J.T. "Ah, well, I'm not sure...that is, it would be better if you come out here. I have a...prisoner who insists on seeing you."

J.T. surged to his feet. "What the fuck? Why isn't he in lock-up?"

Toby's shoulders sagged, and he gave J.T. a look that could only be described as haggard. "Maybe because I don't want *her* brother to kick my ass for locking up his baby sister?"

Oh hell. Oh no, no, no. Fuck it all.

He stalked by Toby and into the small reception area. He came to a dead halt, and Toby ran into his back.

There, standing defiantly by Sandra's desk, handcuffed, was one Nikki Durant. Their eyes met, and her expression positively smoldered. Nikki didn't look at all affected by the heat. No, she appeared cool and composed, and damn if he didn't want to lick her from her pretty polished toes to that delectable, fuckable mouth.

"Jesus Christ, Toby, get those goddamn cuffs off her," J.T. snarled.

"Uh, I would, man, but uhm, she sorta insisted they stay

on."

J.T. rounded on his friend. "Why the hell was she cuffed to begin with?"

"Because if he's going to arrest me, he needs to do it right," Nikki said in her husky, sexy-as-*hell* voice.

J.T. closed his eyes and prayed for deliverance. Then he slowly turned around and gave her a very pained stare.

"I'm afraid to ask. I really don't even want to know. But since you're standing in my jail in *handcuffs*, I feel compelled to ask what you did."

She gave him an innocent smile. His entire body tightened into one vicious knot. That smile could mow down an entire army. Her gorgeous blue eyes widened, and that perfect mouth curved upward.

He mentally traced a line around those plump lips with his tongue. Then he pictured that perfect bow around his dick. More sweat rolled down his back, and he had to shift his position to disguise an erection from hell.

"Maybe you should ask your deputy?" she suggested. "I was merely minding my business."

If it were possible, her eyes widened even further until they shone with an angelic light.

J.T. snatched the keys from Toby and stalked over to where Nikki stood.

"Cut the crap, Nikki." He turned her around and jammed the keys into the cuffs. In another second, he had her free and tossed the cuffs back to Toby. He made a jerking motion with his thumb, and Toby was only too happy to scram.

Nikki turned around and cupped one wrist in her palm, rubbing absently.

"Not too fun, huh?"

Her expression didn't falter.

"Now, want to tell me why the hell my deputy brought you in with cuffs on?"

She lifted one shoulder in a delicate shrug, and it sent her long dark hair sliding forward. The inch-wide pink streak, the one that drove him insane, glared in the fluorescent overhead lighting.

Her palms slid down her sides in a deliberate motion then shoved into the pockets of her jeans. The action sent her waistband lower, baring the thin ring in her belly button.

Sweat beaded his brow. *Why me?* What kind of miscreant had he been in a past life to deserve this kind of punishment?

"Your deputy brought me here because you were here," she said simply. "You're avoiding me."

J.T. blew out his breath. "Come on. I'll take you home, honey."

He immediately cringed as the endearment slipped from his lips. She flashed him a brilliant smile. Hell, she probably thought he was encouraging her.

She closed the distance between them and moved into his space. She pressed against his chest and wrapped her arms around him, burrowing her cheek against his shirt.

His body reacted, jumping to attention. Starving. It was the way he acted around her. And she knew it. Damn her.

"You can't run from me forever, J.T.," she murmured. "Sooner or later, you're going to give in. You know it, and I know it."

She turned her head up and brushed her lips across his jaw. When she would have found his mouth, he turned away and stepped back, out of her arms, away from her warmth and softness. Suddenly the oppressive heat lifted, and a chill settled in its stead.

"Nikki, stop." His voice came out in a husky sound that definitely didn't back up his command for her to halt. It sounded like an invitation, a *plea.*

She laughed softly. Then she pulled away and headed for the door. When she reached it, she gripped the handle and opened it. She paused and turned back to him.

"Don't bother driving me home, J.T. I'll walk."

Then she disappeared out the door, leaving him standing there gawking like a moron at the seductive sway of her hips. And that ass. Sweet Jesus, that ass!

And then he realized that she'd said she was walking home. Alone. In the dark.

Fuck that.

He snagged his Stetson and stalked out the door, glancing down the sidewalk to see her walking with a lazy stride down Main Street. Like any male within a ten-mile radius could resist that come-and-get-me strut? He'd be lucky if he didn't have to beat someone's ass before he managed to wrestle her into his squad car.

He was going to kill Lucas. Not just kill him, but cut him from asshole to appetite and gut him. Six months ago, Nikki's brother had extracted a promise from J.T.

He remembered the moment well. He and Lucas had been standing outside the auditorium at the small university Nikki had just graduated from, waiting for her to come out.

"She wants to move home, man," Lucas said as the two men stood by Lucas's truck.

Something deep inside J.T. flared. A sudden burst of adrenaline spiked through his veins. A warm buzz blew through his head, and he shook it to ward off the reaction to Lucas's announcement.

Playing it cool, he slid his friend a sideways glance. "You don't sound happy about that."

Lucas shrugged. "Barley? What the hell is she going to do in Barley? What's there for her? She always swore she'd get out. Just like I did."

"Maybe she just wants a place to regroup and figure out what she wants to do next," J.T. offered. Hopefully she'd do it quickly before he found himself going down paths better not taken.

"I want you to look after her," Lucas said. "I'm shipping out again. I don't like the idea of her being in that town alone. No one ever understood her or tried."

Shit. He should have seen this coming.

J.T. stared at the grim expression on Lucas's face. Hard, lean and muscled. He screamed military from the standard hair cut to the tattoo etched on his arm.

"Sure, man, I'll keep an eye on her. You know that." Even as the words slipped out, he knew he was damned. He'd just promised to keep an eye on a girl he couldn't control his lust over. Real smart.

"Lucas!"

The feminine exclamation rang out. Both men looked up, and J.T. felt a fist straight to his gut. He honestly couldn't take a breath.

Devoid of the graduation gown that had done a very good job of hiding what was beneath it, she hurried across the parking lot in a pair of extremely tight jeans and a tank top that hugged a luscious set of breasts and bared three inches of her midriff. Her jeans dipped low on her waist, and dangling from her belly button was a very feminine piece of jewelry.

He hadn't seen her in two years, but he hadn't forgotten a thing about how she looked. Or how she made him feel.

Suddenly, agreeing to come to her graduation with one of his best friends didn't seem like such a good idea.

Nikki Durant launched herself into her brother's arms, and J.T.'s mouth went dry. Then she stepped away from her brother and threw herself at J.T. He caught her as she wrapped herself around him. His arms were full of a mouthwatering, gorgeous woman.

Her curves molded to his hard body. Her nipples tightened and poked at his chest. Ah hell, she wasn't wearing a bra. Her swift intake of breath verified she was just as affected as he was.

He stepped back hastily, desperate to put as much distance between him and Lucas's little sister as he could.

Her smile was breathtaking. Her wide blue eyes danced with merriment and mischief. She knew.

After so long of hiding his reactions to her, in one moment, it was all in the open. He tried to conjure regret. Shame. Something other than the prickle of excitement that tightened every muscle in his body.

Hell. He was so busted. Now he just waited for Lucas to beat his ass.

But she turned and waved at someone across the parking lot. Then she looked back at her brother.

"Give me just a second, Lucas."

And she ran across the parking lot, her dark hair flying behind her.

"Was that a pink streak in her hair?" J.T. asked.

Lucas chuckled. "Uh yeah. Her latest method of driving me insane."

J.T. was trying to act casual, but his body was in overdrive. A lot had changed since that night five years ago when he'd held her as she cried. Then she'd been a broken girl, unsure of herself and her place in the world. Now she was a breathtaking woman who seemed very in charge of her destiny.

Lucas turned, his eyes serious. "I meant what I said, man. Look out for her, okay? Nikki...well, she's a free spirit. She'll never fit into a small town like Barley. She never did. People like to give her shit."

His gaze tracked Nikki across the parking lot. "And guys tend to think she's an easy mark because she's so outgoing and...flamboyant. I won't be around to kick some ass, so I'm counting on you to do it for me."

Easy mark? J.T. frowned. He knew Lucas and Nikki didn't have it easy growing up. Even in a poor small town they'd been on the lower rung of poor, and when no one had much, those who had slightly more liked to lord it over those who had nothing.

"They'll look at her and see our mother," Lucas said quietly.

"Don't sweat it, man. I'll make sure she stays safe." *Especially from me.*

Lucas bumped J.T.'s arm with his fist. "Thanks. I appreciate it."

J.T. closed in on Nikki and reached for her arm. Yeah, keep her safe. Who the hell was going to keep him safe from her?

She stopped when his fingers curled around her wrist. Her eyes glittered in the glow from the street lamps, and that pink streak in her hair sparkled and flashed with the movement of her head. Did she have glitter too? Hell.

"Get in the car, Nikki," he said as he swung her around and

herded her back to his vehicle.

"Well, if you insist," she murmured.

His eyes narrowed. She was playing him like a fiddle. He heaved an exasperated sigh as he opened the door and all but shoved her inside. When she was seated, he leaned into the car, his hand gripping the top of the window.

"I am *not* having sex with you, Nikki."

Her lips curled upward in a faint smile. "If you say so, J.T."

Chapter Two

Nikki watched J.T. flop into the driver's seat. Tension radiated from him, and he refused to look at her. His fingers gripped the steering wheel until she was sure his knuckles had to be bloodless. He backed out of the parking lot of the police station without a word and headed down Main Street in the direction of her house.

She suppressed a grin. He was pissed. Maybe she'd gone too far this time.

Nah.

Too far would be showing up naked at his office.

Her eyebrow lifted. That idea certainly had merit. Maybe just a trench coat. She could walk in, crawl onto his lap and let him open her up like a present.

Her nipples puckered and strained then beaded into tight little knots. J.T. was certainly proving more of a challenge than she'd thought. Not that she ever imagined he'd be easy. But she'd known he was attracted to her when she'd hugged up to him at her graduation. She'd felt his cock swell against her and heard his swift intake of breath when her breasts had pressed against his chest. Yeah, he wanted her.

And lord but she wanted him.

She glanced at his profile and narrowed her eyes. War.

She'd declared war as soon as she'd stepped back into this shithole town. Like she'd stick around if it weren't for the fact that J.T. was firmly ensconced in his life and job here?

He was scared of her. She wanted to laugh, but she was afraid he'd be too offended if he knew she was laughing at him. Imagine, little ole Nikki scaring big, bad J.T. Summers. It was hysterical, really.

She released the seatbelt and scooted over so she was next to him. He stiffened and gripped the steering wheel even tighter.

"Nikki," he growled.

She stifled her smile and leaned her head on his shoulder. Her arm snaked around his middle as she nestled closer to him.

"I missed you, J.T. It seemed like every time I came home from college, you avoided me."

"I, uh, missed you too, honey. You always were a fun kid."

She couldn't control the silent laughter. Her shoulders shook as she heaved against him.

"What's so damn funny?"

"You are."

"Glad you think so," he said darkly.

"Does calling me a kid somehow make it so in your mind, J.T.? Come on, I never took you for a coward."

He roared into her driveway a little faster than was necessary and slammed on the brakes, skidding to a halt. He extricated himself from her grip and opened his door.

He sat there, chest heaving for a long second as she pulled away.

"You are a kid, Nikki. You're my best friend's kid sister. I was twelve years old when you were born, for God's sake. When I was getting lucky in the backseat with Jane Seaver, you hadn't even made it to preschool yet. You had just finished

21

kindergarten when I graduated from high school."

Her nose wrinkled as she stared at him. "Well, yeah, if you'd been interested in me when you were in high school that would have made you a complete perv, but that was ages ago, J.T. No one cares now. I'm over the legal age, and you're hardly over the hill. And whether you want to admit it or not, you want me."

She gazed challengingly at him. Let him squirm his way out of that one. If he denied it, she'd call him a big fat liar to his face.

He didn't deny or confirm. He merely got out and walked around to her side to open her door. She accepted his hand, and when he pulled her up, she leaned into his chest and turned her head up so that their lips were close. Tantalizingly close.

For a moment he didn't move, and she almost thought he was going to let it happen. But then he yanked his head away with a soft curse. He curled his fingers around her arm and all but dragged her to the front door.

"Stay out of trouble, Nikki," he said in a resigned voice. "Next time you come into the station in cuffs, I'll let you stay in jail overnight. It's not a joke, and it won't be fun."

She reached up to touch his cheek. "If you're on duty, you could keep me company."

He scowled. "I don't keep the prisoners company, Nikki. Bear that in mind next time you want to play your stupid games."

She arched one brow as she let her fingers slide down his chest. "Game? I'm not playing a game, J.T. You know what I want. I haven't made any secret of that. I've been more honest than you. You want me. I know it, and you know it, but you deny it with every breath you take. So who's playing games?"

Not giving him time to react, she breezed past him and shut the door behind her. She walked over to the couch and flopped down with a weary sigh.

What a night. She hadn't been sure what to do in order to get arrested, and truth be told, she'd been terrified. She'd never even been inside a police station before, much less in jail with handcuffs.

But with J.T. going to such lengths to avoid her, she'd had no choice but to infiltrate his hidey hole. Starting a wee altercation at Tucker's Bar seemed a good idea at the time. Oh, it hadn't escalated to much. No doubt J.T. had put the fear of God into the local men about even looking in her direction.

By the time Toby had shown up, the excitement was over, but she'd insisted he take her in. In handcuffs. She grinned. She'd known J.T. would blow a gasket when he saw her handcuffed. It had been worth it to see the look on his face.

She sighed and closed her eyes as she leaned her head against the back of the couch. He wasn't going to the café anymore. He wasn't going home, apparently, not after she'd shown up there a few nights ago. And now he'd likely avoid his office. Where else could she hunt him down?

The Morgans. She grimaced. No doubt he'd run out to the ranch where he was sure she wouldn't show up.

Her mind raced to figure out a way around his next move. Jasmine was back in town. And married to Zane. Which confused Nikki, because she'd always been sure that Jasmine was pretty hung up on Zane's older brother Seth. She shrugged. Maybe Jasmine had settled. That wasn't her problem. Her problem was making damn sure J.T. couldn't avoid her forever.

She and Jasmine weren't best friends by any stretch, though Jasmine had never been rude, unlike the rest of the good people of Barley. Jasmine had her own difficulties back in the day, but she'd always had the protection of the Morgan brothers and J.T. as well. If Jasmine weren't married, Nikki would be jealous of the fact that J.T. had never tried to avoid Jasmine. In fact...hmmm. Hadn't he hauled Jasmine out of Tucker's Bar on more than one occasion?

Jasmine had to know J.T. pretty well given how close her husband was to J.T. Maybe...just maybe she should look Jasmine up. Give her a visit to catch up. Okay, not that they had any catching up to do. A few hellos in town didn't a friendship make, but hey, she was willing to play nice if it got her closer to her goal of seducing one J.T. Summers.

The heat was ungodly. Hot air blew through her hair as she drove her convertible down the dusty drive of the Sweetwater Ranch. The sun scorched over her skin, leaving her feeling parched and dry. July in south Texas. Only an idiot would live here. And only an idiot would fall in love with a man who had no intention of ever leaving this Godforsaken place.

Oh hello, my name is Nikki Durant, and I'm an idiot.

She pulled up to the sprawling ranch and cut the ignition. How desperate did it make her to come all the way out here to enlist the aid of a girl who might very well tell her to get lost?

With a resigned sigh, and the realization that she'd lost any and all pride when it came to J.T., she hauled herself out of her car and traipsed up to the front door. Right now she'd kill for air conditioning.

She rang the doorbell, and a few seconds later, an older Hispanic lady answered. The lady smiled welcomingly.

"Uh, hi," Nikki said lamely. "Is Jasmine home?"

The woman beamed at her. "I'm Carmen. Come in, come in. Jasmine is in the kitchen."

Nikki stepped inside and closed her eyes in absolute pleasure as the frigid air washed over her damp hair. Carmen pointed across the room and nodded.

Nikki walked nervously toward the kitchen, or what she assumed was the kitchen since Carmen had disappeared. She heard distant voices and quickened her step. When she rounded the corner, however, she put the brakes on, and her mouth gaped open.

Jasmine was in a lip lock with Seth, who was *not* her husband. He had her backed against the counter, and their bodies were molded tightly against each other.

Oops didn't even begin to cover it. Despite the fact that it was certainly none of her business, anger washed over Nikki. She liked Zane. Liked him a lot. He'd been her childhood hero when he'd stepped between her and three other kids who were determined to beat her into a pulp. And the fact that his wife was cheating on him with his brother pissed her off.

"Uh, Jasmine, it appears we have company."

Seth's voice, husky from passion, hit Nikki all wrong. Her eyes narrowed as she glared at Jasmine. Never mind that she'd come here to enlist her help with J.T. Right now she wanted to kick her ass.

"By all means, don't let me interrupt," Nikki said dryly. "Just don't expect me not to tell Zane his wife is fucking around on him with his brother."

To her surprise, Jasmine grinned and cast a sidelong glance at Seth who attempted to keep a straight face.

"Some might say it's none of your business," Jasmine drawled.

"Zane is my friend," Nikki said fiercely.

Seth's eyes widened. "Nikki? Nikki Durant? Is that really you?"

She nodded stiffly. Seth let out a whistle. "Damn, when did you go and grow up on me?"

"Nice hair," Jasmine said, and at first Nikki thought she was being a smartass, but Jasmine looked at the pink stripe with a very interested light in her eyes.

"Don't get any ideas, Jasmine," Seth growled.

Jasmine grinned innocently. "I like it. I was thinking maybe blue for my hair to match yours and Zane's eyes."

Seth groaned and rolled his eyes. "First the belly ring. Then you asked to get a tattoo as a wedding present."

Nikki stared between them in confusion. For two people who should at most have a casual friendship, they certainly seemed to be on intimate terms.

"Are you here to see Zane?" Jasmine asked softly. "He's not here, but he should be back soon."

Nikki shifted uncomfortably. "No, actually I came to see you."

Jasmine's brow lifted in surprise.

"But uhm, maybe it's not such a good idea. I should probably go."

Jasmine grinned. "You gonna go track Zane down and tell him his wife was cheating on him?"

Seth smacked her on the ass. "Stop egging her on, Jasmine."

Nikki frowned. "I was here to talk to you about J.T."

"What about J.T.?" Zane asked as he strolled into the kitchen. His eyes lit up when he saw Nikki. "Nikki, girl! How you doing?"

He swept her up in a bone crunching hug, lifted her off the floor and then plunked her down. He dropped a kiss on top of her head then backed away to look at her.

"Holy hell in a bucket, no wonder J.T. is running scared," he said in amusement.

She frowned even harder. "What's J.T. been saying to you about me?"

Zane grinned then walked over to loop an arm over Jasmine. "Hey, Jaz. Missed you, babe." He pulled her into his arms and gave her a long, lusty kiss that had Nikki turning three shades of green.

Why couldn't J.T. look at her like that? And then she glared at Jasmine as she remembered that not five minutes ago, she'd been kissing Seth just as fiercely as Zane was currently kissing her.

Seth cleared his throat, and Zane pulled away. "Sorry," Zane said in Nikki's direction. "Got a little carried away."

"Not as carried away as Seth and Jasmine got awhile ago," Nikki said acidly.

Jasmine's lips twitched, and Seth had the grace to look away. Zane looked between Seth and Jasmine and then over to Nikki who was still glaring openly at Jasmine.

"Ah," Zane said as if he'd been struck with sudden understanding. "Hell."

"Yeah," Seth said. He cleared his throat. "Nikki is pretty pissed off on your behalf." His lips twitched, and he broke into a grin. "I'd say right now she's considering gutting your pretty little bride."

Jasmine swung her elbow into Seth's stomach, and he doubled over in mock agony.

Nikki stared between them all and wondered what the hell she was missing. They acted like it was some big joke.

"Maybe you two should get lost," Jasmine said pointedly. "She did come out to talk to me. She can catch up with you later," she told Zane. "Maybe after she kicks my ass for cheating on you. You have quite the defender there, sweetums."

Zane grinned and reached out to chuck Nikki on the arm. "Glad someone loves me."

Jasmine rolled her eyes and made shooing motions. Seth and Zane both sauntered out with Seth chuckling the entire way.

Jasmine motioned for her to sit down. "You want something to drink?"

Nikki shook her head. She wasn't going to ask. It was none of her business.

"So, you wanted to talk about J.T.?" Jasmine prompted as she took a seat across the bar from Nikki.

Nikki cleared her throat. "Well, yeah, but I'm not sure you'll want to help me now that I've unsheathed my bitch claws."

Jasmine laughed and flipped her almost-black hair over one shoulder. Then she eyed the pink streak in Nikki's hair. "I'm serious. I think a blue streak would be cool. I really like yours. It's so noticeable."

Nikki blinked. "Well, uhm, sure, blue would look nice."

Jasmine stared at her for a long second, as if measuring her. Then she sighed. "I don't know a lot about you. I mean I've heard Zane mention you once or twice, and J.T. talked about going to your graduation, but I know enough that you've suffered being the subject of talk in this town like I was when I was younger. So I'll say this, hoping you'll remember what it's like to be the topic of gossip and won't go spreading it around."

Nikki stared at her with a furrowed brow, not knowing whether to be insulted or not.

"I'm married to Zane, but in my heart I'm married to both him and Seth. I'm with both of them. I love them both, and they both love me."

Nikki's mouth fell open. Then she tried to close it. Damn.

"Yeah," Jasmine said with a half smile. "Shocking ain't it? Now you know why I don't want it to get around. I suspect some people know or at least think they know, but suspecting and having solid proof are two different things. At least now you won't try to kick my ass for cheating on Zane. As much as I appreciate your apparent loyalty to my husband, I'd just as soon you not feel as though he needs protecting from me."

"Oh damn," Nikki muttered. "I just made a first-class ass of myself didn't I?"

Jasmine grinned. "Nah. You would have only made an ass of yourself if you tried to kick *my* ass in my own kitchen."

Nikki blew out her breath. "Well hell."

Jasmine waved her hand. "Okay, enough of that. Now tell me why on earth you'd want to come out here to talk about J.T.? Aren't you two long-time friends?"

"Not exactly," Nikki said glumly. "He's best friends with my brother. My older, very protective brother."

"Ahh. That explains a lot."

"He's avoiding me, and I figure his next step is to hole up out here, seeing as how I've chased him down everywhere else, including getting myself arrested and taken to his jail last night."

Jasmine burst out laughing. She wiped her eyes with her palms. "Oh lord, now why didn't I think of something like that when I was trying to lasso Seth and Zane?"

"It didn't work very well," Nikki muttered. "Anyway, I was going to come out and appeal to Zane since he's somewhat of an old friend and wrangle an invitation when J.T. retreats out here like the coward he is."

"Any idea why he's avoiding you?" Jasmine asked delicately.

Nikki made a face. "Pick your reason. If you listen to him, he's twelve years older, my brother is his best friend, he promised to look after me for God's sake, like I'm some two-year-old, and then there's the fact that I'm so young and innocent and need protecting from myself."

Jasmine cracked up again. "Okay, despite the fact that you just wanted to kick my ass and the fact that my husband hugged you, I like you, Nikki. I like you a whole lot. I almost feel sorry for J.T."

Nikki grinned. "Oh you don't have to feel sorry for him. I plan to treat him real nice."

Jasmine hopped up from her seat and reached for the cordless phone. She looked at Nikki and held a finger to her lips as she punched the numbers.

"J.T., hey, it's Jasmine. How's it going?"

She paused then grinned. "Hey, I thought you might want to come out for a swim since it's so hot and you have shitty air conditioning in your office. From what I hear, you could use some sanctuary from a certain pretty young thing chasing you around town."

Nikki glared at Jasmine who just grinned and then broke into laughter.

"Oh come on, J.T. Like anything stays secret in Barley? So you want to come out or not? We may or may not be around when you get here, but feel free to let yourself in. We'll be back after awhile, and we can grill for dinner."

Jasmine winked at Nikki and gave her a thumbs-up.

"Okay, J.T. See you later then."

She laid the phone down and grinned at Nikki. "He's on his way out. Now I just need to round up Seth and Zane and give Carmen the rest of the day off. I can give you until dinner to work your magic. Of course you're welcome to stay for steaks, but who knows if J.T. will have the guts to hang around. He seems to have developed a yellow streak where you're concerned."

"Tell me about it," Nikki muttered. "And hey, Jasmine," she said as Jasmine started to walk out of the kitchen. Jasmine turned to look at Nikki. "Thanks. Really. You didn't have to do this, but I appreciate it. Especially since I made a complete fool of myself."

Jasmine smiled. "I know what it's like to want a man who resists you at every turn. Believe me when I say I do. I don't know what it is about the men around here, but once they make up their minds that you're off limits, it's like cracking cement to get them to change them. J.T.'s a good man. The best. And I can see that you're passionate and loyal about people you care about. J.T. needs someone like that. If you can be that person, then I'll do whatever I can to help."

She started to go again but then stopped and turned around with a grin. "Just a thought, but if you want to properly ambush J.T. you might want to move your car around back so he doesn't know you're here when he drives up."

Chapter Three

J.T. pulled to a stop in front of the ranch and wiped the sweat from his brow. He couldn't wait to jump in the pool. There weren't too many safe places left in Barley for him to hide, but he was safe here.

He climbed out and strode to the house in his swim trunks, flip-flops and T-shirt. He knocked then rang the bell, but when no one answered, he opened the door and let himself in. Jasmine had said they might not be here. Which was fine with him. He could use the alone time to work off some serious sexual frustration.

He made his way through the living room and to the glass patio doors. Beyond, the pool shimmered a sparkling blue, and he nearly groaned as he imagined how nice it was going to feel to immerse himself in its coolness.

He shut the door behind him, kicked off his flip-flops and made a beeline for the deep end. But when he got there, his gaze drifted to the lawn chair situated just a foot from the diving board. And to the beautiful, *naked* woman stretched out, sunbathing.

Fuck me. Fuck him. Fuck a duck.

Nikki was laid out, butt-ass naked, her gorgeous tanned skin glistening in the sun. There wasn't an inch of pale skin anywhere on her, which told him she was no stranger to tanning in the nude.

Her slender legs were slightly bent at the knees and parted, just enough to give him a prime glance at her pussy. He groaned. Dear God, this was so unfair.

His gaze drifted higher to her trim waist and the diamond teardrop ring at her belly button. It glittered in the sun and lay in the hollow of her taut belly. Then he settled on her pert breasts. Perfect. Just fucking perfect. Not too large but not small by any means. Just big enough that they stood erect. Not a bit of sag. If he didn't know better, he'd say they were fake, but he'd been up close and personal, and they were way too soft, too fleshy to be silicone.

Her nipples were dark, maybe from tanning, but they were mouthwateringly erect. Brown, darker than her skin. Puckered and pointed. He closed his eyes and tried to stop the inevitable meltdown.

"I expected you a half hour ago," she said lazily.

His eyes flew open to see her watching him with hazy contentment.

Jasmine. Hell. He'd been royally set up and screwed. So much for friendship. Damn women stuck together like thieves.

"I'll just be going," he muttered. How the hell was he supposed to go for a swim with a woody the size of a tree trunk and her lying in the sun gloriously naked?

"Coward," she said bluntly.

He blinked. "Excuse me?"

She sat up, and he couldn't help but watch the way her breasts swayed with her motion. Or the way he'd caught the most spectacular glimpse of her pussy when she'd spread her legs to put her feet down on either side of the lounger.

She pushed herself up and walked to where he stood. His

Drowning in indescribable pleasure.

Yeah, he was a fucking hypocrite, and yeah, he'd do plenty of bitching at himself later, but right now he was going to come all over her mouth.

He closed his eyes, rocked back on his heels and took her head in his hands. Her fingers dug deeper into his ass, and she pressed her face into his groin, sucking him down her throat.

"Oh shit, honey, I'm going to come."

He thought to warn her in case she didn't want him shooting his load down her throat, but she only clamped down on him harder, sucking and lapping hungrily at him.

Fire gathered in his balls, squeezing, burning. Electric sensation shot up his cock, and he swelled larger in her mouth, grew harder until he thought he was going to burst.

The first jet exploded from his cock, and he shouted hoarsely as he came all undone. His hands gripped her head, and he began fucking her mouth in earnest, no longer content to let her do the driving.

Harder and faster he thrust as he filled her mouth with his cream. She swallowed, and it caused her throat to convulse around him, sending another spasm of pleasure rocketing up his dick.

He rocked up on tiptoe as he strained to get further inside her. His legs trembled, and his ass cheeks clenched together until finally the last drop dribbled into her mouth.

But still she slid her mouth up and down his cock, sucking and licking gently at his softening erection. Finally, she released him with a soft plop, and his dick sagged like a tired puppet.

Then she leaned forward and swept her tongue over the top to snag one last drop of semen, and he groaned all over again.

"Nikki, honey, get up off the concrete. Jesus, your knees."

He hoisted her up by her arms, frowning at the scrapes on her knees. He walked her backward until she bumped against the lounger, and he eased her down.

"God, I'm such an ass."

"You have a very nice ass," she said huskily.

He winced and closed his eyes.

"You know, I never pictured you for the selfish type."

His eyes flew open at that.

"Wha?"

Her eyes narrowed, and he honestly couldn't tell if she was teasing or not.

"I figured you for a generous lover, not the type to take your pleasure and leave the woman hanging."

He gaped at her and then realization sank in. His jaw tightened. "Selfish, huh."

She nodded. "Seeing as you've had your fun and here I am aching from head to toe." She shrugged, that delicate little motion that made her naked breasts bob and the nipples quiver. He went tight all over again. "I don't imagine it would take much. I'm so worked up that if you looked at me right I think I'd come."

He looked down to see his dick straining upward again and then over to where his trunks were lying on the concrete by the pool. Hell.

She shifted and parted her thighs, giving him a glimpse of the pink flesh hidden by the dark curls. One tiny hand snaked downward, skittering across her belly then delving into her folds. She moaned and arched her hips as her fingertips rolled across her clit.

He swallowed then swallowed again. He found himself unable to tear his gaze from the glistening, plump flesh bared by her fingers.

"Are you going to make me do all the work?" she murmured.

"No," he croaked. Hell no. He wanted to taste her so bad he was damn near licking his lips.

Sliding his hands up her slender legs and up the backs until he reached her sweet little ass, he gripped and kneaded the fleshy mounds before spreading her legs even further apart.

He lowered himself until he was the one with his knees digging into the hot concrete.

Nikki caught her breath as J.T. inched his way up her body until his mouth hovered over her hand. Her movements stilled and then gently, he pulled her fingers away from her pussy and rested them on her belly.

He moved his other hand between her legs and delved between the sensitive lips and brushed across her engorged clitoris.

She moaned and tilted her hips up to meet his touch. He was finally touching her. Her body tensed in anticipation, in absolute glee. She'd waited forever to have him between her legs, his body over hers.

His taste was still in her mouth, and she savored it. She licked her lips as she imagined his cock thrusting between her legs this time.

And then he licked her. A long, sensuous sweep with his tongue. She cried out as shock splintered through her abdomen. He drew a lazy circle with the tip around her clit then lapped harder at it, drawing it into a stiff, quivering peak.

She thrust her hands into his short hair, gripping him tightly, wanting more, wanting him never to let up.

"You taste so sweet," he murmured against her damp flesh.

He slid one finger just inside her pussy as he sucked lightly at her clit. He eased back and forth, barely rimming her entrance with his fingertip, and then he pulled away and lowered his mouth to suck avidly at her opening.

A cry ripped from her mouth just her orgasm tore through her abdomen with painful ferocity. Her pelvis lifted and bucked but his hands cupped her ass, holding her tightly as he drank deeply from her.

Her fingers balled into tight fists at her sides, and she clenched her eyes shut as another cry erupted from her chest.

Long, warm slides of his tongue coaxed her down from her orgasm. Tiny little shivers continued to quake over her body, and her legs shook like jelly as he gently lowered her back to the lounger.

She opened her eyes and looked hungrily at him, but when he met her gaze, his eyes flickered, and he looked away.

Her heart sank. He couldn't have broadcasted his regret more if he'd yelled it out loud.

She firmed her lips and tilted her chin upwards. No way he'd come around after one illicit encounter. She knew it and refused to feel disappointment over something she'd expected.

Without giving him opportunity to speak, react or shove the entire incident under the table, she swung her legs over the side of the lounger and pushed herself up.

Her bathing suit lay in a crumpled heap a few feet away, and she gathered it up, pulling the bottoms on before arranging the top around her breasts.

When she looked up, she saw J.T. staring at her, his mouth working to say something. She smiled and closed the distance between them.

She rose up on tiptoe and brushed her lips across his

mouth. She pressed in closer, knowing he'd retreat. He stumbled back a few steps, and then she shoved at his chest. Already off balance, he tumbled backward into the pool, an expression of shock on his face.

He came up sputtering, a murderous gleam in his eye. Well, it sure beat regret and pity. She'd take his temper over rejection any day of the week.

"Have a nice swim," she said sweetly. "I'll see you around."

She turned and strode to the patio doors, his furious shouts echoing in her ears. A tiny grin worked at the corners of her mouth. Off balance. He was best kept off balance and unsuspecting.

She just had to keep him that way.

Chapter Four

Two days. It had been two days since he'd seen Nikki. J.T. had steeled himself, sure that because of his temporary loss of sanity, she'd be even more determined.

Instead, he spent every moment in anticipation of her popping out of nowhere. Only to be utterly disappointed. He snorted. Disappointed? More like relieved.

He was edgy and ill-tempered, and his friends avoided him like a good case of crotch rot.

He missed her. It wasn't something he wanted to admit, but she consumed his thoughts. She made him feel... He stopped his train of thoughts before they bordered on the ridiculous.

When Nikki had moved back, he could have listed a dozen reasons why getting involved with her was a bad idea. But at the moment, he was struggling to remember even one.

Then he remembered. She'd never settle here. Lucas was right about her being a free spirit. Why would she stay in a town that had done its best to crush that spirit? No, she wasn't about home and hearth and commitment. Things at his age that he was seriously starting to consider. She was young and on the cusp of unfurling her wings. She'd fly and be beautiful doing it.

He wanted to touch her, her magic, wrap himself around her and lose himself in her vibrancy. He wanted her for himself.

Selfishly, he wanted her to shine for him and only him.

J.T. leaned back in his chair and stared up at the stained ceiling. Rain. The air smelled of it. The slightly metallic smell of rain hitting hot pavement lingered in his nostrils. Wishful thinking. Not a drop had fallen. Yet.

And then he heard it. Big fat drops hitting the tin roof of the building. One, two, faster and heavier. It started light but quickly gained momentum. Hallelujah. He wanted to run outside and play like a kid. Thinking of Nikki did that to him. Made him feel young and silly with a bucketful of smiles.

He got up and walked over to the window. He pulled down the slats of the blinds with one finger and peered out. A short distance away, the sun still shone, a stark contrast to the dark, sullen clouds hanging just overhead. It would be a quick cloudburst, unfortunately, but it should cool things off by a few degrees even if it made the humidity more oppressive.

When he turned back toward his desk, his door burst open, and Nikki hurried in, dripping water all over his floor. She shut the door behind her and stood there, staring at him, her big blue eyes bright as her soaked hair clung to her cheeks.

A smile wavered around her lips as she stared at him. "I kinda forgot my umbrella."

Before he could even offer a greeting, she walked to the center of the room and started shedding her clothes. Hell. He wouldn't have put it past her to have ordered up a rainstorm just so she could walk in here wearing her clothes like a second skin.

Her shirt came off first and landed with a wet plop on the floor. She wasn't wearing a bra.

"Nikki, stop," he growled as he hurried over to retrieve her shirt. He wrung it out and tried to arrange it around her naked breasts. Anything so they wouldn't tempt him so goddamn much.

She shivered as the wet cloth hit her skin. He swore. How the hell could she be cold in this heat? But sure enough, goose bumps puckered her skin, making her delectable nipples strain outward.

He glanced around the room in near panic. No way was he going to have a naked woman in his office. Not only would it get his ass fired, but gossip would run through the town like a hog headed for slop.

Making a quick decision, he yanked open the buttons to his shirt and shrugged out of it. By the time he was done, she'd peeled her jeans off and stood completely nude in front of him.

He clenched his teeth and quickly wrapped his shirt around her shoulders. Okay, so it swallowed her, but that was good considering he couldn't very well shuck his pants and give them to her. He was already dead meat if someone walked in.

Alarmed by that prospect, he started for the door.

"It's already locked," she said huskily, a thread of amusement in her voice.

He frowned. Of course the little minx would have thought of that.

"Nikki, you have to go home. I'm working."

One dark eyebrow rose, and a hint of laughter sparkled in her eyes. "Yes, I can see how busy you are. Want to go play in the rain with me?"

Damn if he wasn't tempted. Then he shook off that insanity and frowned, hoping she'd get the message and hoping she wouldn't, all in the same thought.

Instead she sashayed up to him, his shirt hanging loosely around her. The lapels parted and her breasts peeked out, her nipples playing an erotic game of hide and seek.

She reached for his hand and pulled it upward. His palm grazed one breast, and she stopped, forcing him to cup the plump mound.

"Touch me," she whispered.

Her skin was so soft. Baby fine.

He yanked his hand away. Baby. Of course it was baby soft because next to him, she was a freaking infant.

Undeterred, she dug her fingers into the waistband of his pants and tugged at the fly. It came undone and she reached in, her hand curling around his dick.

"Nikki, honey, you have to stop this." He gripped her hand and pulled it away, holding it as far away from his body as he could. "Go home. We can't do this."

Again she raised one delicate eyebrow. "Oh, but we can, J.T. Who's going to stop us? Your door is locked. No one in their right mind is out in this rain. Except me," she added with a laugh.

She reached for him with her other hand and managed to shove his pants down over his hips. His cock sprang out, desperate for her touch, and she didn't disappoint.

Her fingers brushed over the head then closed around the base. He damn near came in her hand.

What was it about this woman that drove him stark raving mad? All she had to do was touch him, and he lost any and all control. He prided himself on his discipline, on his ability to not cave to his desires. But damn it, this woman made him throw caution to the wind.

Again she fell to her knees in front of him, and her mouth closed hot around his cock. Fire consumed him. Hot, edgy, painful. But so damn good. So. Damn. Good.

He yanked her to her feet. "Not today, honey. No kneeling

for you. I've had about enough of that fake submissive shit."

She laughed, her eyes gleaming as he picked her up and backed her to the desk. He laid her out like a feast, all spread out for him. And damn if he wasn't starving.

"There's a condom in my pants pocket," she said huskily.

His lips thinned as he stared ferociously at her. "I think I can take care of the damn protection." He yanked open his desk drawer, rummaged around then pulled out a condom.

"Why, J.T., one would think you'd been expecting me," she teased.

A dull flush heated its way up his neck. How could she know he'd just bought them? Hell, he didn't even know why he'd bought the damn things. He hadn't had sex in a year, and he certainly never kept rubbers in his desk drawer. Only after she'd come to town with her sexy-as-sin walk and those pouting lips.

Ignoring her smirk, he lowered his head to her breasts, but she placed her palms over his cheeks and forced him higher until their lips hovered precariously close.

"Kiss me," she whispered. "*Me*. Not my breasts."

Her lips were plump and so tempting. He knew he'd be lost if he tasted her. Completely and utterly lost.

She didn't give him a choice. Her head came off the desk, and she fused her lips to his. Hot. Intoxicating and so damn sweet.

Her tongue fluttered over his lips, and without thinking, he parted them, allowing her entrance. Soft and inquisitive, she delved into his mouth, brushing across his tongue, leaving her taste.

He curved his hand behind her neck, thrusting his fingers into her thick hair. He took control of the kiss and swallowed her moan of pleasure. He wanted all of her. She belonged to him.

That thought sent alarm bells clanging in all directions. She wasn't his. What he was doing was wrong. But she felt so incredibly right. And he wanted her. Wanted her so damn bad he couldn't breathe around her. Would it be so bad to exist in the moment and pretend she could be his, even if for only a little while?

And then she shifted and wrapped her legs around his waist, pulling him closer to her. She whispered into his mouth, and it took a moment to understand what she'd said.

"Love me, J.T. Please love me."

Her words tugged at him. Such a simple plea and yet so heartfelt. Could he make love to her and then let her go?

He tore himself from her mouth and slid his lips down the side of her jaw, to the tender skin of her neck. He inhaled her sweet scent as he nibbled his way over her shoulder toward her breasts.

She squirmed and twisted underneath him, and he smiled as he sucked one taut nipple into his mouth. He suckled lightly for a while, teasing and nipping at one breast before he lazily turned his attention to the other.

Her muscles shook and spasmed, and her breaths came heavy. After sucking tenderly for several seconds, he sank his teeth into the firm point. She cried out and arched off his desk.

"Shhhh, honey," he murmured. "We have to be quiet."

She whimpered and ran her hands frantically over his shoulders.

"Take me, J.T. Make me yours," she begged.

He closed his eyes as his dick tightened painfully. She was so fucking responsive. All he had to do was touch her. Making love to a woman who was so tuned into him was a power trip like he'd never experienced. He felt invincible.

His mouth slid down her body, her exquisite, oh-so-tempting body. Her belly ring quivered as his tongue traced a line around it. Pretty and delicate like her. Feminine. He liked it. Even the pink streak was growing on him in a big way. Somehow it just fit.

He kissed a line to her pussy, enjoying the feel of her against his mouth. She smelled as good as she tasted, and he knew he'd never get enough of her.

Reaching underneath her knees, he hooked his arms and pulled her ass to the edge of the desk. She lined up perfectly with his cock, and he was dying to get inside her.

He fumbled with the condom wrapper, suddenly clumsy and inept. His fingers shook as he rolled the latex over his penis. But still, he held back.

Bending to one knee, he parted the damp folds of her pussy and pressed his mouth to her center. She jerked and quivered as he licked and tasted her. She was ready for him.

Rising back up, he pulled her legs wider apart then positioned himself at her entrance. His thumb found her clitoris, so taut and rigid. As he began to gently manipulate the sensitive bundle, he thrust inside her.

She gasped and went rigid around him. Her body reacted, and her muscles seemed to protest and spasm. Her hands flew up to grip his upper arms, and her eyes were wide.

He frowned and cursed under his breath. He'd gone too fast.

"Did I hurt you, honey?" he asked in concern. "I'm so damn sorry."

She shook her head vehemently. "No, don't stop. God, it

feels so good, J.T. Love me please," she begged.

There wasn't a man alive who could refuse a plea like that. He slowly withdrew then plunged forward again.

She writhed underneath him, and she wrapped her legs around him, pulling him tighter against her.

He sank into her welcoming heat, and with each thrust, he felt like he was losing more of himself. It wasn't just physical. He wished to hell it was. He wanted it to be lust, because then when she was ready to go he could let her without regret or a sense of loss. But as he moved deeper into her body, he felt the pull in his chest. Right where his heart lay.

Then he looked into her eyes. There was want and need there. They shone with something, something he couldn't quite describe, yet it instilled such an ache within him. Did she feel it too?

Her movements became more frantic, and her eyes widened. He knew she was close, and he was determined that she go first. He reached down, finding her clitoris. With a gentle touch, he strummed at it as he slid forward again.

Her mouth opened, and he knew if he didn't cover it, she was going to let out one hell of a scream. He almost didn't make it in time. As he clamped his hand over her mouth, his other hand still plucking at her clit, she let out a hoarse yell. Her pussy convulsed around him, sucking him wetly as she orgasmed.

He closed his eyes and ground his teeth together. Oh holy hell, this was big. Shit. Every ounce of blood in his body raced to his cock, swelling outward. Pressure. God, the pressure.

The condom felt like a vise around his cock. He wanted to rip it off to alleviate the tightness. Harder he thrust. Frantically he pounded against her willing body until finally the unbearable pressure blew.

He exploded inside her, the head of his cock damn near blowing off with the force of his orgasm. Mindlessly, he rocked against her, never wanting the feeling to end.

Nikki sucked in her breath as J.T.'s hand slid from her mouth. She wanted to cry out, to scream, but she bit her lip to keep silent. Never had she felt anything to equal their coming together. It was everything she'd dreamed it would be.

She glanced up at J.T. who gently slid out of her body. Their eyes met, and what she saw in his made her heart fall. Regret. Guilt. Everything but the loving acceptance she'd hoped to find.

"J.T.," she said softly as she struggled to sit up on the desk.

He took her hand and helped her up, but he wouldn't look at her.

"I'll get your clothes," he said in a low voice.

"J.T., look at me," she pleaded.

He finally turned his head, and she saw the regret simmering in his dark eyes. But there was something else. Sadness? The pupils were dilated, overtaking the brown orbs and painting his eyes black.

"I'm not going to insult you by offering excuses, Nikki. It shouldn't have happened, but I wanted it. I knew exactly what I was doing. But make no mistake. It can't happen again."

"Why?" she demanded. She pressed in close to him, uncaring of the fact she was still naked. Her pussy was still throbbing from her orgasm, and she wanted nothing more than for him to take her in his arms.

"I'm not having a fling with you, Nikki," he gritted out.

She tensed and tried to keep her anger and frustration at bay. "Who says it has to be a fling? Why can't we have sex?

49

We're two adults, J.T. I'm not a child."

"Maybe I'm not into casual sex," he said calmly. "Maybe I'm at an age where I'm ready to settle down and find something more than a quick fuck."

She flinched and stepped back. "Quick fuck," she said in a low voice. "Is that what I am, J.T.?" She couldn't keep the pain from her voice. She wasn't the woman he wanted to settle with. "I'm good for a blowjob and an easy lay, but not good enough for more." Bitterness crept in. Invaded and slid over her with agonizing speed. Some things never changed in Barley. She'd been a fool to come back.

"That's not what I said, Nikki," he said patiently.

"You didn't have to say it," she whispered.

She yanked on her wet clothes, not caring how they looked. Without a backward glance at him, she unlocked his door and strode out to where her car was parked.

Her eyes were dry. She wouldn't cry. Not over him. Her only consolation was that she hadn't humiliated herself even more by blurting out her feelings.

J.T. shut the door so he could dress. He was standing in his office in the middle of the day, naked and still wearing a used condom.

He reached down to pull it off and froze when he saw the traces of red on the outside of the latex. Blood. What the fuck?

His gaze flew to the desk but all he saw was the faintest smudge of red. God, had he been that rough? Had he hurt her?

But then he registered how tight she'd been. How unsure she'd been as he positioned himself to take her. And her gasp of surprise when he thrust that first time.

Nausea rolled in his stomach. Jesus Christ. She'd been a virgin.

He closed his eyes, and then remembering he was still naked, in his office, in the middle of the day, he let out a curse and yanked his clothing back on.

A virgin. God. He'd taken her virginity, something he had no right to do, and not only that, he'd insulted her. He'd all but called her a whore. Not that he'd ever hurt her like that, but he might as well have said it out loud. All that shit about not wanting a quick fuck.

No, he didn't want a quick fuck with her. He goddamn wanted more. But she didn't. This was all a game to her. He couldn't ever see her settling with a small town, hokey cop in a place that had caused her nothing but grief. Why the fuck had she even come back?

Lucas was going to kill him.

J.T. groaned and rubbed a tired hand over his forehead. He'd promised one of his best friends that he'd look out for his kid sister and protect her from men who thought she was an easy mark. He swore long and hard again. Easy mark? She'd been a goddamn virgin, and he'd been the one who treated her like she was a carbon copy of her mother.

Way to go, asshole.

Chapter Five

If J.T. had wanted Nikki to disappear, he'd certainly gotten his wish. She was no longer there every time he turned around. It was a week later before he realized he'd stopped hiding in hopes that he would see her, but no matter where he went, the café or Tucker's, his house or his office, there was no sign of her.

A midweek conversation with Jasmine yielded nothing other than Jasmine calling him a dumbass and hanging up in a huff.

Where was she?

He couldn't very well keep an eye on her if he never saw her.

"You're a stupid son of a bitch," he muttered. He'd hurt her. He still flinched when he remembered the look in her eyes. He'd been such a bastard.

Of course she wasn't lining up to seduce him. A woman like her didn't need to wait around on a man like him.

But she *had* waited, and he couldn't figure out why. Why him? She had to have had men dying to take her out in college.

Even as he thought it, an image of her mother came readily to mind. And the expression on a much younger Nikki's face the night he'd had to tell her that her mom wasn't coming home.

That night had been a catalyst for so many things. He'd taken Nikki to his home so she'd have a place to stay until Lucas got into town. He hadn't wanted her to be alone in the house she'd grown up in. Not when her mother's boyfriends paid call at all times of the night. When they discovered Tricia gone, who was to say they wouldn't turn their attention on Tricia's teenage daughter?

Nikki hadn't reacted with surprise to the news that her mother had skipped town with a new boyfriend and left Nikki to her own devices. It was that stoic acceptance that made J.T. grieve for the little girl trapped behind Nikki's abrasive façade.

It made perfect sense why she was still a virgin. It didn't take a rocket scientist to figure out she wouldn't want to be tarred with the same brush as her mother.

What didn't make sense was why she'd chosen him to be her first.

He swore and pounded his desk with his fist. Then he glared at the window unit that had quit earlier in the afternoon. Damn repairman was supposed to have been here hours ago. He was tired of sitting here sweating his ass off with the ridiculous hope that Nikki might burst through the door with her million-dollar smile and those big blue eyes shining with mischief.

Instead, all he could remember was the hurt shadowing those gorgeous eyes. Hurt that he'd been responsible for.

Toby stuck his head in the door. "J.T., you might want to head over to Tucker's."

The urgency in Toby's voice spurred J.T. to action. He quickly stood and strode toward the door, his hand automatically checking his weapon at his side.

"What's up?" he demanded.

Toby gave him an uneasy look and J.T. knew. He sighed.

"What's she done now?"

Toby grimaced. "There's a disturbance. Uh, Tucker said Nikki is pretty drunk."

J.T. bit out a curse even as he started for his car. Toby was right behind him.

At first, J.T. wondered if this was just another ploy on Nikki's part, her calling his bluff on locking her up overnight. But when he walked into Tucker's a few minutes later, he quickly hung up that notion.

In a word, Nikki was plastered. And he'd never seen her drunk. Hell, he'd never even seen her take a sip of alcohol.

She was on top of the bar, ignoring Tucker's pleas to come down. She wore a tight miniskirt that afforded anyone in a three-foot radius a prime view of her underwear. He only hoped to hell she was *wearing* underwear.

Her midriff was bare as her tank top rode higher, brushing the undersides of her breasts. She was most definitely not wearing a bra.

She teetered precariously on three-inch heels, and no less than four sets of hands reached up to steady her. A peal of laughter escaped her as she dodged and continued gyrating atop the bar in time with the blaring country music.

She looked like she was having the time of her life. Only J.T. could see the pain flashing in her eyes.

Then one of the guys reached up and yanked at her hand. She tumbled down with a surprised yelp, right into the asshole's arms. He grinned and plastered his mouth to hers.

She began to struggle and kick wildly, but the guy wasn't inclined to let her go. If anything he tightened his grip. Her whimper of fright spilled out. It was all J.T. could hear. No music. No loud conversations. Just her sound of fear.

J.T. exploded into action, shoving men out of his way as he closed in on his goal. Tucker gave J.T. a relieved look as he saw him.

Without a word, J.T. reached out and snagged her wrist. He pulled, but the guy holding on to her was reluctant to let go. Until he saw J.T.'s uniform. His compliance wasn't enough, though. J.T. wanted his blood.

He decked the guy right in the jaw, and he went down, almost taking Nikki with him. J.T. grabbed her and hauled her against him. He shoved her behind him as he waited to see if he'd have any more trouble out of Mr. Obnoxious.

Satisfied that he was out for the count, J.T. turned to Nikki. Her usually clear blue eyes were cloudy with confusion and the haze of too much alcohol.

"Are you all right, honey?" he demanded as he touched her cheek in a gentle gesture. To his horror, her eyes filled with tears. Hell.

He pulled her into his arms then looked over her head to Tucker. "How long has she been at this?"

"A few hours," Tucker said. "Only got bad about a half hour ago."

"Thanks for calling," J.T. said with a nod. "I'm taking her home."

"Give Lucas my regards when you talk to him," Tucker said. "Tell him he won't have to worry about Nikki coming in here again."

"No, he won't," J.T. said shortly. "She'll be back in over my dead body."

Tucker nodded his satisfaction, and J.T. gathered Nikki under one arm, pressing her against his side. He urged her from the bar, keeping her in the protective shelter of his embrace until they were outside.

When he got to his car, he opened the back door and gently helped her in. She offered no resistance and crawled onto the seat, lying down and curling her knees protectively against her chest. He stood there looking at her for a long moment, his jaw clenched until he thought his teeth might break.

J.T. turned and nearly ran into Toby.

"I'll head back over to the station," Toby said. "You go ahead and take her home."

J.T. nodded. "Thanks, man."

"You bet."

J.T. walked around to the driver's side and got in. They rode to her house in silence. He glanced over his shoulder in the darkness to see if she was sleeping, but she was just lying there, her gaze fixed on some distant object. He sighed and turned his attention back to the road.

A few minutes later, he pulled up outside her house and cut the engine. He got out, opened the back door and reached in to pick her up. She offered no resistance and lay limply in his arms as he walked to her front door.

Hell, it wasn't even locked.

"We're going to have a talk about your safety measures," he grumbled as he elbowed his way inside.

Her silence was starting to unnerve him. For a girl who always had something to say, this prolonged no-talking thing was starting to bug the shit out of him.

He laid her on the couch and knelt down beside her. He touched her cheek and ran his finger down to her lips.

"Are you okay, honey?"

Again her eyes filled with tears. One popped over the rim of her eye and slipped down, colliding with his finger. Damn.

"Don't call me honey," she said hoarsely. "I'm not your honey. I'm not your anything. I'm nothing to you. Just an easy lay."

He damn near exploded. Only the fear of scaring her kept him from losing his cool entirely.

"Don't you *ever* call yourself an easy lay," he ground out.

She shrugged. "What else would you call someone who all but forced you to have sex with her?"

Sarcastic and acerbic. It was always how she'd dealt with situations that left her at a disadvantage.

"I have a lot I want to say to you, Nikki, but damn if I'm going to do it when you won't remember it the next morning. So what I'm going to do is get you undressed and in bed. But tomorrow? We're going to talk, and I don't give a damn if you have the worst hangover in history. It won't get you out of this."

She gave him a faint smile. "Sometimes when you talk to me, it's almost like I belong to you. It's nice." Then her smile faded. "But I'll never belong to you. I don't belong to anyone."

She closed her eyes but not before he saw the renewal of moisture.

His chest heavy and aching, he picked her up again and carried her into the bedroom. She didn't stir as he undressed her then tucked her carefully into bed.

For a long moment he stood at her side, staring down at her in confusion. She spoke of belonging to him, of *wanting* to belong to him, as though she held deeper feelings, beyond a crush or sexual attraction.

Had he gotten her intentions wrong all along? Was the brazen, sex-kitten act just a cover-up for deep-seeded insecurities? Okay obviously the sex-kitten act was a farce.

She saved herself for you.

If it were any other woman, he'd read a lot into that fact, but with Nikki, he'd never been sure of anything. She moved too fast, made his head spin and generally kept him in a state of befuddlement.

What if she did want more? What if it wasn't all a game? What if he'd fucked it all up before he realized he'd even had a chance?

He lowered his head and kissed her temple, letting his lips linger there for a long moment.

"I'm sorry," he whispered. "So damn sorry."

After touching her cheek one last time, he turned and walked out of the bedroom toward the living room. He'd crash on the couch, and then tomorrow he'd find out what the hell had prompted tonight's uncharacteristic drunken binge.

Even though he had a bad feeling he knew.

Chapter Six

Nikki woke to a pounding head and a tongue that was dry and swollen, sticking to the roof of her mouth like fly paper. She was naked. In her bed.

Shame crowded into her mind until she wanted to scream. So much for not being her mother's daughter.

She fought to try and remember what happened last night. She remembered drinking too much and having to force herself to swallow the nasty crap. The rest of the evening was fuzzy, though she did remember being pulled off the bar by a guy she'd never seen before.

Fear took hold. Please, please don't let her have had a one night stand with him.

She scrambled out of bed, inspecting it for signs that she hadn't been alone in it. Her stomach lurched as she hurriedly dressed, and she had to breathe deeply to keep from having to hang her head over a toilet.

She brushed her teeth then doused her face with water until some of the cobwebs cleared. Then she ventured out of her bedroom, afraid of what she might find in the living room.

When she saw J.T. sitting on the couch, TV remote in hand, she sagged in relief. No matter what he might think of her, he wouldn't have allowed anything to happen to her.

He turned to stare at her, his expression indecipherable. Unable to hold his gaze, she ducked and headed for the kitchen.

"Oh no you don't," J.T. said as he strode after her.

He touched her shoulder then let his fingers slide over her skin before turning her around to face him.

"How are you feeling?" he asked, though his expression told her he knew damn well how she felt.

"Like shit," she said bluntly.

He nodded. "I'm not surprised. That was one hell of a drunk you threw last night. Want to tell me what's going on?"

She almost laughed. Would have if it wouldn't have split her head wide open. She shrugged indifferently. "Nothing's going on. Just decided to give the public what they expect."

His eyes glittered dangerously. "And what do they expect, Nikki?"

She shrugged again, and his hand tightened on her shoulder. She was pissing him off. Not that it was anything new.

"Drunken whore. Like mother, like daughter." She would have shrugged again, but his grip prevented her.

He cursed under his breath, but the words still stung her ears. "You're not a whore or a drunk, Nikki. Why the fuck would you want people to think you are?"

She lifted a brow and stared straight back at him. "What else would you call a quick fuck?"

J.T.'s face darkened in fury. He spun her around and all but shoved her out of the kitchen and back into the living room. He sat her on the couch and plopped down beside her.

"Cut the crap, Nikki. You were a virgin. I was your first."

She couldn't breathe. It hurt too much. She hadn't wanted

him to know, hadn't wanted him to have that kind of power over her.

Then he cupped her cheek, his touch so gentle, she wanted to cry. He nudged at her chin until she was forced to meet his gaze.

"I hurt you, honey, and I'm so damn sorry. It shouldn't have been like that. It should have been special, not a quickie on my office desk."

"It was my choice," she said defiantly.

"But why was *I* your choice?"

She refused to look at him even though he held her chin as he stared at her.

"Nikki, look at me," he ordered.

She let her gaze flicker back to him. "Does it matter? I didn't even think you'd know. And who would believe I was a virgin anyway?"

"I would," he said quietly. "And damn it, Nikki, you should have told me. I could have hurt you badly. If it had been someone else, someone who didn't have your pleasure or best interests at heart, it could have been a lot worse."

"But it wasn't," she said. "Everything was just fine. My first time was all I could hope for, and now I no longer have my pesky virginity to worry about. I can lose the hang-ups over who the first guy will be and go out and have fun."

J.T. frowned, and he gripped her shoulders and shook her slightly. "Can you be serious for two seconds here? This isn't a game. I know damn well you don't take sex that lightly. Why are you acting so goddamn flip?"

Pain centered in her chest and spread at an alarming rate. Rose up her throat until she couldn't breathe. "I was being serious," she whispered. "There was only one man I wanted. I thought...I thought he would be different than all the others. I thought he could see past who my mother was and see *me*. But in the end, I was just another quick fuck. Nobody important. Certainly no one he'd ever settle down with."

J.T. looked as though she'd just slapped him. He released her chin and stared at her with a combination of shock and horror. And she hadn't thought she could hurt any more than she already did.

She rose abruptly from the couch, folding her arms protectively across her middle.

"I want you to leave, J.T. We have nothing more to say to each other. You won't have to worry. I've gotten the message. I won't be stalking you anymore."

He was on his feet in two seconds, pressing into her space. She backed warily away.

"Now you wait just a damn minute, Nikki," he growled.

They were interrupted by the doorbell. She turned swiftly to answer it, relieved to be saved the confrontation. What else was there to be said? He'd made his point. She got it. No need to beat her over the head.

She yanked open the front door to see Zane standing there, hands shoved into his pockets.

"Hey, Nikki," he said in a gentle voice. "I heard you had a rough night."

To her eternal disgust, she burst into tears.

Zane pulled her into his arms. "Hey now, it's okay. I'll take you out to the ranch. Jasmine was worried about you."

She nodded against his chest.

"J.T. still here?" he asked.

She pulled away and scrubbed at her face. She started to ask how he knew J.T. was here, but then she looked beyond him to see the squad car in her drive. Great. Now the whole damn town would know he'd stayed over. Not that she gave a shit, but J.T.'s reputation would suffer, no doubt.

She turned in time to see J.T. walk up behind her. "You should get your car out of my driveway," she said acidly. "Whatever will people think? You can't have everyone thinking you've been a round with the town whore."

J.T.'s face whitened, and anger glittered in his dark eyes. "That's enough, Nikki."

She turned back to Zane. "Can we go?" she pleaded. She didn't want to stay here another minute.

"Sure," Zane said. "Go on and get in the truck."

"Wait a minute. You're not going anywhere," J.T. said in a frustrated voice. "We've got a lot to talk about."

She ignored him and walked at a fast clip out to Zane's truck. As she got in, she could see the two men talking and then J.T.'s nod. A few seconds later, Zane slid into the driver's seat and started the engine.

He gave her a look of sympathy then reached over to squeeze her hand. "It'll be okay, Nikki. You can stay out at the ranch as long as you need to."

"Thanks, but there's no need," she murmured. "I'm leaving Barley."

Chapter Seven

J.T. sat in his office, his sweltering office, head in his hands, elbows propped on his desk. Nikki had been holed up at the Sweetwater Ranch for two days, and when he'd finally gotten tired of getting the runaround on the phone, he'd driven out, only for Jasmine to refuse him entry. He was seriously tempted to go out with a warrant. But then he'd piss off Seth and Zane and ruin a perfectly good friendship. His only hope was that Nikki would eventually calm down and have a rational conversation with him.

His cell phone rang, and he reached for it, irritated by the hope that it was Nikki. He frowned when he saw an unfamiliar number on the LCD screen. Flipping it open, he brought it to his ear and uttered a brisk hello.

"J.T., it's Lucas. We need to talk, man."

Fuck.

He sucked in a deep breath. "Hey, man," he greeted, trying to keep his voice light and unaffected. "What's up?"

"I need you to tell me what the fuck is going on with Nikki," Lucas said, cutting straight to the point. "She said she's leaving Barley. For good."

J.T.'s stomach bottomed out. "What?"

"You mean you didn't know? I thought you were keeping an

eye on her for me. She's upset, and I don't know what the fuck is going on. All I got out of her is that she's packing up and going. I tried to get her to agree to wait until I could get leave so I could at least help her and find out what the fuck happened, but she's determined to haul ass out of there as soon as possible. I need you to sit on her, J.T. I don't want her going anywhere until I can get there."

J.T. groaned. Christ. He was going to have to come clean with Lucas. No way he could keep his best friend from finding out what happened.

"What aren't you telling me?" Lucas demanded when a long silence ensued.

J.T. sighed. "It's complicated."

"If it involves Nikki, I doubt it's simple," Lucas growled. "Cut the shit and tell me what's going on."

"I think I'm in love with her," J.T. said in a low voice. And then he nearly let his head drop to the desk. What a dumbass. You didn't go around spouting shit like that out of the blue. And where the hell had it come from anyway? Was he in love with Nikki?

Haven't you always been, you dumb shit?

Lucas's silence was starting to unnerve J.T. He was probably coming up with a list of classified methods of torturing J.T.

"What do you mean you *think?*" Lucas snarled. "Either you are or you aren't. Are you the reason she's out at the Morgans' crying her eyes out?"

Crying? Shit. Nikki didn't cry. Or at least she never had before. She had perfected her you-can't-hurt-me exterior. It seemed only J.T. had the power to upset her so badly.

"It's...complicated," J.T. murmured.

"Hell yes it's complicated," Lucas yelled into the phone. "What the fuck have you done? I trusted you, man. I asked you to look after her, not fuck around with her emotions. I tell you what. You stay the fuck away from her. I'll handle this. I'll get there even if I have to go AWOL. You just stay the hell away from her."

J.T. gripped the phone in his hand. No, he'd spent too much time away from her as it was. That had been his mistake. Trying to avoid her, trying to deny the attraction between them. In doing so, he'd hurt her.

"No, Lucas. I'll handle this," J.T. said firmly.

He hung up with Lucas cursing in his ear and threatening fourteen kinds of bodily harm. J.T. took a deep breath as he stood. First he needed to go take a shower. He smelled like a goat and looked like he'd gone three rounds with a Sumo wrestler.

On his way out the door, he opened his cell phone to call Seth. He needed to make damn sure Nikki would still be there when he got out to the ranch. He also needed to make sure Seth knew he wasn't going away this time. He'd arrest the whole damn household if he had to.

Nikki brushed out her long hair then pulled it back into a ponytail. It looked odd without the pink stripe. She'd gotten used to it, even a little attached to it. She shrugged. It had been fun, and she'd done it to get a reaction out of J.T. There didn't seem to be a point anymore.

She dressed in a long T-shirt Jasmine had given her then pulled on her baggy jeans. She felt swallowed up, but then until her return to Barley, she'd always dressed unassumingly with the intention of drawing the least amount of attention as possible.

Squaring her shoulders, she headed down the stairs to say goodbye to Jasmine and Seth. Zane was supposed to drive her into town so she could pick up her stuff from the house and get her car from Tucker's.

Leaving shouldn't bother her so much. It wasn't as if she had any attachment to this town. God, why should she? No one had ever gone out of their way to make her or Lucas feel welcome. Her brother had been right. She should have never come back. There was nothing here for her.

As she hit the bottom of the stairs, Seth met her, a grim expression on his face. There was a hint of concern, and she frowned as she looked up at him.

"J.T.'s here," he said.

Her chest tightened, and no matter how badly she wanted to be calm and cool about it, she couldn't disguise the jump of excitement. Apparently she harbored serious masochistic tendencies.

"He said he won't leave until he sees you," Seth continued.

Her shoulders sagged.

Seth put a gentle hand on her arm. "You don't have to see him, Nikki. Zane and I can make him leave. He won't like it, but it can be done."

She shook her head. "No. I don't want to be the cause of problems between you. You've been friends for too long."

"I can always sic Jasmine on him," he said with a grin.

She laughed, and it was the first time she'd smiled since before Zane had brought her out to the ranch.

"No, I'll see him. I want to say goodbye."

Seth nodded. "You know if you ever need anything, all you have to do is pick up the phone, okay?"

"Thanks," she said in a soft voice. "I really appreciate all you, Jasmine and Zane have done. And I'm sorry for thinking you were such a bastard in the beginning."

Seth chuckled.

Drawing a fortifying breath, Nikki moved past Seth and toward the living room. J.T. was there, pacing, his movements agitated. Zane was there too, and he looked at Nikki in question when he saw her. She nodded that she was okay, and Zane reluctantly left the room.

J.T. looked up and saw her, and she could swear relief flashed in his eyes.

"Nikki, thank God."

He crossed the room and would have taken her in his arms, but she stepped back, putting her hands out to ward him off. It was hard enough to face him. No way she wanted him touching her.

"We need to talk, honey."

"Okay. Talk."

He shook his head. "Not here. Let me take you home. Zane said he was running you to the house anyway. I can do that. We can talk in private, and if afterward you still don't want anything to do with me then I'll leave."

She stared suspiciously at him. "Promise?"

He held up two fingers. "Swear."

She let out a little sigh. "All right. You can take me home. Let me just say goodbye to the others."

"I'll wait out in the truck," he said.

After saying goodbye to Zane, Jasmine, Carmen and Seth, Nikki slid into J.T.'s truck and braced herself for the inevitable lecture. To her surprise, they drove back to town in silence. He didn't even look her way. He kept his hand curled tight around the steering wheel, tension radiating from him in waves.

It reminded her of the way he'd driven her to his house that night her mother had flown the coop. He'd been so incredibly gentle with her but so angry at her mother. Rage had simmered from his big body, and he'd driven home much like he was doing now. Face etched in stone, hands drawn so tight his knuckles were white.

Even with the tension so thick she could barely breathe, a smile softened her mouth. That was the night she'd fallen in love with J.T.

Oh, it had started as nothing more than a girlish form of hero worship, but over time her feelings had grown. This time...this time she'd vowed to do something about the current of attraction that flowed between them.

And it had been a complete and utter disaster.

She sighed glumly and wondered how long it would take for J.T. to say his piece so she could nod and say whatever just so she could leave to lick her wounds in solitude.

They pulled into her drive, and he cut the engine. Not looking her way, he got out and came around to her side. She stepped from the truck, but he didn't touch her as they walked to her front door.

Why was she dreading this so much? Maybe because saying goodbye to the only man she'd ever loved was tearing her heart right out of her chest?

Love sucked. No two ways about it. Maybe her mother had it right. Never give yourself to one man. Much too messy and painful. Play the field. Have it all. Protect yourself at all costs.

She walked into her living room and sank down on the couch. Whatever J.T. had to say, she hoped he'd make it quick.

She was already steeling herself for the apology. The regret he'd show over what happened between them. And then the whole *You're young, you have your whole life ahead of you, you'll find someone else* speech.

Gee, she could hardly wait.

"Nikki, look at me," he said softly.

He knelt in front of her and touched her cheek. That loving gesture was her undoing. Despite her vow not to cry in front of him, not to let him know how much he'd hurt her, tears slipped down her cheeks.

He cupped her face in his big hands and kissed the tears away from both sides of her face. She flinched and yanked away from him. Was he just trying to kill her? Twist the knife a little deeper?

"What do you want, J.T.?"

"We need to talk about us," he said. "I need to know why you waited, why you chose me. I need to know how you feel about me."

She reared back and glared at him. Either he had to be the dumbest man on earth, or he was being unnecessarily cruel. Right now she was thinking it was the former.

"Oh no," she said with a shake of her head. "I've laid it out, put myself on the line too much already. No way I'm giving you that kind of ammo. You have to be the stupidest man I've ever met if you have to ask such a dumb question anyway."

He laughed. The bastard actually laughed. Here she sat dying on the inside, and all he could do was laugh? She shoved angrily at him, but he refused to budge.

"Okay, I can take a hint. You've made all the moves, and yes, I'm a complete dumbass, Nikki. You knocked me for a loop. I honest to God didn't know if I was coming or going when you were around."

"That's easy. You were going. Running," she muttered.

His expression sobered. "Yeah, I know, honey. I'm sorry. More than you'll ever know. But I need to know if you care about me or if this was just a game. I need to know if it was more than just sex and a good time."

She knew she couldn't control the hurt that flashed in her eyes, and he saw it, because just as quickly, she saw regret in his as once again he managed to stick his foot right down his throat.

"I know it must have looked like I was some silly little nympho on the hunt for a cock. But you have to know that sex has never been a game for me. You know what my mother was," she said softly. "I was a virgin, J.T. A twenty-two-year-old virgin. Like those are common these days?"

He cupped her cheek. "But why me, Nikki?"

Well hell, it didn't really matter at this point. She'd lost any and all pride over this fool. In for a penny, in for a pound. Besides, she wouldn't ever have to see him again.

"Because I love you," she said defiantly. "I've loved you forever, J.T., and there was never anyone else for me. I wanted you to be the first...the only."

He opened his mouth to speak as his eyes widened in shock, but she cut him off.

"I know what you're going to say. I'm too young. I don't know what I want. I'm naïve and foolish. You can say all you want, but it doesn't change the facts. I'm *not* naïve or stupid. I grew up a long damn time ago, J.T. But I'll tell you this. I'm through waiting around on you to wise up and pry the corncob out of your ass. I'll go be miserable someplace else."

She was silenced by his lips sweeping over hers,

demanding, hard but loving. So loving and tender. His hands shook as they framed her face.

"I had to be certain," he said in a shaky voice. It was dark and husky, catching and stumbling over the words as he spoke. "I thought I was a fling, a diversion, someone to bide your time with until you moved on."

"Yeah, well who says you aren't," she grumbled.

He laughed again, and then something dark and primitive shadowed his face. "I love you, Nikki. God knows I fought it tooth and nail, but damn if I don't love you with every piece of my soul. I'm afraid to even go back and figure out how long I've loved you. I'm not sure I'd like the answer."

She glanced skeptically at him. Her heart pounded a little harder, but she was too afraid to hope.

"Don't look at me like that, honey. I'm so sorry I hurt you. I swear if you'll give me a chance, I'll never hurt you again. Okay, maybe I will, but I won't mean to, and I'll spend every day of my life making sure you know how much I love you."

Her eyes widened in wonder. "W-what are you saying, J.T.?"

"That you're mine," he said fiercely. "I want you with me always. I want you to marry me. Have my babies...eventually. Well, preferably before I turn forty, because Jesus, how else would I be able to keep up with them?"

"Marry you? You really want me to marry you? You love me?"

He leaned in and kissed her again, his lips moving over hers, his tongue sweeping in, tasting her as she tasted him.

When he pulled away, she saw the truth in his eyes, and it nearly flattened her.

"Marry me, Nikki. Lucas can't very well kill me if I'm his

brother-in-law, right?"

A broad smile attacked her face, pushing her lips upward, so high she could feel it in her cheeks.

"You really love me," she said in wonder.

"I really do," he said with a smile.

He got up from the floor and slid onto the couch next to her. He pulled her onto his lap and held her against his chest, stroking his hand up and down her arm and then her body.

"I'm glad I was your first. I just regret how it happened. On my desk. Jesus Christ, Nikki. You deserve better than that."

The self-condemnation in his voice made the ache in her chest swell even further.

"You could make it up to me," she murmured. "I have a perfectly good bed."

His grip tightened around her. She could feel the tension boiling in his veins. She smiled. He wanted her all right.

Then she felt herself swept into his arms as he charged toward her bedroom.

Chapter Eight

Nikki felt at a distinct disadvantage this time. As J.T. laid her tenderly on the bed, his eyes glowed with...love. God, love!

She felt more in control when she was doing her vamp act. Sexy and wanton like nothing in the world mattered to her. But this mattered. It mattered so much.

It irritated her that she felt so damn vulnerable all of a sudden. Just like the shy virgin she'd been a few days ago.

"What are you thinking?" J.T. asked gently as his fingers brushed across her face.

For a moment she considered slipping back into her she-sex act. But J.T. would see through her like a piece of plastic wrap.

"I'm nervous," she managed to say without choking on the words.

His gaze softened. And then he kissed her. Warm, sweet, his lips moving delicately across hers, like the touch of a feather.

His heat bled into her skin, infusing her with confidence she badly needed.

He reared back on the bed long enough to tug his shirt off. It went sailing across the room, and then he shimmied out of his pants.

When her avid gaze fastened on his cock, she couldn't help but lick her lips. He groaned aloud.

"You have to stop that, honey. I'm only a man. A Neanderthal, even. You can't look at me like that and expect me to act civilized."

She grinned. "Screw civilized."

"I want to take this nice and slow," he said as he eased down over her body. He began working at the buttons on her oversized shirt. "I want to love you like you deserve to be loved. I want it to be good for you, sweetheart."

She raised her head up and kissed him. "It hasn't been bad with you, J.T. It's been wonderful. You're the only one with the hang-ups over how I lost my virginity."

He grimaced as he pulled her shirt apart. "Don't remind me that I took you on my desk."

She pried her arms out of her shirt, and then he went to work on her bra. He shoved it up over her breasts and then lowered his mouth to one straining nipple.

A shiver worked down her spine as his wet tongue circled the puckered nub. He sucked lazily at it. Warmth bloomed in her pelvis. Her pussy burned, and her clit tightened with need.

He lifted himself off her so he could peel her jeans down her legs. His fingers hooked into the lacy band of her underwear, and soon it was gone as well.

He settled back between her legs, his cock brushing against her quivering flesh. She spread herself wider and squirmed impatiently.

But he wouldn't be hurried.

His chest pressed against hers, but he was careful to keep his full weight from her even as she wanted him, all of him. His hands stroked through her hair, and he frowned as he undid her ponytail.

"You got rid of the pink."

"Yeah. It was silly."

He shook his head. "I liked it. It was you. Vibrant. Bright."

"Oh, come on. It drove you crazy."

He smiled. "*You* drive me crazy, honey. And I love every minute of it."

She smiled back. "I'll consider getting it back. Maybe purple this time."

"No, I like the pink. Don't forget the glitter."

"Shut up and kiss me," she growled.

"With pleasure," he murmured as his lips swept downward.

She opened her legs and then circled his waist, locking her ankles at the small of his back.

"Please, J.T. Don't make me wait," she begged. "I want you so much. I've waited so long for this."

His elbows on either side of her face, he arched his hips, bringing his erection into contact with her pulsing entrance.

"I love you," he whispered as his lips took hers again.

She melted against him, his sweet words like a balm. All the pain of the past disappeared, and hope radiated from her soul. Warm, giving, beautiful.

And then he slid inside her. So gentle. So tender. Tears clogged her throat as he paused against her, allowing her time to adjust to his size.

"You okay, honey?" he asked as he looked down at her. There was so much love in his eyes that she was afraid her chest might bust wide open.

She circled his neck with her arms and pulled him down to her. She took his mouth in a hot, breathless kiss, pouring every ounce of her passion, her love, into the gesture.

Their lips tangled, and their mouths moved heatedly as his hips flexed between her legs. He retreated, nearly pulling out completely, and then slid forward in one long, delicious thrust.

She closed her eyes and reveled in the feel of his complete possession. Yeah, what they'd had before was sex. Good sex. But this? This was making love. It was like the first time all over again. Could you lose your virginity more than once?

"You're so beautiful," he said in a hoarse voice.

Her fingers dug into the short hair at the nape of his neck then moved lower, splaying out over his back, digging into his shoulders as her pleasure mounted.

He moved faster now but still with exquisite gentleness. There was an unbearable tightening in her groin as her orgasm slowly built. No flashpoint this time. No sudden surge to completion. Slowly and leisurely, the tension built higher and higher.

Her breath came in agonized spurts as she struggled against the pressure. He was swollen inside her, heavy and engorged. He touched every part of her, sliding against the sensitive walls of her vagina. Each thrust, each time he dragged his cock over her throbbing tissues, she felt an incredible burst of pleasure.

"J.T.!" she gasped.

"I'm here, honey. I've got you. I'll always have you."

"I love you," she whispered. "I love you!"

Her words sent them both over the edge, plunging into deep, dark waters. Pleasure, blinding and hot, splintered deep in her pelvis, rushed outward in twenty different directions.

He tensed against her. His cry split the room. Then her cry mingled with his as they gave in and let go.

He gathered her close in his arms, his weight pressing her into the bed. She wrapped her arms tighter around him so he wouldn't move.

Finally he raised his head and started to move off her. She whimpered in protest and held on.

"I'm too heavy for you," he murmured.

Gripping her around the waist, he rolled until he was on bottom and she was sprawled across his chest.

"But you can lay all over me for as long as you want," he added.

She smiled but was too tired and wrung out to do more than snuggle deeper into his arms. She tucked her head under his chin and kissed the damp skin of his chest.

"Did you mean it, J.T.?" she whispered.

"Mean what, honey?"

"That you love me and want to marry me."

His hand tugged her head upward until her lips were just inches from his frown.

"Never doubt it, Nikki mine. You're stuck with me forever, because there is no way in hell I'm ever letting you go now."

She smiled and kissed away his frown. "Hold me? I just want to sleep for a while. I haven't slept in nights."

He tugged her back down against his chest and smoothed a hand through her hair. "Then sleep, sweetheart. Right here, with me, and know that I love you."

Her eyes fluttered drowsily, and strangely she felt like crying all over again. Happy tears. When had she ever cried happy tears?

They leaked from her eyes and slid over J.T.'s bare chest.

"Hey," he said softly as he lifted her head so he could look her in the eye. "What's that for?"

She smiled a watery smile then leaned down to kiss him. "Nothing. I'm just happy."

He smiled back. "Okay then, that's all right, I guess. Now get some sleep, honey. You're going to need all the rest you can get because I don't plan on letting you out of bed for at least a week."

She dove back into the comforting warmth of his embrace and closed her eyes. Maybe dreams did come true. Even for girls like her.

Chapter Nine

J.T. woke to a sweet, warm body draped across his chest, her legs tucked between his. They were all tangled up like two mating love bugs, and damn if that didn't bring the stupidest grin to his face.

Unable to resist touching Nikki, he stroked a hand through her long hair and frowned again over the missing pink stripe. It had grown on him. Just like she had.

He relaxed and enjoyed the feel of her in his arms, nestled into his body like she was made for him. A perfect fit.

Yeah, he was too damn old for her, but at this point, he wasn't going to argue the blessing of having such a beautiful, vibrant woman swear she was in love with him. And he sure as hell wasn't going to let that keep him from spending the rest of his life loving her in every imaginable way possible.

A noise from the living room made him tense. Had he locked the door when they'd come in yesterday? Hell if he could remember. He knew he'd been pissed that it hadn't been locked when they'd come in, but after that, he didn't remember anything beyond making love to Nikki.

Before he could ponder whether or not he should get up and investigate, the bedroom door flew open, and a very large, very pissed-off Lucas charged in.

He couldn't be sure who was more stunned. Him or Lucas.

Lucas's mouth fell open, and then his face tightened in rage.

"You son of a bitch!"

Nikki jumped in his arms, her eyes flying open.

"Shhh honey, it's okay," he soothed.

"No the hell it isn't okay," Lucas bellowed.

Nikki rolled off of him, grabbing for the covers to hide her nudity. Her face was bright red with embarrassment. She looked downright mortified.

Lucas stalked forward, and J.T. braced himself for impact. Then Lucas stopped and cast a disgusted look down at the bed.

"For God's sake, get some clothes on so I can beat your ass properly."

If he wasn't so sure that Lucas was going to do just that, he'd laugh. He cast a wary glance over at Nikki before rolling out of bed.

Nikki launched herself toward Lucas, the sheet wrapped tight around her body.

"Lucas, no! Stop, please. You can't just barge in here like this and threaten J.T."

Lucas growled, but J.T. noticed he curtailed his anger when he looked at Nikki. His entire gaze softened, and he reached out to touch her cheek.

"I'm going to kick his ass, Nikki, and he knows it. He's been expecting it. Why the fuck else would he be in bed with you when he knew damn well I was coming home?"

"Lucas, please," she pleaded. "I love him. Don't do this."

He put a finger to her lips. "J.T. doesn't need you protecting him. If I don't kick his ass now and get it out of my system, there ain't a hope I'll ever be able to stomach him. He took advantage of you. He was supposed to be protecting you."

"But—"

"Nikki, honey, let it go," J.T. said as he dragged his pants on. "I want you to stay here, okay?" He leaned over and kissed her, hard. "Trust me."

Her eyes were troubled, and her bottom lip was firmly caught between her teeth as he started to follow Lucas from the room.

When they hit the living room, Lucas gestured curtly toward the door. "Outside."

J.T. sighed but followed. This wasn't going to be pretty, but it was necessary. Lucas was one pissed-off son of a bitch right now. Yeah, he could hold his own, but both of them were going to hurt before it was over with.

He barely cleared the door before Lucas grabbed him and tossed him off the porch. He landed with a thump, and Lucas came after him.

"You bastard," Lucas gritted out as he landed a fist to J.T.'s jaw.

J.T. swung, bloodying Lucas's lip and knocking him back. J.T. scrambled up and circled Lucas warily.

"Don't you think she's had enough hurt in her life?" Lucas demanded as they stepped around each other. "You made her cry, you son of a bitch. Our mother couldn't make her cry. All the taunting and abuse she suffered at the hands of this town didn't make her cry. *You* made her cry. I'll never forgive you for that."

J.T. sighed. "Yeah, I did, man. I'm a lousy bastard." He broke off when Lucas swung again. He ducked, but Lucas's other fist connected with his nose.

J.T. went sprawling, but he got up just as quickly and lunged for Lucas. They went down in a heap, rolling in the dirt as they fought for position. J.T. punched him in the gut, and Lucas grunted.

"You don't deserve her. No one in this piece of shit town deserves her," Lucas growled.

J.T. rolled off Lucas and scrambled to his feet.

"You're right, Lucas. I don't deserve her. But I love her. She loves me."

"Oh, so now you love her. What happened to *I think I love her?*"

"I'm a goddamn idiot," J.T. said. "What do you want me to say? I love that girl, and nothing you say or do is going to keep me away from her. You got that? Do your worst, Lucas, but remember that you're trying to beat the shit out of the man your sister loves. I don't think she'll forgive you for that."

Lucas's shoulders sagged, and a murderous gleam entered his eye. "Fucking pussy," he grumbled. "Hiding behind a woman."

J.T. grinned. "There are worse things than hiding behind Nikki. She could take you, I think."

Lucas rubbed a hand through his hair and let out an exasperated sigh.

"Hey, dude, are you AWOL?" J.T. couldn't keep the concern out of his voice.

Lucas smiled. "Nah. My CO has a baby sister too. He was only too happy to let me go kick some ass."

"Well then, instead of me kicking your ass, why don't we go out and have a drink to celebrate the fact that I'll be your brother-in-law."

"You kick my ass?" Lucas sputtered. "I was going easy on you because I didn't want to permanently injure the guy Nikki thinks she's in love with."

J.T. glared at him.

"Married? For real?" Lucas asked as if he'd just caught that part. "You're marrying her?"

"Well, the hope is that she's marrying me," J.T. said. "Now, can we get cleaned up? I'm starving."

Lucas glared at him again. "Don't say another goddamn word about why you're starving or I swear to God, I'll kill you."

J.T. chuckled. "Come on. Let's go. Nikki will be glad to see you."

Chapter Ten

Nikki sat on J.T.'s lap at Tucker's while Lucas navigated his way through the crowd, holding a pitcher of beer. He gave her a decidedly big brother indulgent smile as he plunked the beer down.

"Hey, got room for us?"

Nikki looked up to see Seth and Zane with a grinning Jasmine sandwiched between them. She stifled her laughter when she saw a very bold blue streak down the side of Jasmine's dark hair.

"Hey guys, you're just in time," J.T. said.

"In time for what?" Seth drawled. "Your ass-kicking?"

Lucas snorted. "That already happened."

Nikki reached over and punched him in the arm.

"Nikki has agreed to put me out of my misery and marry me," J.T. announced with what she could only call extreme smugness.

"Hey that's great!" Jasmine said, a wide smile on her face. She leaned over and kissed J.T. on the cheek. "Glad to see you finally wised up."

"Congrats, man," Seth offered.

Zane leaned down and kissed Nikki on the forehead. "Way to go, girl. Guess it's true what they say about determined women."

Jasmine arched one eyebrow. "Oh? And what's that?"

Zane grinned down at his wife. "That they always get their man?"

"Or men," Nikki murmured mischievously.

Seth choked on his laughter, and J.T.'s arm tightened around her waist.

"That's man singular to you, honey. Don't you forget it either."

Nikki grinned and plastered a big, sloppy wet kiss on his lips.

"Can we get on with the beer drinking?" Lucas drawled. "I've had about all the mushy shit I can take for the day."

There was a chorus of agreement from the guys as they all reached for mugs. Nikki sat back and snuggled deeper into J.T.'s arms.

The group crowded around the table, commandeered chairs from other tables, and soon they had one big crowd, laughing and drinking beer.

"Do you think you can be happy here?" J.T. whispered in her ear. "Here in Barley? I know the town hasn't been good to you, but honey, I'll always love you, and I'll always protect you."

She smiled. No, this town didn't hold any appeal to her. But she was surrounded by family, good friends and the man she loved more than anything. What else could she ask for?

The town could go to hell. As long as she had J.T.'s love, she could take on anything.

"I love you," she said simply as she stared into his dark eyes. "Wherever you are, I'll always be happy."

"Funny. I was going to say the exact same thing about you," he said in his deep, tender voice.

She closed her eyes and burrowed her face into his chest. Yeah, dreams did come true. For so long she'd been afraid to dream. Afraid to chase her dreams. But dreams only landed in the laps of the heroines in fairy tales. She didn't want a fairy tale. She wanted the real thing. She'd gone after hers.

And she got it.

About the Author

To learn more about Maya, please visit www.mayabanks.com. Send an email to Maya at maya@mayabanks.com or join her Yahoo! group to join in the fun with other readers as well as Maya: http://groups.yahoo.com/group/writeminded_readers.

Look for these titles by
Maya Banks

Now Available:

Seducing Simon
Colters' Woman
Love Me, Still
Stay With Me
Amber Eyes

Brazen
Reckless *(stand-alone sequel to Brazen)*

Falcon Mercenary Group Series
Into the Mist (Book 1)
Into the Lair (Book 2)

Print Anthologies
Unbroken
The Perfect Gift
Caught by Cupid

Coming Soon:

The Cowboys' Mistress

Color My Heart

Red Garnier

Dedication

This one is for my husband, the man who put the color in *my* heart.

You make everything beautiful.

Chapter One

Why do two colors, put one next to the other, sing?
Pablo Picasso

Billy Hendricks slammed the door of his red Toyota Camry and crossed the parking lot toward the two-story apartment complex. Looked like it was about to rain. Odd for this time of year. Clouds—heavy and angry—gathered in gray clusters above him. Good thing he'd decided not to wash the car today, he thought with a grunt, and slapped the magazine he'd picked up at the corner store to his thigh.

Taking the stairs two steps at a time, he reached the second-floor landing and heard whimpers. A figure was huddled down the hall, looking more like a sack than a human being. Frail shoulders racked with sudden, jerky movements, while sharp, heart-wrenching sobs tore into the air.

Billy moved forward, rolling the magazine into a tube and slipping it into the back pocket of his jeans. "Hey," he said gently, on his knees as he cupped one bony shoulder in his hand. "Are you all right?"

Her head snapped back and a pair of wide blue eyes that shimmered with tears looked up at him through a fringe of wet lashes. He'd expected a kid, but he found a woman.

Young, maybe in her mid twenties, with a tiny nose and a

93

very small, plush mouth. Her hair was cropped, so that maybe looking at her from behind, she'd be mistaken for a boy. Yet Billy found nothing boyish about her face. It was delicate. Pretty. Not sexy, not beautiful, but pretty all the same. It was smeared with mascara and moistened with tears.

"Are you okay?" he asked.

She stopped crying and gave one last sniffle before she wiped her hand across her face. "I'm fine."

Billy required no PhD to know she was far from fine. She looked vulnerable and lost, and by the way her shoulders slumped, he guessed she was in sore need of a friend. "You don't look fine. Can I help with anything?"

She gave him a quick once-over, as if debating whether he could deliver or not. "No, I-I'm fine. Really."

"Do you live here? Are you waiting for someone?"

She put a thumb out and pointed farther down the hall, then grudgingly said, "I'm at 221."

"Really? I'm 229." Strange he'd never seen her before. Or had he? She was small, a bit on the plain side, easily overlooked perhaps.

She tried to return his smile, but hers was brief and broken, the kind you shouldn't even bother with in the first place. "Guess I'd better get back to my place," she said as she scrambled to her feet.

Billy followed her up, noting the top of her head didn't even make it to his chin. Thunder rolled across the skies, the soft pitter-patter of rain hitting cement and the scent of dampened soil stirring in the air. "You sure you're all right?" he insisted, falling into step beside her.

She nodded, and her eyelashes pointed toward the pair of old, unlaced sneakers she wore. Billy scrutinized her profile, wondering if the pain etched on her face had been put there by a man. It pressed all his buttons in the wrong way, making him want to do something violent—maybe even illegal. Her nose was tiny as a button, and her doll-like features provided an interesting contrast to the loose green cargo pants she wore.

She halted at the door, her back to him as she opened it.

Billy lingered there as she entered, waiting for some sort of indication, a sign that she'd be all right.

She turned to him slowly, her eyes downcast. Then her lashes rose and her gaze—now a vivid, electric blue—shocked the air right out of him. And then she jumped him.

Billy staggered back from the impact of her weight, her ravenous mouth all over his face at once. His mind reeled as he clamped his hands on her arms. "Whoa, now hold on a sec."

She held on, all right. She held on tighter. Her arms firmed around his neck and her legs clenched tight around his hips, her ankles locking behind him. Her mouth—which moments ago he'd thought a tiny, delicate thing—felt like it was devouring him.

Every organ inside him froze from the shock while his cock responded with a jolt. *No one* had ever jumped him this way. He'd had come-ons. One night stands. Plenty of girlfriends.

He was tall, well-built, had a smile his female friends claimed was an open "invitation". But never in his twenty-nine years had he been attacked this way.

Her mouth felt hot, wet, frantic. Her hands moved up to clutch his face and hold him still for her voracious kisses. She rocked her hips against his, scraping his erection. She gripped him so tight if she'd had any more force in those slim hands, his jaw might have cracked.

And *fuck*. She made the most amazing sounds. Little mews that put him in a fever. In sudden response to her lusty attack, every fiber in him exploded, and his body fairly screamed at him to touch and taste the wanton female against him.

"Okay, hang in there, sweetheart."

Taking control, he grabbed a fistful of soft black hair and pulled her head back. He kissed his way up her jaw and licked her damp skin as he headed for her mouth. Hungry for it. No, starved.

Her sigh sounded almost reverent. "Oh, yes, please."

"You afraid I'll leave you like this?" he murmured and urged her lips apart with his. Their mouths blended and their tongues met in a decadent, calescent tangle. He pushed and retreated and then swept up to the roof of her mouth to leave no part of her untasted.

She trembled as he ran one big hand down her hips and grasped the side of her thigh. He could feel her warm flesh through the fabric of her pants, the lean muscles in her legs under his palm. Their tongues played, melted, and her smooth vanilla bean flavor warmed every cell in him to a burn. "God, you're so sweet. I'd be a fool to walk away right now."

With a complete lack of finesse and moves made clumsy by arousal, he moved them in and somehow managed to shut the door behind him.

The little package in his arms whimpered as he pushed her back against the door and her hips rocked restlessly against his cock. The tiny hard balls of her nipples strained against her white cotton tank top and his mouth watered at the sight.

With a deep, guttural growl, he charged for one and latched his lips around it, sucking it into his mouth along with the worn fabric. Billy was known to be a casual, laid-back kind of guy, and that was just the way he'd enjoyed sex—until her.

The woman from 221 burned for it.

She was lusty and desperate and she wanted sex now.

Even through their clothes, her pussy felt like fire, scraping up and down the length of his pained dick. The sounds she made would make one think she was dying. All of a sudden as frantic and mindless as the wanton in his arms, Billy set her down and grappled with her cargo pants while she pulled off her shirt.

He couldn't do it fast enough. Get her naked. Get inside her.

He shoved his jeans down to his ankles. His hands trembled as he tore at a foil package—which he always carried with him because frankly, a man just never knew—and then he hauled her back to him, his mouth crushing hers.

She hooked one leg around him, then the other as he boosted her up and braced her back against the wall. Wrapped around him like a vine, she frantically kissed every inch of him she could reach—his neck, his jaw, his ear. His cock twitched hungrily between their bodies and all that fragrant flesh surrounding him made something inside him snap. And Billy knew he needed to fuck her. Fuck her now.

Seizing her wandering lips, he plunged his tongue into her sweet mouth and clutched her hips to push his hard dick inside her. Holy shit, it was glory.

Silky, moist heat curled around his cock as he penetrated her.

She tensed from the intrusion and gave a wanton cry into his mouth.

A deeper, more primal, sound rumbled up his throat when she began to ride him. She clutched him and screwed herself down on him hard, her urgency evident in the sharp tips of her nails digging into his shoulders and her throaty moans and gasps. Her breasts were small, nipples pointy and quivery as she bounced over his cock, her small frame jolting at each impact.

Her whimpers filled the dense sex-tinged air around them. "Please, yes, *yes!*"

Hell yes, baby. Billy pitched his hips forward and met her thrusts, hammering her with his cock again and again. He moved his hands from her thighs to curve tightly around her ass cheeks and gained leverage to push in deeper, fuck her harder, bury himself up to the balls. He'd never fucked anyone so fast, so damned hard. It was as if he knew all she needed was a good quick fuck, and that was just what he was giving her.

When he drew back to gaze down at her, fresh tears stained her cheeks. Her eyes were pressed so tightly shut her pretty features looked slightly distorted.

Billy had an eerie sensation of not being in the room with her.

He got the distinct impression that those helpless whimpers tearing out of her at each thrust were meant for someone else. Not for him.

And he would not have it.

"Open your eyes, sweetheart," he said raggedly. "Open your eyes and look at me."

She did. Their gazes locked—hers damp and hazy, his hot as fire.

And he brushed her trembling lips with his own, and whispered, "Say Billy, baby."

He lengthened his thrusts and dug his fingers into the flesh of her ass. His cock was hard as a steel rod and she was so tight he found himself gritting his teeth to keep from coming. "Say my name just this once," he urged.

She moaned in protest, as if it would be painful to say.

He nuzzled her face with his as his breath tore out of him in hot, haggard pants. "Come on, don't be shy. I'm inside you. I know what you smell like, what your pussy feels like... Say Billy for me."

"Billy." It was just a breath, but once out, it returned with more force. "Oh, yes, Billy."

His balls throbbed, hardened like rocks from the sound of his name on her lips. He grunted, then groaned and quickened his pace, pushing against her slick grip, glorying at the fierce ripples of her pussy around his cock. "You're so tight, so fucking soaked."

And so soft in his arms.

He breathed her in with each strained breath, and her soapy, flowery scent intensified his need. She licked a path up his neck and traced a thickened, pulsing vein up to his jaw. Her mouth felt as scorching as her pussy, and when he captured it, it was to ravage her with a violent kiss she reciprocated in kind.

Undone by lust, Billy threw his head back and roared, pounding her one, two, three more times. He felt the contractions in her pussy, the long, heavy ripples of orgasm that ran across her body, and with one more stroke, he followed her.

"*Fuck!*" Reckless, uncontrollable shudders shook him to the core. And he rode it. Rode his orgasm. Pumping inside her with gradually decreasing jabs. Holding her as tight to him as possible.

Minutes later they remained locked together and struggled to catch their breaths. It took a moment for Billy's mind to clear, but once it did, he had no idea what to do next.

He didn't remember ever being in such an awkward situation before. It seemed as though neither of them wanted to be the first to pull away. Moving meant they'd have to look into each other's eyes and face the reality of what they'd just done. And what *had* they done?

He didn't even know her name. He'd been called a bastard on occasion, but he wasn't completely without scruples.

His cock was semi-hard inside her and his chest heaved against hers. He smoothed a hand down her back and felt the rounded knots of her spine as he pressed a kiss to her temple. "Better now?" he thought to ask.

She made a sound against his neck, a snort maybe. Then her chest began to vibrate and she threw her head back and laughed. Billy smiled, grunted in amusement, then started laughing with her.

Guess it *was* kind of funny. In a weird way.

"Do you have a name to match that pretty face of yours?" he asked when they had sobered.

"It's...it's Hannah."

Chapter Two

I do not literally paint that table,
but the emotion it produces upon me.
Henri Matisse

Hannah Myers added one last stroke of red to the canvas and stepped back to eye her masterpiece. An explosion of red, orange and yellow oil-paint stared back at her. She'd applied it with a heavy hand on purpose, adoring the sight of the bold, rich blobs over the canvas and the way they'd texture her work when they dried.

Yep. This was what she'd intended.

Let the world know she was pissed—and busy getting over Brad Kingman.

This was pure, simple "Fury".

She smiled at both work and title, inordinately pleased. No way in hell she enjoyed making the portraits at the studio as much as the abstracts she painted at home. Portraits were so...there.

At the studio, she put a nose where a nose belonged and couldn't diverge much from what was actually there. Unhappy customers were bad for business, after all, and Hannah needed her job badly. Portraits paid the rent, but abstracts were her life.

A loud knock at the door made her head snap toward the sound. Her heart began to pound. She checked her plastic wristwatch, realized it was 6:34, and plunked her brush with the other brushes in the watered tin can at the foot of the easel.

She untied the apron she wore, then slipped it off and draped it across the back of a couch. Her hands shook as she quickly ran them through her cropped dark hair, hoping to pretty herself up with that meager effort. Giving up when a second knock sounded, she drew in a breath and went to open up.

"Heya, doll."

Hannah stared at the blonde out in the hall. Margie Phils was the last person she'd expected to see. Flooded with disappointment, she stole a look past the older woman's bare, spotted shoulders.

Disconcerted, Margie turned her head one way, then the other. "Waiting for someone, hon?" she asked.

There was no one outside other than Margie. No gorgeous jean-clad hunk with a killer smile and eyes gentler than a whisper. Hannah sighed and stepped back to let Margie in. "I guess not," she mumbled, shutting the door behind her.

But truth was, Hannah had been hoping Billy would stop by. They'd fucked yesterday. And the day before that. And the one before that. Hell, the whole month before, ever since that time she'd gone crazy and almost raped him.

But they hadn't fucked today—and Hannah really wanted to.

Shaking her head for falling into her old ways when she swore to herself she would not, Hannah followed Margie into the living room. It was neat and cozy and bursting with color, and the adjoining open kitchen was decorated with lively pottery that hung from the ceiling.

"I just *had* to talk to someone, sweetie. I hope you don't mind? You know Rob, the electrician? The bastard's married. You hear? Married!" Margie dropped down on the couch with a sigh. "That motherfucker."

Hannah took a chair across from the couch and smiled apologetically.

Margie from 103 looked like everything Hannah didn't want to look like twenty years from now.

So beat-up.

Her clothes permanently smelled like cigarettes. Her boobs had been lifted so many times they'd nearly lost their form. She'd suntanned so much her skin looked dry and spotted. But what most appalled Hannah was the wearied, cynical attitude, the one you got after asking life repeatedly for something and having her fling your dreams back at your face—in shards.

Margie had been married four times, all of them to some kind of devil, and her affairs always seemed to take a turn for the worst. "You watch out for that little heart of yours, Hannah, or you'll end up like me," Margie had once said.

Hannah hadn't been paying much attention. But after getting said heart broken several times, she'd decided there was some genius to those words. The way things had been heading, Hannah's future hadn't looked so bright either. Failed relationships. Liars. Cheaters. Bastards. Hannah had dated them all.

She'd been left so broken, so angry after each. And it had taken the greatest bastard in the world, the one called Brad Kingman, to snap her awake—and make her realize she'd been repeating her same mistakes over and over again. She gave too much, too soon. She trusted, believed, lived in a fairy tale.

Well.

She'd changed now.

She wasn't depending on a man ever again. Even one as wonderful as Billy.

"I'm sorry about Rob, Margie," Hannah finally said, and she really meant it.

Margie sighed, adjusting her strapless tube top before her breasts managed to pop out. "Anyway. I didn't come here to talk about that asshole. I came here to ask if you're going to that thang."

"What thang?"

"You know, the yearly good neighbors party."

"Oh, that." Hannah waved her hand. Truth was, she wasn't too good with crowds. She got nervous. Claustrophobic. She stuttered and blushed and did all kinds of no-nos. And she had no desire to be seen with Billy in public. "I'm not sure, Margie."

"You haven't been to a single one since you've been here."

"I know, I know, shame on me," Hannah said, starting for the kitchen. "Do you want something?"

"Nope." Margie mumbled. As Hannah opened the fridge and poured herself a glass of water, she heard her say, "You know, there are a lot of great catches in the building... There's Lance from 117. Man, that guy is *so* hot. Did you see his new Hummer in the parking lot?"

"How could I not see that yellow box?"

Margie snickered. "I'll just bet he can fuck just like that rowdy car can take on a mountain. And then there's also Yancey—the blond guy? He's got quite a package, though I heard he goes both ways... I'm not sure how I feel about that."

Glass of water in hand, Hannah made her way back to sit, vaguely amused as Margie verbally listed the whole male population of the building. "Then there's Greg, and Phil, and the gorgeous Kent from 205. Of course why would anyone want *them* when there's Billy?"

Hannah nearly spat out her water. She coughed, slapped her chest, then set the glass down on a small round table beside her.

Margie stared. "You okay, hon?"

"I'm fine." Hannah went to pick up her brushes, intending to wash them while Margie talked. Billy. Just hearing the name made her skin prick and every cell in her body grow warm.

She'd barely made it to the sink and ran her brushes under the faucet when a knock came. Her heart accelerated tenfold, as though rather than standing, she were in a full run.

It was Billy outside. Hannah knew, she just *knew*, it was him.

Though every instinct cried out for her to rush to him, she went utterly still as Margie rose and crossed the room toward the door, humming a tune to herself.

"Billy?"

And then, then that rich, familiar rumble said, "Hello, Margie."

Weak-kneed by the sound and not even breathing, Hannah watched Billy step inside—in jeans and a black T-shirt and a smile that just knocked on her heart. His walk was a confident male swagger, his grin oozed charm, and that row of white teeth flashed in a gorgeous, sun-kissed face.

Dear lord, she kept forgetting how gorgeous he was. And the powerful effect he had on her. His dark brown hair had streaks of sunlit gold in it that brought the light out in his eyes and gifted his masculine, strong face with a friendly and approachable quality.

His nose had been broken once as a kid, he'd told her, and the slight arch to it stamped his face with even more character.

His lips were plump and sensual—a perfect mouth if she'd ever seen one.

The truth was Billy was quite simply unmatched in her eyes.

Completely edible material. Beautiful, inside and out. Her knees threatened to fold as his head turned and his warm gaze locked with hers.

"Hannah."

Hannah's smile felt so forced it actually shook on her face. "Billy."

The times she'd cried that name recently, *Oh, Billy, yes, Billy, more, Billy, please,* for some reason replayed in her mind and her nipples puckered under her shirt.

"Do you two know each other?" Margie asked, curiously eyeing one, then the other.

Billy grunted like it was obvious that they did. At Hannah's pointed scowl across the kitchen counter, he then coughed and said, "Well, we *are* neighbors and all."

"We've bumped into each other several times," Hannah quickly said.

Margie's eyebrows shot up. "Bumped into each other?"

Hannah turned red at the visual the words procured and set her brushes down on the counter. "Anything to drink, Billy?" she called, acting all nonchalant from the kitchen. At least she *hoped* she came off as nonchalant. Though one touch of her clammy hands would completely attest otherwise.

Smooth as always, Billy said, "I'm fine, Hannah. Thank you. I'm just here for some...flour."

"Oh, I'll get that for you in a second, I'm just getting this cleaned." Like hell. She didn't want him to leave. She wanted him to kiss her, hold her, touch her, make hot, noisy love to her.

"So whatcha been doing lately, Billy boy?" Margie asked.

"Not much, Margie. You?"

While they went back and forth with idle chit-chat, Hannah made a show of wiping the kitchen counter with a bedraggled cloth. She didn't want Margie to see them together, or to suspect anything. As soon as people thought they had a relationship, they'd start asking stupid questions like, "*When's the wedding?*" But dammit, Hannah didn't want Billy to leave either.

She'd been waiting for this moment all day.

He kept stealing glances in her direction, and just the way his eyes sparkled with mischief when they met hers made her hurt all over. Flushing red, she wiped the pristine, bone-colored counter with more vigor.

She wasn't at all comfortable with the way she responded to Billy—getting all itchy, lusty and achy in his presence. Her relationships up until now had been emotional roller coasters—with crashes at the end. She had no intention of a repeat. Billy knew that. Hannah had made it clear to him from the start. Or at least...from the second start.

And yet here she was, her panties soaked by the sight of him, her skin breaking into a sweat.

Hannah shouldn't have even fucked Billy in the first place. If she hadn't been so utterly devastated that time out in the hallway, she probably wouldn't have. But she had—and for one reason or another, she couldn't stop. But damn it, complications made for lousy company.

"So, Billy, you coming to the party?" Margie's question snapped Hannah out of her thoughts.

"The one tomorrow, you mean?" he asked as Hannah finally

relented from her task and slowly approached them.

"Yeah," Margie said. "Hannah's not sure she can make it, but I've been counting the days for months."

Billy's thick-lashed eyes unsettled her like two loaded guns aimed right at her. "Why can't you make it, Hannah?"

Hannah sighed. Arguing seemed pointless when she was so clearly outnumbered—plus she had no single, valid reason to provide. "I'll try, okay?"

A wily smile curved his lips. "I'll see that she does, Margie."

"Well good." Margie slapped his back in a manly way. "Now I'd better get back to my place. If you need anything, Billy, you come to Margie. I'll take care of you, honey, plus my kitchen's always stocked."

Billy's deep, vibrant chuckle as he accompanied Margie to the door made Hannah's sex twitch needily. He was just so amazing. Every itty bitty thing about him.

"Bye, Margie," Hannah remembered to say before the door closed, and she was left alone with Billy. Finally.

Feeling the heat creep up her neck, Hannah got busy and set her clean brushes beside the oil paint tubes at the foot of her easel.

When she straightened, Billy had drawn up behind her and his body warmth enveloped her like cashmere. His arms went around her waist and his chin came to rest on her shoulder. "Hey, you."

Her pussy clenched, her stomach moved, her heart sped. She breathed out a frail, "Hey."

"What's this I see?"

In silence, Hannah scrutinized her work at the same time he did. She was no Van Gogh. No one was going to pay millions of dollars for her works once she was gone. But it was her work, her little way of expressing what words could not manage to say. At least she felt it that way.

"Wow," Billy said at last. "It's pretty vibrant and...angry." He cocked his head and pressed his lips to her ear. The mist of his breath sent tickles down to her bare feet. "Who are you angry with, Hannah?"

She shifted with unease, suddenly feeling as if he'd forayed into her soul. "Me," she said.

"You? Come on, why would Hannah be angry at Hannah?"

No matter how much the temptation, Hannah was *not* going to dump her personal trash on him. She'd done that in every other relationship she'd had—and had learned her lesson the hard way. She and Kleenex had a long history together. And among the insightful, less-than-welcome lessons she'd learned, one stood predominantly from the rest: never trust a man who wants to sleep with you. Period.

Turning in his arms, she gave him a noisy kiss right smack on the lips. "No reason Hannah can't take care of." She smiled one of her best smiles. "Now what was it you were here for? Milk? Sugar? Eggs?"

He grinned—the grin that made her toes curl. He said, "Flour." Then, sheepishly, "I'm afraid I'm running out of excuses." He grazed her cheek with his knuckles before his palm cupped her jaw, the pad of his thumb stroking her lower lip. "I wanted to see you."

That husky confession did all kinds of things to her.

And all she could think of was how easy it would be...to let her guard down.

Let him in.

Tell him about her childhood, her fears, her dreams.

And be disappointed and hurt all over again.

No. She wouldn't ask for anything, wouldn't expect anything, and she would certainly not upgrade him to knight-in-shining-armor status like she'd been inclined to do with every man she'd been involved with before. There were no more of those nowadays. All she could do to safeguard herself was to keep this as casual as it was intended to be.

"You know, you might come in handy after all," she said, lightening the mood as she took a step back to scrutinize him. "I need a canvas."

"A canvas?" Oh, that look of disbelief on his face was priceless.

"Yep." She nodded with a satisfied grin. "Strip."

He arched his brows daringly. "How about I put that stuff all over you?"

"How about you shush and take your pants off?"

He chuckled, then pulled his T-shirt shirt over his head and unzipped his jeans.

Billy had an amazing body. Sculpted. Tan.

His torso was beautiful, athletic, arms and shoulders rounded with muscles, every inch of him lean and solid. His abs were perfectly defined. A path of fine, silky curls started at his navel and fanned to a wider, darker thatch below. His hips were narrow and led to a pair of long, powerful legs dusted with silky dark hairs. His penis was large, broad. The sight of it stiff and swollen as it snapped free, the skin stretched so tight it gleamed, set off needles of hunger inside her. His deep-set eyes smoldered as he watched her and tossed back the last of his clothes.

His voice was a low rasp. "Your turn."

Unable to resist him, she stepped forward, close enough to touch him. "I've wanted to touch you," she confessed. His skin felt smooth under her fingers as they danced up his chest, then down to trace the muscles on his abs. "We're always in such a hurry."

His restless hands pulled on the hem of her shirt and his breath stirred the hair at the top of her head. "I want you naked."

Her pussy contracted into a painful ache between her legs. Hannah had never wanted anyone as much as she wanted Billy. She'd never ached this way, or come as violently as she did with him.

Usually she worried too much on what she looked like naked, if she moaned just right, if her partner was finding pleasure, to really get into the act herself. But with Billy she couldn't even *think*. She could only feel—a burning hunger, a need. Pure, unrefined lust.

"Come here, let me feel you," he said once her clothes lay scattered across the floor. She stepped into his powerful arms, skin against skin. Her sensitized nipples brushed against the hardness of his chest and her pussy squeezed in tiny spasms of anticipation.

"Billy."

"I've wanted to do this all day," he murmured, his mouth on her neck as his big, solid hands moved between their bodies to cup her breasts. Shivers danced down her spine as his thumbs stroked her nipples, going around and around the pebbled peaks, then over them, grazing, pressing.

He guided her back as easily as though they were dancing a waltz and then flattened her rear against the wall, a few feet away from where her easel stood. He ran his hands down her hips as his gaze drifted to the silky V of dark hairs glowing damp at the apex of her thighs. "Open your legs for me."

Breathless with impatience, Hannah spread her legs apart,

111

surprised when he began to retreat. On a startled gasp, she asked, "Where are you going?"

He shot her a wolfish grin as he knelt down and lifted a slender paintbrush. "You put ideas into my head." He waved the slender brush in her face as he returned and paused a few inches from her, the brush poised to strike with the feathery tip toward her.

He smiled in mischief and circled her nipple with the tip, still damp from when she'd cleaned it. Hannah gasped and shuddered from the cold, moist feel of it—and the contrast it made to her fired-up body.

"You like that, don't you?" His voice was as arousing as the brush tip as he proceeded to do the same to the other puckered peak.

One would never guess Billy was no master painter. He moved the brush with slow, expert strokes. His teasing play made her muscles shake so badly she could barely stay upright.

Heat curled inside her and burned in her womb. With her head back against the wall, her chest heaved with every labored breath. "Billy, please."

"Legs wider, Hannah, I'm going to brush this baby right into you."

Hannah gasped when she felt the tip graze her clit, slowly teasing and brushing across the tender nub, up and down.

Her limbs trembled as pure, raw lust thrummed in her veins, clenched around her core. The damp coldness and gentle strokes of the brush tip on that throbbing, sensitized part of her blew her mind. Her heart thundered inside her and the air hissed out of her lungs. Her hands flattened against the wall behind her, offering her much-needed extra support. "Billy—"

"Hold on, sweetheart, I'm really loving this."

When she looked at him with heavy, misty eyes, she saw that his cock twitched against his abdomen and droplets of semen ran down the tip.

He dragged the brush lower, stroking the turgid, pink lips and the very entrance of her slit until she shuddered wantonly. Then he knelt and lowered his mouth to her clit. His lips enveloped the wet little nub and his mouth suctioned, pulling it into his heat. His tongue flicked it, up and down, up and down.

Hannah moaned and arched up to his mouth, shuddering with cold heat as something sleek and long entered her pussy. Not his finger...not his tongue...but part of the brush handle.

Gliding in and out of her creamy pussy.

Hannah screeched and her nipples stung so fiercely she had to clamp her hands on them and squeeze, her head thrashing against the wall. "Billy, fuck! Oh God, Billy."

"Hannah, sweetheart. I could come just looking at you like this."

Hannah was ready to come. More than ready. She was feverish. Moaning. Pinching her nipples. Pumping her hips against the sleek, wooden brush handle. Crying out each time Billy sucked on her clit.

His words vibrated against her sex. "I'd love to sink this baby right into your ass while I shove my cock into your pussy. Would you like that, darling?"

The thought of the brush buried in her backside while Billy pounded into her with his hard shaft thrust her right over the edge. Her sex clenched around the brush handle and a cry tore out of her as she exploded.

"Thatta girl, come for me, Hannah." The hot, gruff words were spoken against her clit before he rolled it under his tongue and worked her through her orgasm. Spasms rocked her, waves and waves of pleasure crashed through her, loosening her muscles, shooting through her veins.

Withdrawing the brush from inside her, he cupped the inside of her thighs and delved his tongue into her wet pussy— hot and creamed—stroking her walls and causing even more tremors to come forth. She clutched the back of his head and pumped her hips, trembling in what seemed like a never-ending bliss. He drank her up with wild thirst and growled when she gave one last sobbing cry.

Minutes afterward, Hannah smiled up at the ceiling, laboring to breathe. Billy came up to kiss her. She could taste herself in his mouth, and the frantic hunger in him.

His hands shook violently as he cradled her cheek and stabbed her mouth with deep, ravenous thrusts of tongue. Hannah pushed him back at arm's length and noticed the quick flare of his nostrils, the sheen of sweat across his brow. His chest heaved. His arms were stiff by his sides and corded with tension. He seemed so tightly wound-up he looked ready to explode.

"Give me that, Billy. This is *my* brush," she teased as she snatched it from him. "Now stand still, it's my turn to please you."

"Are you going to paint me, Hannah?" His voice was so gummy she barely understood him.

She pushed him back against the wall. "I'm going to color you everywhere. And torture you because deep down, I'm evil."

"I'm shaking."

Hannah chuckled. She knew him well enough by now to know he meant that as a joke, but Billy wasn't smiling. He trembled head to toe, was flushed and tense and breathing heavily. The hungry twitches of his cock gave Hannah a perverse pleasure to know she did that to him. "Shh. Quiet or I'll lose my concentration," she admonished.

He groaned. "Come on, Hannah, I'm dying here."

And this was naughty, wicked fun! "I think I'm going for orange here," she said, brush in hand. She leaned forward to tease one small, brown nipple with a circular stroke, and repeated the motion with the other.

"And blue here." The feathered tip traveled down his chest, then slowly traced a circle around his navel.

"Then definitely red here." She lowered her hand to brush up and down the thickset column of his cock. She deftly drew a line around the bloated crown and watched it jerk under her ministrations. A drop of semen emerged and she swiped it up, then spread it across the ruddy head. Billy's breathing had turned harsh, irregular, and scorching heat emanated from his body.

"Then I'd go for purple here," she continued. His abdomen quivered on a quickly held breath when she reached his balls and swiped across every inch of the generous sac. She was so wet again, she could feel a trickle of cream down the inside of her thigh.

He curled a hand around her wrist. "That's enough," he said in a gruff voice.

"But I'm just getting started!"

He took the brush from her and dropped it with flair. "I've been wanting to fuck you all day. Come here, Picasso." With one arm, he hauled her until she was flush against him. His lips crashed down on hers and his kiss seared her until her bones melted again.

"You wanted something in your ass, didn't you, darling?" he huskily said.

One coiled arm kept her pinned to his body as he delivered a series of rough, wet kisses up her jaw to her temple. He smoothed his other hand down her back and traced the length of her spine with the tip of one finger. He paused at the small of her back and stroked down the dent between her buttocks. "Do you think this will do?"

Hannah shuddered as a light, feathery stroke caressed the outside of her ass. Her pussy watered and tightened with little contractions. "Yes."

"Let's give it a try, hmm?" He gently pushed against the tight entrance. The unexpected pressure as he entered caused her to arch against him with a mew. He nipped her earlobe, and she could hear by his voice how perilously close to losing control he was. "Does it feel good?"

She nodded jerkily, gradually adjusting to his finger sliding deep into that part of her. The slight pain made the pleasure so much sweeter. The hungry contractions in her jealous pussy felt almost unbearable. Hannah placed her hands on his chest and wiggled against him, wanting more. His cock, his mouth on her, more of that breaching finger.

He started moving in and out, visibly straining for control as he blasted hot puffs of air against her temple. "Yeah? That good, Hannah?"

Her legs felt weak, her ass stretching to each in-and-out motion. Gasping, she rubbed her hips against the stiff cylinder pulsing between their bodies. "Yes, God, yes, it's good."

"*You're* good," he rasped, and ground his cock against her. "So damned good, baby."

"Billy please." She reached between their bodies and grabbed his cock. "I want—"

"Wait right here," he ordered.

He left her to search his clothes, then came back—all feline grace and flexing muscles—to lean against the wall and roll a condom down the length of his cock, the rubber stretching to hug every wide inch of him.

Hannah loved to watch him put it on, the way his big, tanned hands efficiently slid along his shaft as the rubber unrolled. "My dick's so hard for you, baby," he whispered.

Hannah burned, sweating, shaking, craving him more than ever. She placed her hands on his shoulders and frantically rubbed her breasts against his chest, her pussy pulsing and soaked. "Billy, I want you inside me."

He lifted his hands to her cheeks. He stroked her lips, her jaw, her temple. His gaze glowed with fierce need, but his caresses felt so tender she wanted to sigh. "Look at you," he said in a hoarse, textured whisper, "all flushed and ready for me."

He boosted her up and she instinctively curled her legs around him. His hands cupped her ass and gently lowered her to his cock. She felt the folds part, stretch as he came in. He entered slowly, letting her feel the slide of each inch, until she felt full with Billy wide and massive inside her. His hands squeezed her buttocks as he groaned. "Oh fuck, sweetheart, you're so tight."

She whimpered when he began to play again in the outskirts of her ass, teasing the entrance with tiny strokes of his finger. Hannah wiggled in his arms. "Put it inside me, Billy, please, put it inside me."

"You sure? Because I'll be pounding you hard."

Hannah gripped his shoulders and could barely exhale a breath as his finger pierced into her ass, causing her to arch. "Oh God, it feels so good."

"Oh yeah? You like that?" He curled one arm snugly around her waist as he withdrew to the head, then plunged back in with a deep thrust. "As good as this, Hannah?"

Nothing was as good as this. As good as Billy. Sheathed inside her.

Her pussy squeezed around him with a slow, milking rhythm, drawing his length in deeper. Her hands trembled violently as she cupped his face. "Billy, kiss me."

He did kiss her. He covered her lips with his and swept his tongue into her mouth, the heat and taste of him invading her.

His kiss consumed her as his tongue stabbed her in rhythm to his thrusts.

Compared to the first time they'd fucked—more like rutted like animals—the pace he set now was painfully slow. A sharp awareness knifed through her at each deep glide of his hot, satiny cock inside her. She felt weightless, and her mind swam in a haze of sensations. His soapy, sweaty scent filled her lungs until she felt invaded everywhere inside.

"Let me see how we're doing back here," he whispered, his breath warm on her face. She felt his finger leave her for the barest second, then return with a harsh plunge.

She screamed, riding him viciously, needing to come now—now that her ass stretched and her pussy burned. He twisted his finger inside her and she sobbed with pleasure, her nipples throbbing with pain.

"That feel good, baby?"

"Yes, oh yes, Billy, do it again."

He twisted into her ass again, causing her to push back against his hand, desperate to take in more when he was only sliding in about half of it. She whimpered when it almost hurt, the pleasure acute, sharp, tearing inside her. "Oh, God!" she cried.

"Take it in, Hannah, take all of me in." Lodging that finger in deep, he rammed her pussy with harsh, rampant thrusts that rattled her to the bones. "Oh fuck, I love fucking you."

She screeched as the pressure built inside her, a ball of fire ready to burst. "Yes, *yes.*"

"Fuck me, baby. Harder. Make me come. That's right, make me come, Hannah."

Hannah fucked him like her life depended on it. She screamed a sharp, ear-splitting cry when her orgasm hit her. Torrents of pleasure crashed across her body, shaking her to the core. Billy plunged in deep and followed her. His head fell back with a roar, his body jerking uncontrollably.

Hannah felt herself soar, suddenly blinded with colors. Bright fiery reds and vibrant purples and greens and blues...so many blues...

The hues were fiery, magnificent, as they exploded before her eyes, creating a masterpiece that a simple hand could never create. Like those colors, emotions tumbled inside her, torn loose from their confinement.

The way you make me feel, Billy Hendricks...

As he buried his nose into her hair and breathed in her scent, Hannah couldn't shake off the eerie sensation of being owned.

It took a while to gain complete control of her senses, and in the meantime she gloried in the safe, protected environment of Billy's arms.

He pressed his lips to her temple and murmured, "Urghm."

She giggled. "Is that supposed to mean something, Billy?"

"Yeah." He spoke at last, drawing back to look at her. "It means at what time should I pick you up tomorrow? Take you downstairs to the party?"

Hannah stiffened in his arms and her stomach cramped. "We-we said we'd keep it casual."

He flashed her a grin. "I thought we could renegotiate."

And suddenly the weight of his arms around her felt an

119

entire world heavier.

Holding her breath while a thousand thoughts scrambled inside her, she carefully unwound her body from his. She avoided his gaze, took the discarded brush to the kitchen sink and ran the water to clean it. "I don't think so," she finally said.

Billy remained against the wall, then he sighed dejectedly. His arms spread by his sides and he shook his head. "Hannah, this isn't doing it for me."

No, no, no, *no*!

Twisting the faucet closed, she set the brush down on the counter. Her eyes met his, her lips starting to tremble. "We said no dates, no staying the night, nothing except...sex. A casual summer fling sort of thing."

He took a cautious step forward, his voice threateningly low. "I know what we said, Hannah."

It seemed incredible how, with that inexorable look on his face, his dark brown hair mussed from their lovemaking, his naked body glistening with sweat, and having come twice in his arms, Hannah could still want him so much. Her breasts felt full and her body sang to his presence, and she had a crowded sensation in her chest she couldn't seem to ease no matter how deep a breath she took.

Seeking the extra support, she braced one hand on the edge of the counter to her right as she carefully weighed each word. "Billy, please let's not ruin this. If I *do* go to the party, just remember we're...friends. Okay?"

He said nothing but rather stared at her for the longest moment with an expression so intent she felt like cringing. Then he let out a long, put-out sigh and bent to pick up his clothes.

He dressed in record speed and Hannah watched with a sunken heart as he made his way to the door.

He stopped before opening it and gazed at her with a solemn, heart-wrenching look on his face. "I know someone hurt you, Hannah," he said in a deceptively soft murmur, "but I'm not him." He quietly shut the door behind him.

Based on the horrible feeling that gripped her inside, Hannah had the distinct impression things had just taken a turn for the worse.

Chapter Three

The world today doesn't make sense,
so why should I paint pictures that do?
Pablo Picasso

Music stirred the nighttime air, mingled with the sounds of laughter and voices. Wearing a simple black dress and a pair of black pumps she hadn't worn in ages, Hannah descended into the lit, sparsely decorated back gardens of their complex. The warm summer breeze stirred her hair and the knee-length skirt of her dress.

Flattening a hand on her thighs to keep her skirt in place, Hannah scanned the crowd littered across the lawn and glimpsed Margie's familiar face pop up inside the pool.

The older woman's words had skidded through her mind most of the night. Yes, there were a lot of good catches in the building.

The tall, blond Lance over by the punch bowl, the muscled Kent with his short, army-cut black hair lounging in his trunks beside the pool. And Billy. Of course Billy. His gorgeous face like a beacon amid strangers as he stood among a group of friends, amiably chatting.

Hannah froze when she spotted him and her nipples pricked in an instant. Lance might have the Hummer, but Billy

Hendricks had *every*thing.

Killer looks, personality, charisma.

He was so easy to be around.

Even now, among a group of six, he somehow managed to involve everyone in the conversation. His eyes met those of the person who spoke, his smile warm and engaging. Billy was kind. He was tender and sweet and...

Hannah stopped herself, wanting to pull her hair out in frustration. Damn it, she *knew* this would happen. She was falling for him. Hard.

Harder than ever.

Just the sight of him with his hair damp from a recent bath and those clean-cut khaki slacks slung low across his hips made her want to run to him. She had heart palpitations, weakened limbs and trouble focusing. In short, she was done for.

On her way to The Brad Kingman Disaster all over again.

She'd end up as his doormat. And not just that, but as his personal bank, too. He'd drain her of what little savings Brad— the king of bullshit himself—hadn't managed to wheedle out of her, maybe even use the same story of opening a business so they could get married. And then she'd find him in bed with a bombshell redhead—maybe even the same one Brad had fucked. And then. Why yes, then Hannah would be devastated. Again.

That time she'd walked in on Brad and his slut, getting comfy in a sixty-nine on his bed, Hannah hadn't even reached her apartment before she'd fallen apart.

And then this tall, muscled god had appeared, with faded jeans and a solid blue T-shirt. His expressive brown eyes had glistened in concern and his smile had been simply breathtaking. All Hannah had wanted right then and there was...

She wasn't sure exactly.

Maybe to know someone found her desirable. Maybe to feel connected to someone, if only for a few minutes. Maybe she'd wanted revenge, to prove to herself and to that bastard Brad that she wasn't going to let him break her.

She'd never expected to continue with the affair.

But she hadn't been able to stop thinking about Billy after that first time. Billy's deep baritone, speaking to her as he'd filled her, slammed his cock into her, played like a song in her head. Interminably.

All night she'd replayed his words in her head and suffered the effect those same words had caused all over again. Then she'd fretted over what she'd do when she saw him next. How embarrassing it would be. And yet by the second day, the thought of not seeing him seemed much worse.

Four days and three sleepless nights later, she'd decided it would be best to keep it friendly. So she'd gone by his place to ask for sugar. Like none of the three doors between them had some. He'd opened the door shirtless and wearing only his jeans, stared at her for a long moment, then he'd stepped back to let her in.

Gone speechless, Hannah had held out her tiny sugar cup with trembling hands, her every cell blooming to his presence.

His gentle yet penetrating gaze never left her face as he pushed the door shut behind her, slowly pried the cup out of her grasp, and wrapped his free arm around her waist. "Yeah. Me too," he'd whispered before he kissed her.

Oh, God, how well he'd fucked her that night...and each one after.

Yes, Billy was different.

But Hannah recalled having thought that of *all* the other guys.

Now her savings were next to zero, her pride still smarted from the blow of that no-good cheater, and if it hadn't been for Billy—she'd be in therapy by now and gone flat broke from it. But now she was needy for him instead of some psychiatrist and ached for the steady, solid feel of his body against hers, intoxicated by the way he made her feel. Hannah could not let that happen.

They'd said it would just be sex, not exclusive, not obligatory, just sex.

She snickered to herself. She'd bite her toes if what they had was just sex. Because here she was, a breath away from believing in happily ever after again.

Well. She hadn't worn this stupid dress for nothing. And as Margie had said, there were excellent catches in the building. Other than Billy.

"Don't think I've seen you before," a masculine drawl said from nearby. Turning toward the voice, she watched the tall, green-eyed Lance approach, a drink in each hand, and he slowly extended one out to her.

She accepted the offering, saying, "Hannah." She cocked her head toward the building behind her, adding, "221", and a dazzling smile to go with that.

"Lance," he said then.

Very sultrily, as if she'd been waiting for him her whole life, she whispered, "I know," and lifted the foam cup to her lips, studying all six feet of Lance with womanly appreciation. "Nice to meet you, Lance."

"Oh, the pleasure is all mine."

Was it really?

She stared at him with eyes that sparkled like those of the besotted. The solution to her problem was suddenly so obvious, Lance could've worn a sign on his forehead that read, "Your Way Out of Incoming Disaster".

Wishing to God this wouldn't be a mistake she would regret for like, forever, Hannah leaned forward and placed a hand on his shoulder. "So, Lance, is there anything real to drink around here?"

Ignoring the conversation around him, Billy watched Hannah as she laughed over something Lance said. He could hear her rich, throaty laugh all the way across the patio and he suspected she'd intended it that way. He sat on one of the foldout chairs across the lawn, his drink untouched over his knee, a hand curled around it.

Every time Lance brushed her arm or bent to touch her waist, Hannah kept stealing glances his way—as if to check if he was watching.

Hell yeah, Billy was watching.

And for a moment he felt like sending his chair flying high into the air—in Lance's direction.

Hannah had asked him to act normal at the party, friendly, so Billy had stayed away. He'd figured he wouldn't be able to keep his hands off her, so distance had seemed the wiser choice. And here he was, sitting like a trained little dog waiting for a sign to go fetch.

The thought made him grunt.

Her obsession about people not knowing about them bordered on the insane. And now, hell, now she was coming on to Lance. Right in front of Billy. Evoking a million spirals of emotions inside him, none of them welcome. Much less pleasant.

Billy wasn't stupid.

He knew she'd been hurt.

He knew she was trying to get over some heartless bastard and move on with her life.

He could see the anger that lingered inside her in each of her paintings, but he could also see, *feel*, her passion.

What they had between them wasn't normal. It was sizzling hot chemistry and more. Her reluctance to embrace it, to admit that what they had was the kind of thing a million people waited a lifetime for, was driving Billy crazy.

He couldn't quite make out the way she made him feel, but he'd never felt this way before. He ached to hold her, protect her, make love to her—not just fuck her. He'd had her so many times he'd lost count. And yet each time he did, he wanted more. All of her, all the time.

At work, Billy usually found himself daydreaming about her, anxious for the clock to move the little hand to the six, the large hand to the twelve, so he could get off and finally get to see her.

But Hannah was so guarded, spoke so little about herself. Maybe at one point in his life, more than one woman had annoyed the hell out of Billy by going on and on about what she needed, how everyone including her parents had failed to give it to her, etcetera, etcetera, etcetera. But where Hannah was concerned, Billy wanted—no, *craved* with every fiber in his being—to know more.

He wanted to know whose pictures had occupied the empty photo frames in her living room. He wanted to know who'd inspired her to paint that blinding, violent masterpiece he'd

127

seen yesterday. He wanted to know why she'd let Billy inside her body, but not her mind, her heart.

He wanted to know *her*, damn it!

This arrangement sucked.

"This is just sex, occasional, no-strings, and certainly no involvement beyond," she'd said that second time they'd "bumped into each other".

"That's fine by me," Billy had said. And it *had* been fine—for like five days. Now it wasn't fine. Nope. It was not fine at all.

And the message Hannah was getting across wasn't very heartening. She was flirting with Lance, leaning close to him, whispering into his ear, right in Billy's line of vision. And as much as Billy hated watching her, his cock felt like a baseball bat. His balls were heavy, an aching pain inside his underwear.

He narrowed his eyes, bile rising up his throat. She was trying to drive him away. Trying to show him they didn't mean anything. *He* didn't mean anything. Of course.

Clenching his jaw together, he rose to his feet and set his drink down on the chair seat. Damned if he was going to sit here all evening watching her. Damned if she thought she could drive him away. And damned if she wasn't asking for it.

He wound his way across the lawn, ignoring a string of salutes and inquisitive gazes as he headed for her.

Now Lance chuckled over something she said and Billy seized the moment to draw up behind her. "I know what you're trying to do," he murmured into her ear, cupping her hips and letting her feel his erection—the erection *she* had given him. "You're trying to make me jealous, drive me away, aren't you?"

She'd gone stiff. Mute.

Well, good. Because he wasn't through talking.

He grazed her earlobe, his voice but a whisper. "Guess

what, Hannah? I am so hot for you I'm near bursting. Even if you go on and fuck him, I'm *still* not going anywhere." He pressed a wet kiss to her ear, his lips lingering against the delicate shell of her earlobe. "I'm in for the long haul."

"Billy, please, not here."

He barely heard the words; she spoke so low.

"Not here? Are you afraid of a show, Hannah? You're doing fine all by yourself—you're so hot you'd come now if I touched you, wouldn't you? It excites you...my watching you."

"Yes."

A shudder coursed through Billy at that breathy word, lust tightening his muscles. "Ask him up to your room."

"No, I—"

"Look at the front of his pants, sweetheart. He's hard for you. You've been working him all night. I'll bet if I stick my hand under your dress right now, you'd be wet as a seal. You *want* to fuck him. You want to see if he can make you feel what I do, don't you? You want to try someone else, see if he does anything for you?"

"Yes, yes, all right, I do!" she cried.

His balls drew up against him at her admission, his veins near bursting with blood. "Then ask him up. Suck his cock, fuck his cock—do whatever you have to do, Hannah. And I'll still be here when you're through."

He felt a slight tremble run down her spine. "You...you don't mean that."

"The hell I don't."

"I—" She shook her head. He could feel the tension in her muscles, her body vibrating against his front as she tilted her head up to Lance and blurted, "Lance, w-would you like to come up for a minute?"

Lance had been witnessing their exchange with mild interest and now he watched as Billy coiled one arm around her. One hand came to rest over her breast in a proprietary way, and Billy squeezed, gently enough not to hurt her, but rough enough to make her whimper.

Lance stared at his hand as Billy's grip loosened and he started kneading her over the dress. Then his gaze rose and clashed with Billy's dark one. The blond's eyes were red, his voice slurred by too many drinks. "Billy coming too?" he drawled.

Billy snorted. "Oh, I'm there all right. I am *so* there, you have no idea."

Lance answered that with a shrug, then he tossed back the rest of his drink and straightened, crushing the foam cup in his fist. "Lead the way then."

Billy's smile felt strained as he put one hand across the small of Hannah's back and gave her a slight push. "I'm right behind you."

Hannah could barely walk on her high heels as she crossed the living room to switch a lamp on by the window. An echo roared inside her ears and her heart rammed her ribcage so hard she feared she'd collapse.

Lance hovered by the door while Billy grabbed a chair from the adjoining dining room. He turned it around, straddled it and rested his arms across the back. "Got any lube around here, Hannah? You know, in case ole Lance here wants to play a little dirty?"

She wasn't fooled by the casual note in his voice—his eyes could have burned two holes through her.

"Y-yes."

"Come on in, Lance, she won't bite you much." Billy waved him forward as Hannah quickly disappeared into her bedroom. She kept the lube—brand-spanking new, never before used—in the drawer of her nightstand. Because Billy certainly got her wet enough.

She'd barely reached for it when the men's footsteps sounded behind her.

Oh God, what the hell was she doing...?

"I'll take that," Billy whispered. His chest touched her back as he curled a hand around the lube. "I'll take you too," he huskily added and cupped her breast with his free hand, scraping his jaw up her neck. "Hell yes, I'll take you."

A tremor started at her nape and rushed to the small of her back as his mouth grazed her skin. A damp, lingering kiss up the side of her throat drove her temperature higher, his breath moistening her skin. "Do you really want to do this, Hannah?" he murmured. His thumb had started to circle and now it grazed her hardened nipple through her dress.

Hannah held on to her resolve even though her knees felt like pudding and she had no real idea of what she was doing. She knew, deep down, Billy was more than enough for her—and yet she needed to prove to herself otherwise. No, she did not need Billy. Her world wouldn't collapse if he stopped wanting her. Any other man would do. Really.

"Yes, I'm sure," she said.

I'm sure I want this. I'll come with Lance's big cock inside me. I'll come just as I come with you, Billy, and I'll like it just as much or even more. I'll make sure of it.

Billy grabbed the fabric of her dress and pulled it up. Out of habit maybe, Hannah unconsciously lifted her hands as he drew it up her waist, her chest, her arms, until it was gone. She heard his breath catch and her own came in little spurts.

When she turned around, a mass of nerves and lust and wanting, she wore nothing but a pair of sleek black satin panties.

And there was Lance.

Tall and unmoving as he stood by the window. His green eyes were trained on her and they glimmered at the sight of her.

"Such a prize, isn't she?" A cold edge sharpened Billy's words as he curled an arm around her waist and briskly slipped his hand into her panties. She sucked in a breath when he pried her lips open and inserted a thick finger inside her. He drew it out as quickly as it entered, and she loathed the fact that she felt bereft of it.

"She wants you to fuck her," Billy told Lance, and he sounded so strained Hannah wondered if it had been painful to say that. "And she wants me to watch."

Lance's hands flexed at his sides and his Adam's apple bobbed up and down as he swallowed. "Fine by me," he agreed.

He slowly unbuttoned his shirt and shrugged it off his wide shoulders. His belt hit the floor with a resounding thump and then his solid black slacks and underwear followed.

Hannah gaped when Lance's cock popped out with a tremulous jerk, a cock that did the big Hummer the man drove justice. It rose along his chiseled abdomen, dark-veined and tall, above a set of balls that looked painfully swollen. He took a step forward, his gaze leveled on hers. "Come here, I want to kiss you."

Hannah's body missed the heat of Billy's as she stepped away from him and into Lance's arms near the foot of the bed. His body felt warm, as hard as Billy's. But not Billy's.

Lance bent his head, his lips searching hers, finding hers, taking hers. The unfamiliar taste of him should have been exhilarating. But instead Hannah missed the sweet, familiar

132

taste of Billy's mouth. She forgot about it when she felt the definite evidence of Lance's arousal scrape against her stomach. His aroused groan trickled across her skin, tightening her muscles. His hands ran down her back and palmed her ass, pressing her closer.

"Hmm, sweet," he murmured into her mouth, filling his palms with the flesh of her buttocks.

She didn't hear Billy come forward, but she heard his words, whispered into her ear and vibrating with eroticism. "Does he taste like me, Hannah? Does he turn you on like I do? You're going to kill me—making me watch."

Hannah's heart stopped beating. But she pushed the words aside and began to kiss Lance with more vigor, moaning into him, rubbing her body against his. "Lance, fuck me."

She heard Billy's choked sound beside her, felt a pang of longing strike deep in her core as Lance pushed her back on the bed.

"Let me taste your pussy," he said, his voice slurred. His hands pushed her weakened legs apart and held them open as he knelt before her and lowered his lips to the very heat of her.

Hannah's spine arched over the bed and her gaze widened in shock as Lance's tongue invaded. Her eyes locked with the pair of tortured brown ones she wanted to forget.

"Billy," she gasped, as the throbbing in her nipples intensified to an acute pain.

He didn't move, just watched her, towering over the right side of the bed while Hannah... Hannah had Lance's blond head buried between her legs, moving briskly, eating her, gobbling up her pussy. A small muscle flexed in the back of Billy's jaw and his gaze glowed on her face.

Hannah ached for him, deep in her gut, she ached. "Billy..." she breathed, and reached out to touch him, her arm not long enough to reach.

"I'm here, Hannah. I'm just watching like you want me to."

"Oh God…" It was Lance she must need, Lance she must want. Not Billy. Not him. Not this much.

Billy looked tortured, like a man witnessing a crime, powerless to stop it. "I wish it were me sucking that pussy," he rasped.

Lance growled, seemingly having heard. He surrounded the pearl atop her slit with his mouth and sucked it in. Hannah let out a moan, writhing under the incredible force of his suction.

Billy's thick, textured voice felt like a stroke on her skin. "I want to fuck you so bad, Hannah."

"Billy…" Hannah gazed up at him, loathing herself for being artist to that pained expression on his face. "Billy, I want you both."

One of Lance's hands found her creamed slit. He pushed one finger in, causing her to clutch the sheets by her sides and buck up to him. His mouth held her prisoner, his tongue playing with her sensitive nubbin, but now he also plunged one long finger into her sheath, stroking the slicked walls inside her. Her body rose from the bed, almost twisting with pleasure. "Lance…oh God, you're so good…"

Billy lowered himself onto the bed beside her. "How good is he, Hannah?"

Hannah's hips bucked against Lance's face, his sweet torture almost too much to bear. She spoke through panting breaths, her head thrashing as his tongue penetrated. "Good…so good…Lance…oh God, I want you. I want your big fat cock in my mouth."

Billy took her face and his hands trembled, his breathing ragged. "Where do you want his dick, Hannah? In your pussy, up your ass, where?"

Hannah couldn't bear it. She couldn't stand the pleasure, tension, building inside her. Hot, fiery, overwhelming. Lance's tongue worked her nub with quick, merciless flicks while he stabbed her cunt with his finger.

And Billy...oh God, Billy.

Her face rolled side to side as she gasped for air, her nails raking the sheets, gripping, pulling. "I-I want him in my mouth and I want you up my ass, Billy...*please.*"

She whimpered when Lance lifted his head. Her pussy mourned the loss of him, weeping for more sucking, more fucking, more. The tall, blond creature's voice rasped like gravel as he spoke. "All night I've watched your mouth and pictured me pushing my dick into it."

Hannah whimpered when he rolled her onto her stomach. Billy captured her by the waist and hauled her up to her hands and knees.

The mattress shifted under Lance's weight as he knelt close to her face, his cock in his hand. "Suck it, little one, suck that dick, nice and long."

For some ungodly reason, as if for permission, acceptance, or just a need to see his reaction, Hannah's eyes whipped sideways to find Billy's wild, tortured gaze staring back at her. "You wanted this." It seemed as though every tight word he spoke was kicked out of him. "You wanted to drive me crazy— now you have. So suck him."

She trembled—breathless, eager, a little desperate—and parted her lips wide open, accepting Lance's cock as he held the base and shoved it into her mouth. She moaned as the long column filled, the tip meeting with her throat. Her clit burned with moist heat, her pussy soaked with juices.

Billy moved to the foot of the bed, one hand burrowing

between her legs. His fingers pried through her curls and he inserted one, then two fingers inside her. "You've never been this wet," he said in a heady whisper.

His other hand started to tease the entrance of her ass with his thumb. He circled the ring of muscle, teased, caressed, pressed in. "So tight here. Open up, Hannah, my dick goes right here, right in this tight little ass...just like this." His thumb bit into her ass and tore through her entrance, penetrating deep.

Hannah's body jerked, near bursting from want, sensations, from the biting feel of two big, aroused males. Lance's cock jabbed into her mouth and splattered her tongue with the emerging drops of semen that dribbled down the tip.

Lance moaned as if in a daze, the mixture of booze and lust slurring each word he spoke, making his moves slow. "She your girl, Billy?"

Billy kept toying with her pussy, his thumb circling inside her ass, opening her. "Shut up, Lance."

"Shut up?" Lance's chuckle vibrated in his cock, in Hannah's mouth. "Does this bother you, Billy, her sucking my cock?"

Billy's answer was silence.

"Would it bother you if I came all over her face, spread my come all over her chin and lips?"

Hannah could feel Billy's jealousy, the tension in him as his hands stopped caressing and paused over her heated entrances, then left her completely. He remained quiet, breathing so harshly she could almost feel his breath on her back, the electric charge radiating from his body.

Making a low, male noise of pleasure, Lance pulled out his cock and slapped it repeatedly to her lips. "Like that, do you, sweetheart?"

"Yes, yes, yes." She opened her mouth, wanting to take in his cock, the whole length of it in her mouth, but he kept slapping her parted lips with it fast. And all she could think was, *Touch me, Billy, touch me more, don't leave me, don't stop...*

Lance halted all of a sudden, his penis glistening as it hovered close to her damp lips.

She cocked her head and met his hazy green eyes. "Your boyfriend looks like killing someone," he said, his chest heaving.

Hannah shook her head. "He's...not...my—"

She yelped as Billy's cock parted her ass and pushed into her.

It was smoothed with lube and damp, advancing through the tight channel as one of his hands flattened on the small of her back and pressed her down, pinning her there, for his invasion.

Hannah mewled, torn by a shattering sensation of stretching more than she could bear.

"Take it in, Hannah," Billy's hot whisper reached her. "There you go, nice and slow."

His cock felt wider than ever. Her ass clamped hungrily around it, adjusting to his size while squeezing. Hannah gasped for air and gyrated her hips a little, suddenly wanting more, wanting him deeper, to move faster, for him to fuck her ass harder.

Before she could even ask for it, he did. He pulled back and rammed back in. The air wheezed out of her, the sound silenced by a bulky pole of muscle poking into her mouth.

"Suck me, pretty," Lance cooed. Hannah's eyes drifted shut. Silent moans gathered in her throat as she followed the lead of Lance's hands on her hair and bobbed her head up and down his cock.

Billy growled and moved inside her. Slowly at first, and then he started to pound.

Her nails sank into the mattress and her breasts jerked to the jarring, rampant thrusts behind her. Her clit felt so sensitive the stroke of air caressed, aroused, teased the little nub into tingles of pleasure that ran through every nerve, atom, inch of her.

Billy's hand traveled from the small of her back up to her hair.

He grabbed a fistful and pulled her head back so Lance could pound her mouth more freely. His other hand curled around her hips and sought her hot spot until his fingers were stroking her pussy, slickly gliding in and out. The mattress screeched, quicker as Billy's thrusts accelerated, his fingers fucking her fast.

He made low grunting noises, having lost all semblance of control as he drilled her, fucked her pussy with his fingers.

Hannah's hips moved against his hand and rocked back to his cock, her mouth working eagerly on Lance. Sensations raced across her and left her gasping, burning with carnal need that felt agonizing. Lightning surged inside her, hot, blinding, tearing through her organs. All while Billy fucked her. All while Lance fucked her mouth. "Oh, oh, *oh!*"

She exploded in spasms and her mouth bit reflexively on Lance, tearing a growl from him and a shot of come as he came with her. Billy part grunted, part groaned out her name as he smashed into her rear and began to shudder.

Several wild, racking convulsions later, the three of them fell on the bed. The bedroom echoed the sounds of their haggard breaths.

Billy drew Hannah to him and curled his body against the

back of hers, spooning her. She felt her hair stir as he pressed a kiss to the top of her head.

"Still here, Hannah. I'm still here."

He murmured that so softly she wondered if he'd even intended her to hear. Hannah's insides grew tight as she closed her eyes and fought the beginnings of tears.

A silence settled among them, disturbed moments later by the sound of faint snoring.

Uncoiling herself from the arms and legs tightly wound around her, Hannah slipped into a robe, not glancing back at the sleeping men as she tightened the sash around her waist and went out into the living room.

A new blank canvas stared back at her from the easel and she stared at it for a long moment, her heart crammed inside her.

This was no summer fling.

She was in love with Billy Hendricks. Completely. Irrefutably. In love with Billy.

Lifting a single brush in hand, Hannah went on to paint the catastrophe.

Chapter Four

I dream of painting and then I paint my dream.
Vincent Van Gogh

Hannah had dreamed of being in love, being loved, of having a wonderful relationship with someone. Of knowing what her partner liked and being known completely in return down to the tiniest, most insignificant details—like her liking strawberries and limes but not lemons, and her favorite toast was wheat.

She might have had it, might still have it. If she'd stop being a coward. She shouldn't judge Billy by someone else's sins, much less Brad Kingman's. Billy wasn't just different—he was unique. She'd never met a man more deserving of her affections. In fact maybe she didn't deserve his.

She stared at her masterpiece. Morning sunlight seeped in panels of light through the shutters on her living room window, lightly dancing over her work like museum lights. She'd used every tube, every color at her disposal, and even ran out of red. Now contemplating her soulful rendering, she realized this was exactly what she felt—what Billy made her feel—and yet her reluctance to admit it kept her from truly embracing it.

She'd turned her life into one of the portraits she was paid to do.

Hannah shook her head, saddened by the thought. A portrait wasn't what she dreamed of, or what she'd wanted from her life. She'd wanted a wild, unpredictable, fiery abstract. Filled with passion, fury, lust, laughter, tears even.

Playing on the safe side left her with nothing. Her breath left her in a rush when she heard a loud thump on the bedroom floor, followed by a grumbled, "Fuck."

Soon Lance appeared out in the living room, clutching his clothes to his chest and looking disoriented. He paused when he saw her and opened his mouth long before anything actually came out. "H-Hannah—right?" He seemed unsure of her name and unsteady on his feet. Warily, she nodded.

Lance shook his head in confusion. "Did something happen here?"

Billy rushed into the living room, buttoning his pants and still without a shirt, and his gaze sharpened when he spotted her. "You all right, Hannah?" he asked, standing a few feet away from Lance.

Oh, Lord, now what?

Hannah nodded, gone speechless.

"What in the hell was I doing in bed with Billy?" Lance demanded, and flung his clothes at the floor, glaring at her first, then at Billy.

Billy blinked, then roared with laughter. "Buddy, believe me," he said, slapping his back. "I'm not interested. But thanks."

Lance didn't look appeased with his eyebrows slanting above his eyes. "Would one of you please tell me what in the devil's name happened here?"

"You mean you don't remember?" Hannah asked, trying to recall how many cups of beer she'd watched him drink last night. The fact that she'd lost count seemed proof that whatever the number—it had been a lot.

Before Lance answered, Billy jumped in, "If it had been memorable, trust me, a guy like you would remember. Now here, let me get your clothes for you. Thatta boy. And take some aspirins, got it?"

Lance accepted the pile of clothes Billy deposited in his arms, then lifted his gaze to stare at Hannah. "I fucked you, didn't I?"

Hannah wrung her hands together and inhaled a deep breath before managing to nod.

Lance didn't do much as he digested the news. He heard it and didn't give any reaction away. Until a sleek blond eyebrow rose. "Well, did I pass?"

This was, by far, the weirdest morning of her life. Feeling as though her tongue had frozen in her mouth, Hannah nodded again.

Lance smiled then, a crooked smile that showed a hint of a dimple on one cheek. "I'd hate to under-perform in front of such a pretty lady."

Hannah would not look at Billy. She felt flushed enough as it was. And she could *feel* his gaze on her. Hot. Bothered. "You didn't. It was...interesting."

"Great, maybe we'll have a repeat," Lance said, back to oozing charm. "Mind if I use the bathroom to get dressed before I leave?"

"No, go right ahead." Her cheeks were really on fire now. Neither Billy nor Hannah said a word when Lance disappeared, and Hannah did her best to avoid Billy's gaze.

She wanted to tell him a thousand things and yet she feared none of them made sense. *Billy, I hope I didn't drive you away, I have no idea what I was thinking and I've fallen for you hard...*

Billy already held the door open for Lance by the time he emerged, all dressed, coolly raking a hand through his hair. "You know, you're absolutely right, I do need an aspirin—happen to have any handy here, Hannah?"

Hannah could sense Billy's growing frustration, his desire to be left alone with her, but she wasn't at all sure she was ready to face him. What could she say, where would she even start?

She quickly fetched an aspirin from one of the kitchen drawers, where she kept a medicine kit handy, and handed it to Lance with a glass of water.

"Thanks, beautiful." He kissed her smack on the lips, leaving her winded as he returned the half-empty glass and strode for the door. Now it was Lance who slapped Billy's back. "You look peaked, Billy. I suggest you take some of those aspirins too. See ya later, boy."

When Billy slammed the door shut behind him, she heard his softly muttered "*son of a bitch*" and watched him shake his head in annoyance.

She didn't have the strength or courage to look him in the eye as he started forward, so she went to the window and peeked out at the streets through the blinds. Her heart pounded like a hammer inside her, her nerves alert to his every move. He was coming closer...closer...but then, he didn't reach her.

A few feet to her left, Billy paused before the easel and stared at her rendering for the longest of minutes. Hannah grew faint. Suddenly she *needed* him to like it, needed his approval, a hint of him understanding it. And she found herself holding her breath as he regarded it.

When he didn't say a word for a while, her mind raced with thoughts. Maybe it was badly coordinated. The colors overlapped too much. The layers were too thick and it was too bright and puzzling. Maybe it was better off in the trash!

"I want you to do that to me," he whispered, and cocked his head toward her, his lashes rising to reveal those mesmerizing brown eyes.

Hannah was sure she'd misunderstood him. "That?"

She let go of her breath and came to stand next to him to stare at the canvas and make certain they were discussing the same work. She gasped when she saw it with fresh eyes, not even believing she'd allowed him to see it. "That? But that's a mess!"

He took her shoulders in his hands and subjected them to a gentle pressure as he turned her to face him, his knowing gaze grabbing hold of hers. "I love your mess, Hannah, and everything else about you."

With that he knocked the breath out of her completely. She swayed against him. "Billy…"

His gaze glimmered on her, full of tenderness as it danced across her face, touching her lips, her nose, finally settling on her eyes. "I want you to paint your colors all over me, anywhere you want, anytime you want."

"Oh. Billy."

It was all she could say as his thumb pressed her lips, sealing the top and bottom one to keep her from saying anything else. "You don't have to say anything. I'll wait as long as I have to. And when you're ready…you can just paint something to let me know. Right here." With his free hand, he tapped his bare chest with his knuckles. "Right over here."

Hannah stared at that beautiful hand as it flattened over his chest, knowing exactly what lay there, alive and beating under his bronzed skin and rigid muscles. "You want me to use real paint, right there?"

A heart-stopping grin teased the corners of his lips. "Yeah, I thought color would be nice."

Her smile barely fit in her face and her heart pirouetted inside her. "Close your eyes, Billy."

Hannah picked up a brush as his lids fell closed. She unscrewed the orange paint tube and surveyed his beautiful features while she swiped the feathery tip across the top. All through the summer she'd cheated herself out of dozens of nights she could have stayed over and slept with Billy, and oh, how she wished she could remedy that tonight.

Her hand trembled slightly as she rested the heel of her palm on his chest and curled her wrist for each paint stroke, using her detail brush with the thinnest tip and inwardly thanking God oils took days to dry, so she could wash the paint away from him later. "Ready," she said once finished.

His eyes popped open and he glanced downward, taking a moment to read the words, which to his eyes were upside down.

Love you.

A thousand expressions crossed his face as he looked up again. Dazed, he shook his head, tousling his bedroom hair even more. "I have to say, Hannah, I like your choice of color," he said, in a voice uncommonly low and raw.

She stared up at him without a hair on her whole body moving, completely perplexed. Did her confession do nothing to him at all? Had she misread him? Had she again done what she'd avoided this whole time? Stupid, stupid, stupid—

"Come here, you."

A powerful arm secured her against him and she gasped at the abruptness of his move. Her hands flattened on his chest, the heel of one palm getting smudged with paint as she stared up at him in confusion.

His eyes felt endless as he searched her gaze. "I have to say I like your choice of words even better."

Hannah's heart all of a sudden grew wings. She felt herself smile, her feet gone weightless. "Oh?"

"Yep." Ever so slowly, he kissed her forehead, the tip of her nose, her lips. "I love the color, the words...and I love the artist. I want no one else coloring me but you."

She yelped in surprise when he lifted her into his arms and kissed her on the mouth. "Come on, Picasso, I'm itching to put *my* signature on you. I'll have no more Lances touching my girl."

Hannah laughed and suddenly realized what maybe deep down, she'd known from the start. "You know, Billy, as Margie once told me. Why would I want anyone else when there's you?"

"Margie said that?"

"Yep."

"I ought to have married the woman."

"Billy!" Hannah slapped his arm.

He smiled and made his way to her bedroom and kissed her, a kiss as passionate as it was tender, his tongue tasting her. "No more kidding," he whispered, setting her down on the bed. "I need to have you."

As his hands worked to untie her robe, she cupped his jaw, his day's growth of beard raspy against her palms. And with her heart in her eyes, as bright and fiery as any of her paintings, she whispered, "No one. There's no one like you, Billy."

About the Author

Red Garnier writes fun and sexy erotic contemporaries as well as paranormals, which can range from dark and emotionally intense to fun and sweet as cherries. To learn more about Red Garnier, please visit www.redgarnier.com. Send an email to Red at redgarnier@gmail.com or visit her at her blog at http://redgarnier.com/blog/.

Heat of the
Moment

Elle Kennedy

Dedication

To Lori

Chapter One

Why was it that heat waves always made her want to have sex? Shelby Harper wasn't certain, but she suspected it had something to do with the spike of body temperature and the constant sheen of sweat that coated her body, clinging to her breasts, sticking to her legs. It made her want to rip her clothes off and wander around naked until the end of time. And thinking about being naked logically led to thoughts of sex, right?

Or hell, maybe it wasn't the heat wave at all. Maybe she really shouldn't have taken the tequila shot that cute Navy lieutenant had tempted her into. But she'd never been able to say no to a man in uniform...

Too bad the guy was married. He really had been pretty appealing, with that clean-shaven jaw and those playful green eyes.

Fighting a smile, Shelby reached for another ice cube from the plastic cup sitting on the smooth countertop. Though most of the ice had already melted, she managed to find one cube still intact, and slowly ran it over her collarbone. The ice felt heavenly against her fevered skin. A cold shower might have felt even nicer, but she'd already taken one this morning and she was trying to conserve energy.

"Jesus, Shel, turn on the air conditioning. I'm dying of heat here," a sexy male voice drawled.

The ice cube slid out of her fingers and down her shirt, landing directly in the left cup of her lacy pink bra. Her nipple instantly hardened, though it was hard to tell if it was a result of the ice or the sight of John Garrett standing in front of the bakery counter. When had he come in here? Her shop was divided into a bakery and a café area, the latter being where most of the customers had holed up all evening. She hadn't even noticed John—no, he liked to be called Garrett, she reminded herself—she hadn't noticed *Garrett* walk into the bakery. Not surprising, since he was a SEAL with the Navy and possessed the eerie ability to make himself invisible until he decided to materialize out of nowhere.

At the moment, however, he was the furthest thing from invisible. Wearing a pair of olive green cargo pants that hugged his long, muscular legs and a white T-shirt that was pasted to his rock-hard abs thanks to the heat, he was really, *really* visible. He shot her a grin that was even sexier than that husky voice of his, adding, "I'm hot."

Oh yes you are...

She quickly silenced the naughty voice inside her head. Yes, Garrett was hot—he was the walking, talking and breathing definition of tall, dark and handsome. And yes, his body was to die for, with all those perfectly sculpted muscles that didn't come from a gym but from swimming with sharks and hanging off helicopters—or whatever it was he did as a SEAL. But no matter how good he looked, she knew fantasizing about this man would get her nowhere.

Truth was, Garrett wasn't interested in her. A year of flirting and that one pathetic attempt she'd made at asking him out to dinner confirmed this sad truth. Whether she liked it or not, he'd apparently tucked her away in friend territory long ago. Which was probably a good thing, because did she really want to hook up with Garrett anyway? She'd played the part of military girlfriend before, and look how well *that* turned out. Not only had Matthew, her ex, been away for months at a time, but apparently he'd been doing more than playing GI Joe when he was gone—he'd been fucking every female he happened to encounter.

"Earth to Shelby."

She lifted her head and saw Garrett was still standing there, still staring at her. Jeez, this heat was making her space out.

"Sorry, what did you want?"

"Air conditioning," he prompted.

"Forget it."

"Come on," he said with another grin, and then a wink. Man, how did he get away with *winking*? Most men looked like complete idiots when they tried to wink. "Give me five minutes in front of the air conditioner, full blast, just to cool off."

"Increased use of air conditioning during heat waves causes power outages," she reminded him. "Which is why half the city is experiencing a blackout. I'd rather be all sweaty than without power for five days."

She was pretty grateful, actually, that her bakery was the only place in a ten-mile radius that had power, all thanks to the backup generator she'd decided to switch on. No way was she going to put a strain on the generator by cranking the A/C. She hated using it as it was, but she had an entire refrigerator full of cakes that needed to be delivered tomorrow morning and she'd be damned if all those cakes spoiled because John Garrett wanted a little bit of cold air. She'd already done him and his Navy buddies a favor by opening the café on a Sunday evening. The lit-up front window drew the men like flies to honey. To them, electricity meant television, and television meant the ability to see the big game between the Padres and the Dodgers.

He lifted a brow. "You're all sweaty, huh?"

Figured that he'd latch onto that one teeny part of her response.

"Yes, Garrett, I'm sweaty. It's a billion degrees out there, in case you've forgotten."

"Which only supports my idea about the air conditioning."

"Forget it." She set her jaw and crossed her arms over her chest to show she meant business. "Find another way to cool off."

A loud cheer came from the adjoining room, followed by the sound of palms slapping against palms in high-fives. The Padres had obviously scored another run.

"The game's almost done. You could take a quick dip in the ocean after you leave here," she said, trying to be helpful.

But Garrett didn't seem to be interested in cooling methods anymore. His chocolate-brown eyes narrowed, glittering with a mixture of amusement and curiosity as he studied her chest. "Are you...uh, lactating?"

Huh?

She quickly glanced down, suppressing a groan when she saw the round water stain that had seeped from her bra right through her thin yellow tank top.

"Ice," she blurted.

"Pardon me?"

"An ice cube fell down my shirt."

He gave a husky little laugh that made her nipples harden again. Damn it. Everything about this man was way too appealing. His warrior body, his messy dark hair and teasing eyes, his laughter. She'd been attracted to Garrett from the second he'd sauntered into her bakery last year to buy a cake for his commander's birthday. He'd requested the most obscene message to be written in icing, and from that moment on, she'd been a goner.

Maybe she was through with dating military men, but she knew that all John Garrett had to do was ask and she'd have her clothes off in a nanosecond.

But he didn't ask. He *never* asked. In the year she'd known him Garrett hadn't shown one iota of interest in getting naked with her.

"You should take off your shirt."

Until now.

She managed a startled laugh. "Really? Why is that?"

His smile was boyishly innocent. "Because it's all wet. Or, if you'd prefer, I could get a couple more of those ice cubes and rub them over your right breast. You know, so you match."

She laughed again, this time to cover up the zing of arousal she'd just felt at the words "rub" and "your" and "breast" coming out of this man's sexy mouth. He was obviously joking around. He had to be. Because although she'd imagined Garrett's hands on her breasts countless times before, she knew the fantasy would forever stay in her imagination. If John Garrett wanted her, he'd have made a move a long time ago.

So instead of responding to his flirty remark, she said, "You'll miss the end of your game."

Something that resembled disappointment flickered in his dark eyes. "Yeah." He coughed. "You're right. I should, uh, head back in there. Sorry I came in here and bugged you."

What? He thought he was bugging her?

She opened her mouth to tell him he could hang out with her a bit longer, that she wasn't trying to shoo him away, but he turned around before she could say a word. She got a glimpse of his taut backside disappearing through the doorway leading into the café and then he was gone.

Well.

Shelby leaned her elbows on the counter and rested her flushed face in her hands. What exactly just happened here? She replayed the entire scene in her mind, starting with the way Garrett walked in and demanded she turn on the air conditioner and ending with his offer to *rub* her breasts. And then, of course, his abrupt departure.

Had she done something wrong? Had she not flirted enough? She would have flirted more, but she hadn't seen the point. She'd tried it before, and Garrett always brushed off her suggestive remarks, making it obvious that he wasn't interested but never making her feel as if she were inadequate or anything. He genuinely seemed to like her, but after a year of friendship it was clear he wasn't into her the way she was into him.

"You don't want to get involved with him anyway," she muttered to herself.

The reminder helped, but only a little. Yeah, she wasn't interested in dating an officer again, but...but damn it, she really wished John Garrett would have sex with her.

"Another shot for our lovely hostess?"

She looked up and found Paul, the married lieutenant, by the counter, yet again holding the tequila bottle and a shot glass in his hands. The guy was obviously trying to get her drunk, and she wondered if she ought to tell him that no amount of tequila would convince her to sleep with a married man. Nah. He'd find out soon enough, especially if he did something stupid, like grope her. If he did that, then he'd also find out she was pretty damn good at kicking him in the balls.

"I'm already feeling tipsy," she admitted, eyeing the bottle warily.

"Tipsy, shmipsy! It's the first heat wave of the summer! It's a special occasion."

Had he just said tipsy shmipsy?

Trying not to laugh, Shelby tucked an errant strand of hair behind her ears. "No thanks, I'll pass." She couldn't go upstairs until the Padres game ended, but drinking herself stupid was no way to pass the time until everyone left. And it wasn't like another drink would help her forget that John Garrett, her long-time fantasy, was in the other room, *not* wanting to sleep with her.

No amount of tequila could make her forget *that*.

"Face it, she's just not into you," Carson Scott said with a shrug.

Garrett forced his gaze to stay glued on the television and not drift in the direction of the doorway separating the café from the bakery. His peripheral vision caught a flash of movement— Shelby rounding the counter to chat with Lieutenant Paul Aston and his tequila bottle. Oh shit. Did Lieutenant Asshole actually think he had a flying fuck of a chance of getting Shelby Harper into bed? Dream on, brother.

Shelby would never mess around with a married man. Or at least that's what Garrett kept telling himself.

Because in all honesty, the thought of his sweet, sexy Shelby burning up the sheets with Lieutenant Asshole, or any man for that matter, caused jealousy to spiral down his chest and seize his intestines like a death vise.

"You might as well quit pining over the girl," Carson added, lifting his beer bottle to his mouth and taking a long swig.

"I'm not pining," Garrett said defensively. "I'm just..." His voice drifted, his brain unable to come up with an alternative description for the way he felt about Shelby.

Fuck. Fine. Maybe he *was* pining, just a little. But who could blame him? Shelby was pretty fricking amazing. Look up the definition of sexy California girl in the dictionary and Shelby Harper's picture would be there, complete with her wavy, sun-streaked blonde hair, her big blue eyes with those incredibly long eyelashes, and that slender athletic body she kept in shape by surfing out at Coronado Beach every morning. Most of the officers who met her thought she was the typical West Coast blonde, complete with the dumb part, but Garrett had only needed five minutes with the woman to know she was the furthest thing from dumb *and* typical.

Shelby Harper was smart as hell. Funny as hell. Nice as hell.

And there wasn't a chance *in* hell that she'd ever get naked with a guy like him.

"Look," Carson said after Garrett's silence had lasted a bit too long. "You've spent the last year acting like a choirboy, coming in here whenever you're on leave and buying those fancy-pants mocha latte Frappuccinos without ever telling Shelby that what you *really* want is to get inside her pants."

"You can't tell a woman like Shelby Harper you want inside her pants," Garrett replied with a frown, reaching for his own beer. He took a slow sip, but the liquid was already room temperature, and room temperature meant about ninety degrees. He forced himself to swallow the tepid beer, then pushed the bottle away.

"Why the hell not? She fills out a pair of pants pretty fucking nicely."

She sure did...

He forcibly shoved all thoughts of Shelby's tight ass out of his head and said, "I can't treat Shel the way I treated all the SEAL groupies I hooked up with. She's...classy and...*nice*. She deserves more than a couple sleazy come-ons."

"Well, since you've been striking out since day one, maybe a couple sleazy come-ons are what you need."

"I, uh, kinda tried that," he admitted. "Just now." A groan rose in his throat. "I offered to fondle her tits and she—"

Carson hooted. "You did *what?*"

"—pretty much ordered me to get out of her sight," he finished.

And now...now she was cozying up to Aston, who was obviously trying to get her drunk enough so she wouldn't care if he was married or not.

"Look, although the fondling line is gold," Carson chuckled again, "maybe it's time you accepted the fact that she's not interested. And do you blame her? This place is right near the base. Think of all the Navy personnel—and groupies—who come in here. She's probably heard all about your reputation, man."

Garrett clenched his teeth, fighting the urge to hit something, but deep down he knew Carson had a point. He was by no means a saint, and no doubt Shelby had heard some wild stories about him, most of them true. At best, she knew his past was a revolving door of women. Lots of women. At worst, she was aware of his wild streak, maybe even the threesomes, some with none other than Carson Scott, the guy sitting right beside him. But his reputation was the precise reason why he'd tried taking a different approach when it came to Shelby Harper. He hadn't been overly flirtatious, hadn't acted disrespectfully, and he certainly hadn't made it obvious just how badly he wanted her naked beneath him while he drove his cock inside her and made her scream his name while she came...

Shit, definitely not a good idea to be thinking about stuff like that. He was already hot enough thanks to this heat wave.

Next to him, Carson wasn't finished with his lecture. "Shelby's not a wild chick, Garrett. Like you said, she's nice, wholesome, you know, the kind of woman who'd probably freak out if you suggested, I don't know, trying something other than the missionary position. She's got a body that won't quit, sure, but there's this whole Pollyanna thing going on. Maybe it's the freckles."

"I like the freckles."

"Yeah, me too. But I'm telling you, women with freckles are ridiculously vanilla when it comes to sex. I speak from experience, man."

Garrett had to laugh. "Let me guess, your little black book has an entire section reserved for freckle-faced women."

The other man just grinned, which made Garrett wonder if Carson really did categorize his conquests...nah, even Carson Scott wasn't that sleazy.

His brain suddenly stumbled over the word sleazy, and he had to wonder if that's how Shelby saw him. He hoped not, but he wouldn't be surprised if she thought that. Even though he'd bid goodbye to his wild ways, his reputation *did* precede him. So did his rep as SEAL, though Shel didn't seem all that impressed with his line of work. Most women were ready to rip their clothes off when they found out he was a big bad SEAL, an all-American hero. Yet he got the feeling Shelby viewed his job as a turn-off. Garrett knew she'd dated a Marine a couple years ago and that the relationship had ended badly, which was why he'd always made a point not to talk about his work. Not that it helped. Seemed like nothing he did impressed the woman.

"You don't want to have sex with Shelby Harper," Carson was saying, still sipping on his beer.

He rolled his eyes. "Cuz she has freckles?"

"That, and she's too fucking sweet. She's definitely not the type who'd be uninhibited in the bedroom." Carson laughed. "Can you ever see her going for kinky sex, or hell, a threesome? Shit, I'd love to be in the room and see her face if you ever suggested something like that."

Another cheer from the front of the café echoed through the room. Garrett shifted his head and saw a couple of petty officers high-fiving over a homerun from the Padres.

Not interested in the game, Garrett turned his gaze back to Carson, but not before he caught another flicker of movement in the corner of his eye. He quickly glanced at the doorway leading to the bakery, but it was empty. Okay. He could've sworn he'd seen a flash of yellow—Shelby's clingy little tank top perhaps?—but when he peered into the next room he saw she was by the counter, still chatting with Lieutenant Asshole.

Another wave of jealousy slammed into him like a tsunami, even fiercer than the first. Goddammit. He hated the raw emotion Shelby, with her vivid blue eyes and mouthwatering body, evoked inside him. It killed him, how much he wanted her. All she had to do was bat those long eyelashes in his direction, give him the slightest hint that she was interested, and he'd be by her side in an instant. No, screw *by her side.* One word—and the word was *yes*—and he'd be so deep inside her pussy that neither of them would be able to walk again for days.

The thought made his cock twitch.

Damn, he needed to get out of here. If it weren't a million degrees out there, he might have left. Gone home, taken a quick dip in his condo's pool and slid into bed. But spending the rest of the night in the dark, sweating out this heat wave, was seriously unappealing. Shelby's café was the only place with power, and besides, as annoying as it was watching her with another man, at least he could keep an eye on her while he was here. Make sure she didn't get plastered and do something stupid, like the lieutenant.

Yeah, that's why you're sticking around, a small voice taunted.

Fine, so maybe a part of him was hoping Shelby would get plastered and do *him.*

A guy could dream, after all.

Chapter Two

Can you ever see her going for kinky sex, or hell, a threesome?

Shelby kept running the words over and over again in her head, wondering if she'd somehow imagined them. It was hard enough to think in this sweltering heat—add to that a shot of tequila and you got one struggling-to-function brain.

But no, she couldn't have imagined it. She'd heard Garrett and Carson, loud and clear, as they'd discussed her. Scratch that—as they'd discussed all the reasons to *not* have sex with her.

It really was quite insulting, that they'd been indulging in locker room talk about her in her place of business. And yet a part of her was...flattered. Jeez, what was wrong with her? How could she possibly be flattered by the fact that Garrett and his buddy thought she was *vanilla*?

At least it answered the question she'd been asking herself the past year. John Garrett didn't want to sleep with her because apparently she wasn't wild enough for him.

Oh, she knew he liked her. He'd made that pretty clear during his chat with Carson. But he also made it clear that he thought she was sweet. Not sweet, as in "man, she's got a sweet ass" but sweet as in "I don't want to fuck her because she's obviously a huge prude in the sack".

"I am *not* a prude," she mumbled to herself.

"What was that, hon?"

Her head jerked up and she realized Paul was beside her again. "Oh. Nothing. I didn't say anything," she lied, suddenly wishing this man would just disappear.

One of the other officers was throwing up in the café restroom, so she'd let the lieutenant use the bathroom in the upstairs apartment, where she'd lived for the past two years. Paul's absence had allowed her to eavesdrop on Garrett's conversation, but now she kind of wished she'd never been nosy enough to lurk in the doorway. The last thing a woman wanted to hear was that the man she had the hots for didn't think she was wild enough for him.

"So what do you say we kick all these losers out and go upstairs?"

Okay, so maybe *that* was the last thing a woman wanted to hear.

She shot the lieutenant a pointed look. "What would your wife have to say about that?"

He looked startled for a moment, then glanced down at the gold wedding band on his left hand as if remembering it was there. Uh, yeah, buddy, maybe take the ring off before you try to hit on a woman who isn't your wife.

"My wife and I are actually separated," Paul said quickly.

Yeah right.

"I'm sure the separation must be very painful for you," Shelby said politely.

"So, the going upstairs idea..." He looked at her with a hopeful expression.

She just stared at him.

The hope dissipated like a puff of smoke. "Right." He

shrugged. "Can't blame a guy for trying."

She opened her mouth to retort that, yes, she *could* blame a guy for trying, especially a *married* one, but he scurried off before she could speak.

Trying not to roll her eyes, Shelby watched as Paul ambled into the café, muttered something to the officer he'd arrived with, then left her establishment without a backwards glance.

"Jerk," she muttered to herself.

"Please tell me you had something to do with Lieutenant Asshole running off like that." Carson Scott appeared in the doorway, grinning.

"You guys call him Lieutenant Asshole?" she said with a laugh.

"Either that, or Sleazebag Paul. It's hard to pick one, seeing as he's both an ass and a sleaze. We tend to alternate."

Shelby peered past Carson's impossibly broad shoulders, trying to catch a glimpse of Garrett. Apparently the game had ended, because most of the men in the other room were pushing back their chairs and heading for the door. A few approached the doorway, poking their heads in and thanking her for opening up the bakery. She just smiled, waved and wondered where the hell Garrett had run off to. Probably to find a woman who was into kinky sex and threesomes.

Too bad. Because if he'd ever bothered to ask her, he might be surprised to know that she was *exactly* that kind of woman. Just because she'd never acted out any of her fantasies didn't mean she didn't have 'em.

"So we're taking off," Carson was saying. "But we thought we'd help you clean up a bit before we left. Garrett took the beer bottles out to the recycling bin. I came in here to get a rag so I could wipe down the tables."

She was genuinely touched. "You guys don't have to do that."

"It's the least we could do. You didn't have to open the café up tonight but you did. Might as well repay you with some clean-up."

He shot her a crooked smile, and a flicker of heat sparked inside her belly. Carson really was an attractive man, she realized. She'd been lusting over Garrett for so long she'd barely noticed what any of his friends looked like, and for the first time, she actually took the time to look at Carson Scott, really *look* at him. And she definitely liked what she saw. Dirty blond hair, cut short but not short enough that he looked like all the crew cut boys who walked around Coronado. His eyes were blue, his features classically handsome, and he was as ripped as his friend Garrett. Obviously you couldn't be a Navy SEAL without possessing one of those hard, sleek bodies that never failed to make a girl drool.

"Do I have icing on my chin or something?" Carson teased. "Damn, I knew I shouldn't have eaten one of those cupcakes you brought out to us."

"No, nothing on your chin," she said, cheeks warm as she turned away and stopped checking him out.

She rounded the counter and grabbed a rag, then walked back and handed it to him. Trying not to stare at his ass, she trailed him into the café and watched as he efficiently wiped down all the tabletops. Carson had just finished when Garrett returned, the chimes over the door jingling as he walked inside.

Shelby's heart immediately did a couple of jumping jacks. Damn it. Why did John Garrett always manage to make her pulse race?

"Thanks for having us," Garrett said, his voice slightly gruff.

"No problem." She swallowed when she saw him edge back toward the door, suddenly anxious for him not to leave.

She still couldn't believe he thought she was vanilla, and maybe it was crazy—fine, it *was* crazy—but she got the feeling a golden opportunity was staring her square in the eye. That tonight would be her one chance to show him that she wasn't the sweet freckle-faced prude he obviously thought her to be.

"Well...good night," Garrett added.

Their gazes locked, and she could swear the air hissed and crackled with mutual attraction.

Fine, it was probably the heat making the crackling noise, but still...

She broke the eye contact, slowly glancing over at Carson, who'd dropped the rag on one of the tables and was moving toward his friend.

Don't let them leave.

The urgent voice inside her head caught her off-guard, but only for a second. Because after that second was up, she realized that she really *was* looking at a golden opportunity. A delicious, ridiculously tempting opportunity.

She's too fucking sweet. She's definitely not the type who'd be uninhibited in the bedroom.

God, it would be so wickedly satisfying to prove them wrong. Show Garrett that his wild ways didn't scare her and that she was perfectly capable of taking him on. Taking them *both* on.

Heat simmered in her belly, radiated in her limbs and made her weak with...desire. Oh God. She'd always imagined what it would be like. Two men. At the same time. The guys she'd dated in the past would have been aghast if she admitted to that particular fantasy. Even Matthew, who had seen nothing wrong with sleeping around on her, would have been horrified.

Was she crazy? Perverted? Suffering from heat stroke?

Maybe, but who the heck cared? They were all adults here. And yeah, maybe she was a little tipsy from the tequila, but like Lieutenant Asshole had said, tipsy shmipsy. What was so wrong with acting wild and crazy every now and then?

If wild was what she needed to be to show Garrett she could rock his world, then why not?

"See you later, Shel," Carson said.

Garrett's hand was on the doorknob.

"It's still early," she found herself blurting. "You guys should stay and hang out a while longer."

His hand froze and he glanced at her over his shoulder. "You want us to stay?"

She managed a feeble shrug. "Sure. Sleazebag Paul left his tequila bottle here. We might as well put it to good use."

Both men just stared at her, but Garrett's hand *did* drop from the door handle...

"Besides," she added, "it's so hot out there."

"Pretty hot in here, too," she heard Carson murmur.

She met Garrett's gorgeous brown eyes and offered a little smile. "So what do you say?"

Garrett decided he was dreaming. Because, really, there was no other explanation for what had just happened. One moment he and Carson were about to leave Shelby's café, the next she'd somehow convinced them to stay and put a quarter-full tequila bottle to good use. He didn't know why he'd agreed, but somehow he had, and now here he was, watching Shelby Harper toss her head back and take a shot.

Fuck, she was sexy. Her blonde waves cascaded down her shoulders, her delicate throat bobbing as she swallowed back the fiery liquid.

She made a face, then handed the bottle and shot glass to Carson, who was more than ready for the challenge. Carson swiftly took his shot and passed the bottle over.

Garrett glanced at it for a moment, debating. He had no idea what Shelby was trying to accomplish. Was she trying to get him drunk? Was she planning on jumping his bones if he did? And if so, why the hell had she asked Carson to stick around too?

Something niggled in the back of his mind, but he forced the absurd idea away.

No. *No.* Freckles or not, Shelby definitely wasn't the type who'd go for a three-way romp.

Was she?

"C'mon, *Johnny*," Shelby teased after he'd hesitated too long. "Scared of a little tequila?"

Uh-oh, she'd called him Johnny. He'd once told her how he felt about the nickname. His exact words had been, "I hate it. I kick the asses of people who call me that". But he didn't want to kick Shelby Harper's ass at the moment, not by a long shot. She looked so damn good in that tight yellow tank top with her fair cheeks flushed from the heat and the alcohol. He wanted to kiss her. Badly. So badly he could practically taste her on his lips.

But rather than jumping across the table and capturing her mouth with his, he met her challenge and downed some alcohol instead.

The tequila burned its way down to his gut, warming his body and easing the knot of tension coiled inside him.

"God, it's so hot," Shelby said with a groan, fanning herself with one dainty hand. Then she smiled and shot to her feet. "We need ice."

Garrett admired her tight little ass as she hurried out of the room. She was wearing a filmy blue skirt that was practically transparent, and if he looked hard enough he could see the outline of her panties. Wait. The skirt moved and...yeah, she had a thong on.

Oh Jesus.

Trying not to groan, he shifted in his chair, but no matter how he arranged himself his pants still felt exceedingly tight.

"So...I think she's trying to seduce us," Carson murmured. He looked a little startled, as if he couldn't quite believe this turn of events. "I guess I stand corrected on the freckles thing."

Garrett swallowed, not believing it either. He'd been thinking the same thing, and hearing his best friend and teammate say it confirmed his own suspicions. "She's had too much to drink," was the only reply he could come up with.

"She's not drunk, man. Walking in a straight line, not slurring her words..." Carson's mouth stretched out in a smile. "I think she knows exactly what she's doing. And exactly what she wants."

He wanted to argue, but Shelby returned with a plastic bowl filled with ice and flopped down in her chair again. When she reached for an ice cube and began trailing it down her neck, Garrett decided Carson was right. Shelby knew precisely what she was doing. And her plan obviously included making her two companions as hard as granite.

A little moan slid out of her throat as she rubbed the ice along her collarbone, leaving a path of glistening moisture on her silky skin.

Garrett shifted again, but it was futile. He had an erection of monstrous proportion, and it only continued to grow the longer Shelby dragged that ice cube over herself. She lifted her wavy blonde hair up and cooled the nape of her neck. Ran the ice up and down her bare arms. Brought it back to her collarbone, then—oh sweet Lord—slid her fingers under the neckline of her tank top.

It amazed him to realize that he was jealous—of the fucking ice cube. He could see her palm moving beneath her shirt, hear her sighs of contentment as she rubbed the ice over the tops of her perky breasts, and all he wanted to do was push her hand away and take over.

"You guys are missing out," she teased, gesturing to the bowl on the table. "Seriously, take some ice and put it down your shirt. It feels like heaven."

Carson chuckled. "Can't speak for Garrett, but I'm having more fun watching you."

Shelby made an irritated sound and pulled her hand out of her cleavage. The ice had melted, and her fingers were wet, making Garrett want to lean forward and lick the moisture off with his tongue. And when he finished licking her fingers, he'd tear that shirt off her body and lick everything beneath it. And then...then he'd get down on his knees, lift that skirt up to her waist and lick under there too...

Quickly averting his gaze, he clenched his fists, stunned to realize he was unbelievably close to coming. He'd almost blown his fricking load, in his pants, without so much as touching Shelby.

The woman was far more dangerous than he'd ever suspected.

"Look how nice it feels..."

He slowly uncurled his fingers and lifted his head just in time to see...yup, Shelby was running an ice cube along

Carson's jaw line.

Garrett watched as she leaned in closer and traced Carson's mouth with the ice. The lucky bastard was enjoying every second of it and Garrett didn't blame him. He'd be pretty happy too if Shelby had her fingers on his mouth. Which raised the question—would he be getting a turn? Because damn, he really, *really* wanted one. But she seemed pretty content teasing Carson to oblivion, and then she leaned even closer and...

Kissed him.

She was *kissing* his best friend.

And Garrett, fucking strangely enough, was as turned on as he was envious. He couldn't help himself, couldn't tear his eyes away from the sight of Shelby's mouth pressed against Carson's. Her tongue sliding between his friend's lips and delving into his mouth. The soft moan she gave when their tongues met.

Shockwaves of heat pulsed in Garrett's groin.

Fuck.

Fuck.

What was happening? He'd wanted this woman for an entire year, and here she was, kissing his buddy. Kissing, and running her fingers through Carson's hair, and...was he imagining it or had she just slid her other hand onto Carson's lap?

"Whoa," Carson muttered, and Garrett knew he hadn't imagined it.

Shelby did indeed have her hand on his friend's crotch.

"What are you doing?" Carson asked hoarsely.

Good question.

Shelby withdrew her hand and leaned back in her chair, but Garrett saw the hint of a smile tugging at her lush lips.

"I'm going to be honest," she finally said, shifting her gaze between the two men. "I think we should go upstairs to my apartment. All three of us."

Carson's head swiveled in Garrett's direction.

Garrett, however, kept his gaze on Shelby. "Are you serious?" he squeezed out.

"Oh yeah." She shrugged, demurely clasping her hands together on her lap.

"But...why?" he had to ask.

Her smile transformed into a naughty grin, her ocean-blue eyes sparkling with desire and amusement. "Because I want to, of course."

Because she wanted to. It was such a simple, no-nonsense answer, and yet Garrett couldn't wrap his brain around it. Who was this wild-eyed vixen and what had she done with his sweet, freckle-faced Shelby? Shelby, the woman who baked cakes for a living, who actually cared enough to ask him how his day was, who could brighten up his world with just one small smile.

He'd spent the last year getting to know her, holding off on asking her out because he didn't want to make it seem like all he wanted to do was jump her bones. And now here she was, flat-out offering to jump *his* bones, along with the bones of his closest friend.

Part of him was distressed. Dismayed that he'd obviously gotten her all wrong, that she was only looking for a good time like all the other women he'd been with.

But another part of him, the turned on part, was dying to go upstairs with her. So what if she wanted Carson to tag along? Garrett had craved this woman for so long that at this point he was willing to do anything to get her. *Take what you can get*, his body was telling him. His head, too, seemed to be in agreement, pointing out that the offer wasn't likely to stay on the table for long. A few more moments of hesitation and she'd probably kick him out and choose to go upstairs with Carson instead. Just Carson.

"Let's do it then." The words came out before he could stop them and once he'd thrown them out there he couldn't take them back. His legs were unusually shaky as he stood, but he managed to keep a composed front. Glancing at Carson, he added, "You up for it?"

His buddy looked momentarily surprised, shooting him a look that said, "Are you sure about this, man?"

It was actually kind of nice, that Carson would request permission. Carson Scott was the type of guy who did what he wanted, when he wanted it, but when it came to his friends he was oddly considerate. Since Garrett hadn't made his feelings for Shelby a secret, it wasn't surprising that Carson would respect them.

He knew all he had to do was give an imperceptible shake of the head and Carson would hightail it outta there, but if he telepathically ordered Carson to get lost, would Shelby still want *him*? Or was a threesome a prerequisite for tonight's fantasy?

He looked over at Shelby, whose arousal was clearly written all over her flushed face, and realized the answers to either of those questions didn't matter. He was going to take what he could get. One on one, two on one, it didn't fucking matter. Not as long as he got to be with this woman.

And so he offered Carson a small nod of reassurance, because really, if a kinky ménage was what Shelby Harper had in mind, then that was exactly what he'd give her.

Chapter Three

Oh God. Garrett and Carson were actually coming upstairs with her. So they could have sex. So the *three of them* could have sex. She hadn't thought they'd actually agree to it. Garrett had almost fallen out of his chair when she'd suggested it. For a moment she'd even thought he'd get up and walk out the door. But whatever reluctance he might have felt had faded the second he'd stood and said *let's do it.*

Thank God for the tequila swimming around in her blood, that's for sure. She wasn't drunk by any means, but the slow burn of the alcohol and the lightness inside her head definitely made it easier to climb up the narrow staircase leading to her apartment. She didn't dare turn to look at Garrett, who was directly behind her, his breath warming the back of her neck.

She almost jumped two feet in the air when she felt his lips brush her ear. His voice was gruff as he said, "Sure you want to do this?"

They reached the door and she pushed it open, walking inside the dark living room without answering the question.

Did she want to do this? Should she back out, tell them it had been the tequila talking and that no, she had no intention of getting naked with them?

She stopped, leaned against the wall and stared at the two men who'd followed her inside, both gorgeous in their own right.

Garrett, with his dark hair and rugged good looks. Carson, fair and blond with his chiseled GQ-model face.

She could ask them to leave, claim this was a mistake, but her body's reaction to them made it hard to open her mouth and say the words. God, what was wrong with her? Her nipples were as hard as icicles, her panties were soaked, and every cell in her body begged for the chance to be taken by these two sex gods. Two hard bodies pressed against hers, two pairs of hands touching her, two mouths kissing her, two cocks—

"Shel?" Garrett prompted.

She swallowed. It was unbelievably hot in the apartment, making it hard to breathe let alone think. Open a window, that's what she needed to do. Or turn on the fan sitting on the coffee table. But she couldn't bring herself to move. Her pussy was throbbing, her clit so painfully swollen she had to squeeze her thighs together before she keeled over.

"So how do you want to do this?" she burst out. There, she'd finally said something. Which meant she couldn't back down now, because the *something* she'd said pretty much made it obvious she intended to do this. And jeez, did that throaty femme fatale voice actually belong to her?

"It'd help if you took off your clothes," Carson returned with a sexy chuckle.

Garrett said nothing, but his piercing brown eyes were narrowed with arousal, as well as another emotion she couldn't quite put her finger on. She wished he would come over and kiss her. She already knew what Carson's kiss tasted like. Slow, teasing, languid. Would Garrett's lips feel as soft against hers? Would he be gentle? Or would his kiss be rough, greedy?

Suddenly she couldn't wait to find out, but since they obviously expected her to get naked before they touched her, Shelby reached for the hem of her tank and pulled the thin material up and over her head. Her bra was practically pasted to her body, drops of sweat already forming between her breasts. Her fingers were shaky as she unhooked the front clasp and shrugged the lacy bra off her shoulders. Neither man said a word, but their eyes widened with approval at the sight of her bare breasts. The palpable appreciation jumpstarted her confidence, and her hands were no longer trembling when she gripped the elastic waistband of her flowing skirt and took that off too. The thong came off next, and then she was naked and on display for the two sexiest guys she'd ever encountered.

Carson's soft whistle broke through the silence. "Jesus, Shelby," he hissed out. "You're fucking gorgeous."

Heat spilled over her cheeks. Both men were completely dressed, and there she was, standing in front of them without a stitch of clothing so they could openly admire her. And under their scrutiny, her nipples tightened, her breasts grew heavy and a rush of moisture pooled between her legs. Maybe it made her the slut of the century, but she couldn't wait to get started.

Evidently Garrett felt the same urgency, because before she could blink he had stepped toward her and was pulling her naked body to his clothed one. She stared at his mouth, knowing her excitement was written all over her face. "Kiss me," she whispered.

He quickly complied, pressing his lips to hers. His mouth was hot, firm, insistent. Oh yes. Carson had kissed her like he had all the time in the world, his mouth lazy, but Garrett was more intense. His kisses were rough and hungry and passionate, as if he wanted to devour her. Well, she wanted to devour him too. So she did, sucking hard on his tongue and shamelessly rubbing against his lower body.

Breathing hard, she tugged on the hem of his T-shirt and pulled it over his head. Underneath the shirt, his chest was all muscle, a wide expanse of hard ripples and smooth golden skin, with a dusting of light brown hair leading to the waistband of his cargo pants.

Her mouth went dry, her hand unsteady as she reached out and touched that incredible chest. She brushed her finger over one of his flat, brown nipples, eliciting a ragged sigh from his throat.

She was trying to decide if she was bold enough to lower her head and suck on his nipple when she felt a warm pair of hands stroking her bare back. She nearly jumped, then realized it was Carson, obviously eager to join in the fun.

Oh God, this was surreal. Her naked body sandwiched between these two big men, Carson's hands squeezing her ass, Garrett dipping his head and kissing her again. Shivers of arousal danced up and down her spine, and a resulting moan slid out of her mouth.

Garrett chuckled softly, then planted his hands on her waist and turned her around, pressing his groin into her ass as Carson filled her mouth with his tongue.

She could feel Garrett's erection nestled between her ass cheeks, and when Carson pulled her closer and parted her knees with one hard thigh she could feel the ridge of his arousal too. She sighed, pushing her ass against Garrett and reaching down to rub Carson through his khakis.

"Take your pants off," she murmured.

She was addressing both of them, but Carson was the only one to reply. He offered her a lopsided grin and muttered, "Do it for me."

She found herself glancing over at Garrett, who simply glanced back, his dark eyes flickering with raw heat. "Don't keep the man waiting," he said with a faint smile.

Drawing in a slow breath, she tugged at Carson's zipper. It

lowered with a metallic hiss.

Shelby hesitated, unsure of what to do next. This was all so new to her, the entire experience seeming more like a figment of her dirty imagination than a real-time occurrence.

"Help me out here," she said with a nervous laugh. "What comes next?"

Carson's blue eyes twinkled. "I do." He took her hand and guided it inside his pants. She took another breath, gathering every ounce of naughty courage she possessed, and finally wrapped her fingers over his cock and started stroking him.

He groaned, and she saw him fumble with his waistband, attempting to push his pants down. "Help me out here," he mimicked, his features taut with unrestrained lust.

Sinking to her knees, she pulled down his khakis and boxers, wondering if the blood drumming in her ears was a result of the tequila she'd drunk downstairs or the hard cock that sprang up against her face. God, he was big.

She circled his tip with her index finger and he shuddered. "Shit, that's nice," he said hoarsely.

She shifted her head and saw that Garrett was now leaning against the arm of her old patterned sofa. He was still clothed, still watching her with those sexy dark eyes.

She squeezed Carson's shaft, then met Garrett's gaze at the same time she took his friend's cock into her mouth.

With a moan, Carson tangled his fingers in her hair and guided her, pushing his erection deeper into her mouth. Garrett's eyes narrowed, and the fire she saw there nearly made her keel over backwards. Swallowing hard, she finally broke eye contact and focused on the delightful task of sucking Carson's dick.

She ran her tongue along his shaft, flicking over the

sensitive underside. He groaned in approval, still holding her against him with one warm hand. Her pussy throbbed as she licked him from base to tip, her body growing hotter and tighter the longer she moved her mouth up and down his cock. The room was quiet save for Carson's ragged breathing and the sound of the suction her mouth was making over his dick.

"Bedroom," came Garrett's gruff voice.

She tore her lips away from Carson's cock, realizing for the first time that they hadn't even made it to a bed yet. She was on her knees in the middle of her living room, Carson's erection hovering in front of her face while Garrett watched from the couch. The scene was so deliciously dirty that she almost sagged forward, the carpet scratching her bare knees. He was right. They definitely needed a bed.

Shelby couldn't remember getting up, couldn't recall how Carson ended up lying on her bed while she kneeled between his legs and continued driving him wild with her tongue, but somehow they got there, and suddenly Garrett's hands were stroking her from behind. The mattress sagged, the springs creaked, and she gasped when she felt his fingers tugging on her nipples.

God, was it possible to be this turned on? There were too many things going on at once. Carson's cock in her mouth, Garrett's palms on her breasts, his erection pressed against her ass.

Then Garrett's hot breath was fanning across the nape of her neck. "You want me to fuck you while you suck Carson's dick?" he muttered, rolling her nipples between his fingers.

All she could do was whimper.

He gently tipped her forward and she gasped when he slid one finger into her already sopping-wet pussy. "You love this, don't you, Shelby?" he taunted, then pressed his lips to her neck.

Pleasure surged through her. She felt like a volcano that had been dormant for decades, only to erupt out of the blue, with such force, such power, that it covered everything, everyone, with hot smoldering lava and to hell with the consequences. She pushed her ass into Garrett's exploring finger, her lips still wrapped around Carson's dick.

A delighted cry tore out of her throat when Garrett worked another finger into her pussy. He slid those two long fingers in and out of her, so hard and deep that she almost bit down on Carson, who obviously sensed her inability to multitask and gently pulled her up.

She found herself sprawled over Carson's rippled chest, her breasts pressed against his defined pecs, while her ass jutted out to accommodate Garrett's talented fingers.

Carson pinched her nipples, rolling the rigid peaks with his fingers. He smiled when she let out a soft sigh, then tugged on her hair and angled her head so they were at eye-level, so he could brush his warm lips over hers. His tongue slid into her mouth, dueling with hers, stealing the breath right out of her lungs. Her body was overcome with sensation—Garrett's fingers inside her, Carson's hands squeezing and playing with her breasts, the hot tongue inside her mouth and the cock twitching against her belly.

"Do you like having John finger you while my tongue is in your mouth?" Carson whispered against her lips.

"Yes," she squeezed out.

"I'm going crazy here," he added, his features creased with pure hunger. He grasped one of her hands and dragged it down to his cock, urging her to jerk him off.

Garrett's husky voice drifted from behind. "Will you come if I keep doing this, baby?" He added a third finger into the mix

181

then began stroking her clit with his thumb.

"Eventually," she managed to utter, her mind spinning from the tornado of pleasure assaulting her body.

"Eventually?" Garrett made a tsk-tsk sound. "Can't have that. We want you to come now, don't we, Carson?"

"Oh yeah."

Garrett pulled his fingers out and she almost wept with disappointment. A second later she was weeping with delight, because suddenly she was on her back and Garrett's head was between her legs. His warm mouth covered her pussy, his tongue flicked over her clit and...oh yes...his fingers were back too. The pleasure was so intense she could barely keep her eyes open, let alone stroke Carson, who'd shifted and was now lying next to her. He didn't seem to mind that her hand had stopped moving. Instead, he just pushed that hand away and lowered his mouth to her breast.

"Come on, Shelby," Carson murmured. "I want to see you lose control."

Within moments he got his wish, because it was pretty darn hard *not* to lose control when these two men were driving her mad with their tongues. With Carson sucking on her aching nipples and Garrett licking the hell out of her, Shelby exploded. Her orgasm seized her body in a rush of blinding pleasure that had her crying out uncontrollably. The room spun, the mattress sagged, the air became too thick to breathe as she shuddered on the bed from ecstasy she'd never even thought possible.

She whimpered, trying to wiggle away from Garrett's unwavering tongue but he gripped her hips with his hands and kept her in place. Continued to finger her and suck on her clit until the world tilted again and a surprising second orgasm tore through her.

Oh God.

When the waves of release finally ebbed, she could barely move. She heard the sound of Carson's soft chuckle against her breasts, Garrett's ragged breaths against her pussy, and wondered if it was supposed to feel this good. God, why hadn't anyone ever told her how good it would feel to have two men make her come?

"You okay?" Garrett asked with a touch of humor in his voice. He lifted his head from her thighs and sat up, lightly stroking her stomach.

"I'm...great." She blinked herself out of her orgasmic trance, noticing that he still had his cargo pants on. "Take those off already," she complained.

Without addressing her grievance, he pulled a condom out of one of the many pockets lining his pants. Flicking the square packet at his friend, Garrett said, "I've only got one."

A tiny pretzel of disappointment knotted in her belly. As appealing as she found Carson, he wouldn't have been her first choice as the winner of the one-condom raffle. But she didn't voice her frustration, not wanting to shatter any macho egos here.

Carson easily caught the condom that had been thrown to him and then uttered words that had her disappointment dissolving into delight. "There's a couple in my wallet. Think my pants are somewhere in the living room." He grinned at Shelby as if to remind her she'd been the one to dispose of those pants.

"I'll grab 'em," Garrett said, then disappeared out the door.

Shelby stared after him, admiring the way his pants hugged his sexy ass. The moment of admiration was brief, though, because the next thing she knew Carson was covering her body with his.

He kissed her, and gone were those lazy kisses he'd been giving her when Garrett had been sucking on her clit. Carson's

183

tongue filled her mouth and then he drove his cock into her without warning.

That first thrust stole the breath out of her lungs. A small moan found its way out of her mouth, reverberating against Carson's greedy tongue.

"God, Shelby, you're so tight," he muttered.

His rough, erratic pace drove her wild and she arched her hips to take him in deeper. God, this felt fantastic. Was it wrong that it was this damn fantastic? She'd been lusting after Garrett for so long that the way her body responded to Carson Scott almost felt like a betrayal.

But Garrett didn't seem betrayed as he walked back into the bedroom. He paused in the doorway for a second, watching as Carson fucked her, and then finally, *finally*, Shelby saw him start to unbutton his pants.

She tore her mouth away from Carson and watched as Garrett approached the bed again, pulling down his zipper as he walked. She couldn't unglue her gaze from him, mesmerized by each small movement. His hands pushing his pants down. His fingers on the waistband of his black boxer briefs.

Watching her watch him, he slowly removed the boxers, smiling faintly when her eyes widened. His cock jutted out, long and thick and rock hard. Bigger than the cock currently pumping inside her.

"Like what you see?" Garrett asked gruffly.

She managed a nod, her mouth too dry for her to speak. Then she moaned, because Carson had slowed his pace and was teasing her body with deep, leisurely thrusts the way the sight of Garrett's erection teased her eyes.

Garrett moved closer to the bed, his dark eyes so unbelievably intense that Shelby felt the first swells of orgasm flutter to the surface. She sucked in her breath, her inner muscles clamping over Carson's cock. She was seconds away from losing control again, and Garrett obviously knew it because in the blink of an eye he was on the bed, kneeling in front of her and parting her lips with his erection. His tip slid into her mouth and the masculine taste of him was all it took.

Shelby exploded again.

"Jesus," Carson groaned. "Keep squeezing my cock like that...yeah, Shel...just like that."

She couldn't seem to stop moaning, the sounds muffled against Garrett's dick. As shockwaves of pleasure rocketed through her body, she lapped at him with her tongue, his husky groan only heightening each wave of her orgasm.

"Fuck, I'm going to come," Carson hissed, his fingers curling tightly over her hips.

She opened her eyes in time to see his features grow taut, his eyes glaze over with sheer bliss. Carson pushed into her, once, twice, his thrusts erratic, and then he exploded too.

She felt him shudder from the climax and she had to pull her mouth away from Garrett's cock in order to smile. She'd driven guys to climax before, but Carson's orgasm brought her to a level of satisfaction she'd never experienced. He'd doubted her sexual abilities when he'd called her vanilla, and she wanted to shout out from the rooftops that the freckle-faced good girl had just made Doubting Carson come. And come hard. The ragged breaths rolling out of his chest were enough to widen her smile into a full-blown grin.

"You okay?" she teased, tracing his strong jaw line with her fingers.

He stared down at her with heavy-lidded eyes. "Oh yeah. That was...amazing."

She was still smiling as Carson slowly withdrew and stumbled off the bed. He rolled off the condom with one hand

and shot her an unbelievably satisfied look before ambling into the bathroom.

And then she was alone with Garrett. Whose cock was still inches from her mouth. Whose eyes were still glimmering with raw hunger.

She arched one brow at him before leaning closer and flicking her tongue against his cock. He groaned when she sucked the drop of pre-come from his tip. Tangled his fingers in her hair and tried to pull her even closer.

She quickly leaned back, enjoying the disappointment she saw flashing in his dark eyes.

"So Carson gets to have all the fun?" he grumbled.

She responded with a soft laugh. "Actually, Carson was just my warm-up." Again, that throaty voice slipped out of her mouth as if it belonged to her. "Now I'm *really* getting started."

"Oh really?"

"Yep."

With another laugh, Shelby sat up and climbed onto his lap, pressing her palms on his extraordinary chest and forcing him to lean back against the headboard of the bed. Then she twined her arms around his neck and kissed him.

Chapter Four

Oh Christ. Garrett didn't think he could ever get enough of Shelby Harper's sexy lips. She kissed like a fucking dream, her mouth pliant and warm, her tongue slick and eager. If he died right now, with Shelby's curvy naked body in his lap and her tongue in his mouth, then he'd die an unbelievably happy man.

"I love your lips," she whispered, surprising him by voicing the identical thought he'd just been having.

She pulled back and dragged her index finger over his bottom lip, her touch gentle. She was looking at him like he was a juicy Thanksgiving turkey she couldn't wait to dig her teeth into. Blue eyes glimmering with heat. Cheeks flushed with arousal.

His gaze slid south and sure enough, her nipples had pebbled into two tight peaks. Had she been this turned on for Carson? It was absurd, that he would be thinking about that now, making jealous comparisons, but he couldn't help it.

Shelby was so different from the women he'd shared with Carson. She might've surprised the hell out of him by suggesting a threesome, but Garrett was certain she didn't do things like that often, and his jealousy slowly transformed into satisfaction. It was obvious she was enjoying herself—she'd already come three times, for fuck's sake—but there was no doubt in his mind that she was enjoying this part of the night a lot more. Him and her. One on one. Kissing the way he'd wanted them to kiss for more than a year now.

"And your tongue," she added breathlessly, pulling back for air. "I love your tongue even better than your lips."

He chuckled softly and swept his hands over her tailbone. Her skin was moist with sweat, and he was about to offer to turn on the ceiling fan when a cell phone rang. At first Garrett thought it was his, but his pants were sitting at the foot of the bed, and the ringing sounded like it was coming from the living room.

"Shit," Carson said as he came out of the bathroom. "That's me."

His friend was still as naked as the day he was born, but Garrett wasn't particularly fazed. He'd seen Carson naked dozens of times, and the sight of his friend's cock or bare ass no longer made him uncomfortable.

Carson hurried out of the bedroom, his footsteps echoing in the hallway. A moment later, his muffled voice drifted in from the living room as he spoke to whoever had just called him.

Garrett turned to find Shelby staring at him, her expression one of curiosity. "You guys do this, um, threesome thing often, don't you?" she said awkwardly.

He shrugged. "We were a lot wilder a few years back, before we finished the SEAL training. We don't do this kinda thing too much anymore."

She looked surprised. "Really?"

He offered a *what-can-you-do?* smile. "People tend to grow up. Besides, we're out of the country a lot, which makes it hard to, you know, get shitfaced and do the whole ménage thing."

"So...why tonight then?"

Deciding that honesty was probably the best policy, he

raised his hand to her cheek and stroked her soft skin. "I wanted to be with you. And you wanted a threesome so..." He let his voice drift.

She was quiet for so long he was surprised when she spoke again. "I wanted to be with you too, John." She averted her eyes. "I would've wanted it even if Carson weren't here."

Before he could respond to her startling confession, the sound of footsteps interrupted him. Carson reappeared in the doorway, a frazzled expression on his face. "Jenny's car broke down." He had his pants on, but they were unbuttoned and he zipped them up while bending down to retrieve his shirt from the floor. "My sister," he explained when he caught Shelby's questioning expression.

"Is she all right?" Garrett asked. He wasn't surprised, though, since Jenny made it a habit of calling her big brother whenever she needed to get out of a jam. Which was often. Trouble seemed to follow that woman around like a stray dog.

"Car overheated," Carson replied. He poked his head through the neck hole of his shirt and straightened the hem. "She claims she'll die of hyperthermia if I don't come and help." He rolled his eyes, adding, "I, personally, think she doesn't have enough money to pay for a tow truck. She blew her last paycheck on a pair of six hundred dollar shoes—who the fuck pays that much money for shoes?"

Carson drifted over to the edge of the bed, where a very naked Shelby was still straddling Garrett's lap. With a faint grin, Carson dipped his head and planted a light peck on Shelby's forehead. Garrett immediately experienced another flicker of jealousy, but he smothered the irritating emotion.

"I just want to say that you, Shelby, were absolutely incredible. I'd also like to say we'll do this again sometime, but I highly doubt Garrett will agree to share next time." Carson chuckled. "He likes your freckles too much. Not so much your fancy coffees, but he totally digs the freckles." He moved away from the bed. "I'll see myself out."

With a mock salute, Carson left the room. A moment later, the sound of the front door latching echoed throughout the apartment.

And then there Garrett was. Alone with Shelby. Naked with Shelby. Just like he'd always dreamed.

He shifted his gaze back to her gorgeous face, wanting to kiss her again, but her perplexed expression made him reconsider. "What did he mean about you not liking my coffee?" she asked slowly.

Garrett managed a noncommittal shrug. "Nothing. Carson rarely makes any sense." He tried to stroke one of her amazing breasts but she swatted his hand away.

Then she crossed her arms over bare breasts, as if covering herself up would force him to have this conversation. He almost laughed. She had no idea how distracting her body was, covered up or not.

"You don't like my mocha lattes," she blurted out, her eyes widening with horror.

Garret sighed.

"But...you buy one practically every day you're not at the base or off on assignment. You've probably spent hundreds of dollars buying coffee from me. And the cakes—" She gasped. "Do you even like cake?"

He couldn't help but smile. "Yes, Shelby, I like cake. And yes, I might prefer good old black coffee to the elaborate concoctions you sell, but..."

"But what?" Her voice was soft.

"But I'd drink antifreeze if it gave me a chance to see you, all right?"

Something dawned in those dazzling blue eyes of hers. "You come in just to see me?"

"Afraid so."

"Because we're...friends?"

He sighed again. "That too. But mainly because I have a huge fucking thing for you and I've been trying to figure out how to tell you for about a year now."

The silence was so great you could hear fifty pins drop. His admission had obviously stunned her, because she just sat there, staring at him, her firm thighs cradling his still-hard dick. The silence dragged on for so long he wondered if he should repeat the words, maybe in a different language this time since she honestly didn't seem to comprehend what he'd said.

She spoke before he could. "You have a thing for me? Even though you think I'm vanilla?"

He blinked. "What? Who said—aw shit, I knew you were listening in the doorway when I was talking to Carson." He searched her face, suddenly wondering if...had she actually...? "Did you bring us up here to prove something to me?"

She didn't answer, but the telltale blush on her cheeks said it all.

"Jesus, Shelby!"

Frowning at his harsh tone, she crossed her arms tighter over her chest and said, "It wasn't the only reason. I really did want...I've always...it was a fantasy of mine, okay?" She looked defensive as she said it. "Maybe it makes me a big slut in your eyes, but I've always wanted to experience...you know, two guys."

Now she just looked embarrassed. She tried to climb off his

lap, but Garrett gripped her hips and rolled them both over so that she was lying on her back and he was propped up on his elbow, looming over her. Again she attempted to wiggle away from him, so he simply quieted her with a long kiss. She gave a sharp intake of breath before kissing him back, her warm tongue sliding into his mouth.

"I'm not judging you," he murmured when he pulled his mouth away. "And I don't think you're a slut, not at all. I just don't want you to think that you need to, you know, screw my friend in order to make yourself more appealing in my eyes. Truth is, you've always been pretty damn appealing to me."

"Then why didn't you ever say something?" Her eyes were soft as she reached up and touched his chin. "I've been flirting with you for a year, Garrett. You could've given me a sign that you were interested."

She'd been flirting with him for a year? Jeez. Maybe if he hadn't spent so much time trying to figure out a way to ask her out he would've picked up on that flirting. As it was, he felt like a complete idiot for missing the signals she'd apparently been transmitting his way.

"I didn't want you to think I only wanted sex from you," he finally confessed.

"So all that stuff about my freckles and me not being into kinky sex...?"

"That was Carson trying to convince me you weren't interested in me because of my reputation for being a, uh..."

"Man-ho?" she supplied.

He leaned down and kissed the mischievous smile right off her lips. "My man-ho days are over. I was serious when I said I want to be with you."

"This, coming from the guy who just watched his best friend have sex with me."

"I'll admit, that made me jealous as hell," he said gruffly, tucking a strand of blonde hair behind her ear. "But I thought...well, like you said, it was a fantasy of yours. And now that you've gotten it out of your system, maybe we could focus on *my* fantasy."

Her eyes twinkled. "And what would that be?"

"You."

He brushed his lips over hers, and this time when she deepened the kiss he didn't pull back. No more talking. Right now all he wanted to do was lose himself in Shelby's warm body and sweet lips. He licked his way from her mouth to her neck, sucking gently on her skin and inhaling the intoxicating scent of her. She smelled like flowers and lavender and, ironically enough, vanilla. But Carson had been dead wrong earlier, because there was nothing vanilla about Shelby. No other woman had ever managed to turn him on this fiercely.

He moved his mouth from her neck down to her breasts, drawing one nipple between his lips. He flicked his tongue over the pebbled nub, enjoying the way she moaned and tangled her fingers in his hair to bring him deeper. He suckled on her other nipple and got another moan for his effort, and then Shelby's fingers had left his hair and were stroking his cock until he could barely see straight.

"You'll make me come if you keep doing that," he growled.

"I thought man-hoes had excellent restraint."

"I meant what I said about those days being over. I haven't been with anyone for more than a year, Shel."

Her hand dropped from his dick, her expression both startled and wary. "Seriously?"

"Seriously," he confirmed.

The look in her eyes told him she wasn't sure whether to

believe him, and again he decided to put an end to all the talking. They could discuss it all later—right now he just wanted to enjoy being naked with Shelby.

The heat in the bedroom was palpable, both from the heat wave outside and the sparks sizzling between them. Inhaling some much-needed oxygen, Garrett slid his hand between her legs and touched her clit, then lower, groaning when he found her pussy soaking wet.

"Damn it," he squeezed out.

"What's the matter?" He could hear the smile in her voice.

"I'd planned on going slow."

"And you're speaking in the past tense because...?"

"Because the plan was shot to hell the second I felt *this*." He palmed her then pushed two fingers inside all that wetness. "God, I need to be inside you."

He grabbed the condom lying next to them and rolled it onto his dick, and a second later he was on top of her, driving into her sweet heat to the hilt.

"Johnny," she gasped, so much pleasure loaded into her voice he didn't bother reminding her how much he hated being called that. Truth was, the name sounded sexy coming from Shelby's lips.

He slid his hands underneath her and cupped her firm ass, pushing himself in deeper, buried so far inside her pussy he thought he might be hurting her. But her soft groans and the way she tilted her hips spoke otherwise, and soon he was pumping into her without an ounce of finesse. He felt like a horny teenager again, needing to drive his cock into her over and over again, needing to explode in a climax that was one year in the making.

Shelby didn't seem to mind. If anything, she was moving

more erratically than he was, meeting him thrust for thrust, begging him to go faster, and, when fast didn't seem to be enough for her, harder.

"John...I'm going to...oh God..." She dug her fingers into his back, which was now soaked with sweat, and proceeded to fall apart beneath him.

The look of ecstasy in her eyes as she came was enough to send him flying over that same cliff. White-hot pleasure shot down his spine and grabbed hold of his balls, and then he was coming too, his heart damn near bursting, his eyes blinded by the light exploding in front of them.

"Jesus." He gasped out a breath, trying to put what he'd just experienced into more eloquent words. "That was...Jesus."

Apparently Shelby wasn't capable of talking any more than he was, because she simply gave a contented sigh and wrapped her arms tighter around him.

He knew he must be crushing her, so he gently tried rolling off, but she held him in place and murmured, "Stay."

Smiling, he slowly withdrew his still-hard cock from her tightness, never moving off her while he took off the condom. Then he planted a soft kiss on her lips and said, "Don't worry, I don't plan on going anywhere."

Chapter Five

Shelby woke up the next morning to the sound of rain pounding against the bedroom window. She and Garrett hadn't bothered shutting the curtains last night, and she turned her head and watched as fat raindrops streaked down the glass. Looked like the heat wave had finally broken.

The heat level between the sheets, however, was still at record-breaking levels.

"Don't you ever stop to rest?" she asked as Garrett slid one warm hand underneath her panties and teased her clit with his fingers.

"Nope." He snuggled closer to her, looking ridiculously adorable with his dark hair tousled from sleep and his brown eyes twinkling with mischief.

She still couldn't believe he'd stayed the entire night. Somehow she'd been expecting him to freak out or something, decide he'd made a mistake by sleeping with her and jump out of bed in horror. She thought she'd wake up to find his side of the bed empty, the imprint of his body the only sign that he'd actually been there.

But here he was. Playful and awake and not in the least bit remorseful about what they'd done. It was obvious the only remorse he felt was over the fact that she was still wearing panties, but he quickly took care of that.

"We should really get up," she said reluctantly as his fingers continued their exploration.

He grabbed her hand and dragged it to his crotch. "I'm already up."

A jolt of desire shook her body when she felt his hard-on. Oh yeah. He was definitely up.

She curled her fingers over his shaft and slowly began to stroke him, all the while wondering what had come over her. The alarm clock on her nightstand read nine a.m. She had an entire refrigerator of cakes that needed to be delivered, and yet she couldn't stop touching Garrett, couldn't dissuade her body from responding to those talented fingers of his and the way his thumb circled her clit and... Screw the cakes. Who needed so much sugar this early anyway?

She kicked the tangle of bedcovers off her legs and climbed onto his lap. "Fine. You talked me into it."

Laughing, he reached up and cupped her chin. His warm hands pulled her face toward his. A second later his lips covered hers. The kiss was gentle, a flick of tongue, a nip of teeth, and then he moved his mouth to her neck and lightly sucked on her skin.

Heat curled inside her, then spread through her body, leaving sizzling shivers in its wake. Garrett's morning stubble chafed her skin but the small abrasions only turned her on more. She loved his rough masculinity.

"God, I don't know how I went a whole year without touching you," he groaned into her neck, wrapping his arms tightly around her waist.

She inhaled the spicy scent of him, threaded her fingers through his hair and forced his mouth back to hers. This time his kiss was loaded with hunger and she responded eagerly, pushing her tongue into his mouth and savoring the taste of him. She'd never experienced kisses like this before, hot and hurried and so damn erotic that even her tongue began to tingle.

Leaving one hand on her hips, he moved the other around and lowered it between her legs. Never breaking the kiss, he stroked her deftly, massaged her clit, and then pushed a finger inside her, until the dull ache of desire filled her veins and her thighs trembled.

"No, not yet," she breathed, trying to push his hand away. "I want you inside me."

She reached for the nightstand, where a lone condom sat, just waiting to be torn open. She was suddenly grateful she hadn't let Garrett use it when he'd woken her up with a kiss in the middle of the night. Carson had only had two condoms in his wallet, and since she'd wanted to conserve them she'd rewarded Garrett's wake-up kiss with a blowjob that would go down in history—no pun intended—and now she was glad she'd had the foresight to be condom-stingy.

"You're a sex maniac," Garrett teased as she ripped the corner of the packet and practically threw the condom at him.

"Look at who I've got in my bed. I waited a year for you too, you know."

He rolled the latex over his impressive hard-on, tilting his head as he said, "I still can't believe I missed all those signals you were sending." His hand moved back between her thighs and he groaned when he felt how wet she was. "We could've been doing this ages ago."

She straddled him again and guided his cock where she wanted it. "Sure, but don't you think it was worth the wait?"

He thrust upwards. "Oh yeah."

God, she didn't think she'd ever get used to having him buried inside her. It felt so good, so *right.*

She whimpered when he withdrew, wiggled around in an attempt to bring him back where he belonged, but he wouldn't let her. Chuckling softly, he flipped her onto her back and took control, teasing her opening with the tip of his cock.

"I told you I want you inside," she complained.

"Yeah, well, I want it to last. I want you so bad I'm about to explode."

"Then explode."

He shot her a rogue grin. "Not until you do."

She gave one final attempt at getting her way, but he grasped her wrist with his fingers before she could reach for his dick. Then he took her other wrist, shoved both up over her head and locked them together with one strong hand.

"Now be patient," he ordered, his dark eyes flickering with both arousal and amusement.

"Yes sir."

Very slowly, he rubbed his cock over her opening again, dragging it up and down her wet slit. Each time his tip brushed over her clit she shuddered. And each time she arched her hips he withdrew and shook his head with disapproval. He was still restraining her hands, but his hard grip only drove her wild. She kind of liked being at his mercy, lying beneath him while he did whatever he wanted to her feverish body.

Her breasts started to tingle, her nipples hardened, her pussy clenched, and yet he still didn't enter her. His torturous teasing became too much, her body was too primed, and when he finally plunged into her there was no stopping the orgasm.

It hit her like a freight train. Rushed through her blood, clamped onto her muscles and sucked all the breath right out of her lungs. She heard herself moaning but the sound was muffled by the roar of her pulse in her ears.

Garrett didn't slow down, didn't let her recover. He just tightened his hold on her wrists, biting down on her neck and filling the room with husky groans that signaled he was close.

She wrapped her legs around his waist, her bare feet resting on his taut backside as she lifted her hips off the mattress to bring him in deeper. Keeping her eyes open, she watched as his features strained and his eyes grew heavy-lidded from his impending release.

"Come on, Johnny," she murmured, loving the expression on his face, loving that she was the one who put it there.

He buried his face in the curve of her neck, his cock began to pulsate, and then—*oh yes*—he was coming inside her. She could feel his heart racing, thudding against her breasts like an erratic tribal drum. He groaned, thrust one last time, then grew slack.

"Jesus," he wheezed out. "Is it just me or does it only get better with us?"

Finally letting go of her wrists, he rolled over and pulled her on top of him. She pressed her face against his chest and hooked one leg over his muscular thighs. They lay there for a few long moments, neither of them speaking, neither of them moving, until Garrett reached down and laced his fingers through hers.

"It was definitely worth the wait," he murmured, answering her earlier question.

Her heart leaped up and did a little flip-flop. God, she was outrageously into this man. She'd never imagined he could be so tender, so sweet. She wished she could lie in bed with him forever, hold his hand and kiss him and wake up to his sexy face every morning for the rest of her life.

"Let's stay here forever," he mumbled, echoing her thoughts.

She stroked his rippled chest and planted a kiss on one flat nipple. "I'd love to." The image of a refrigerator full of cakes floated into the foreground of her brain. "But I can't," she added reluctantly.

She shifted and his fingers instantly curled over her hip. "No getting up."

A sigh slid out of her throat. "I have to."

"I forbid it."

Laughing, she disentangled herself from his embrace and got to her feet. Her legs almost gave out on her, the sweet aftershocks of her orgasm still fluttering through her body. "I'm serious. I have an entire refrigerator of cakes that need to be delivered." The alarm clock now read ten-thirty. Damn. She was already cutting it close. A lot of the cakes needed to be delivered by noon.

"Can't you do the deliveries later?" Garrett grumbled.

She smiled at the disappointment flashing in his eyes. "I really can't. But if you want, you can be my driver and hang out with me all day."

No sooner were the words out of her mouth than Garrett's cell phone went off. He swore softly, leaning over the side of the bed and reaching for his cargo pants. He fished his cell out of one of the pockets, frowned when he saw the number on the screen and lifted the phone to his ear. "Garrett," he said briskly.

Shelby watched as he listened to whatever was being said on the other end of the line. He didn't say much, except a couple "Yes, sirs", and a quick, "I'll be right there". And then he hung up the phone and the disappointment in his eyes deepened into regret. "That was my commander," he told her.

"Oh." She swallowed. "I take it you have to go?"

He nodded.

"Overseas?"

He was already getting out of bed and fumbling for his clothes. "Probably."

She swallowed harder. "How long will you be gone?"

"No idea, babe. It could be hours, days, weeks, months..." Voice trailing, he pulled on his pants and zipped them up, put on his shirt and headed for the bathroom.

She heard him turn on the faucet, then flush the toilet. He was gone only for a moment, but a moment was all it took for old memories to launch a tired attack. She couldn't remember how many times she'd woken up in the morning—or in the middle of the night—to the sound of Matthew's cell phone ringing. How many times she'd bid him goodbye, only to spend weeks worrying that he'd get shot in the middle of the jungle or get blown up by a land mine. Not that she'd had to worry. Oh no. Matt had been in constant danger, sure, but it turned out most of the danger came from the prostitutes and random strangers he hooked up with in whatever foreign country he'd been deployed to.

Question was, did Garrett share the same habits?

It was an unwelcome thought, not to mention a silly one. Raking both hands through her hair, she leaned against the wall next to the bedroom door for support, wishing she could exorcise the insecurities out of her brain, out of her heart. She had no right to worry about what Garrett might or might not do when he was on assignment. She wasn't his girlfriend or anything, and besides, seeing as she'd had sex with one of his closest friends last night, she really wasn't in a position to judge or reprimand.

"I'm a SEAL, Shel." Garrett's quiet voice filled the room, and when she lifted her head she saw him standing in the doorway of the bathroom, obviously aware of the distress in her eyes.

"When the team gets called, we've got no choice but to go wherever they want us."

"I know." Shoot. Did he notice the wobble in her voice?

Yep, he noticed. His expression softened as he stepped toward her and pulled her into his arms. His body was solid and warm against hers, his lips soft as he kissed her on the forehead. "I'll be back before you know it. And then we can continue what we started last night, okay?"

"And will you be starting a similar, um, enterprise with someone else, you know, if you meet a woman when you're gone?" The words came out before she could stop them, and from the flash of hurt she saw in his eyes, she knew she should've worked harder to rein in her fear and insecurity.

Garrett's hands dropped from her waist. "I can't believe you asked me that." He turned away from her, heading to the bed where he'd left his cell phone and tucking it into his pocket. "You honestly think that low of me?"

Whoa. When he turned back, the hurt on his face had tripled, his features now creased with both disbelief and anger.

"I..." She tried to find the right thing to say, if there even was one. "The guy I dated before...he used to fuck around whenever he was away, okay?"

"No, not okay." A muscle twitched in his handsome jaw. "I'm *nothing* like Matthew—yes, I know all about Matthew, your Marine, and yeah, I'd heard rumors that he couldn't keep his dick in his pants. But I don't do shit like that. I don't screw around on women I happen to care about."

"Garrett..." The fire in his eyes made her reconsider. Closing her mouth, she simply sighed and waited for him to get it all out.

"You think I'd say everything I said, about wanting you, about how crazy I am about you, and then turn around and fuck a stranger? Never mind that I'll be on the job, most likely in a remote corner of the world where the only women I'll encounter would rather strap bombs to their chests than fuck Americans, but damn it. You think I'd do that to you?"

She drew in a long breath, suddenly feeling ridiculously foolish for comparing this man to her ex. Garrett might have a wild past, but she believed him when he claimed to have been celibate for the last year, and in that year, he'd shown up at the café almost daily, buying lattes he didn't even like just so he could see her. And last night...God, last night he'd actually watched her have sex with his best friend just because he wanted to let her have the fantasy, because he wanted to be with her. And the way he kissed her...it was packed with way more emotion than anything she'd ever experienced.

Damn it, she really was an idiot.

Obviously Garrett agreed, because he was already making a swift move for the door. "Fuck this," he muttered. "Obviously our friendship this past year has taught you nothing about me. Obviously everything that happened last night—and mere minutes ago—didn't make any impact on you either. If you don't want to trust me, fine, don't trust me. Screw you, Shelby. I won't jump through hoops over something some other jerk did."

"Garrett—" But it was too late. He was already gone, and jeez, but the man could move. She'd barely made it two steps out of the bedroom after him when she heard the door of the apartment slam shut. A few moments later, the distant sound of an engine starting filled her ears, and then there was nothing but the light pounding of the rain against the windows.

Chapter Six

Garrett had just slung his duffel over his shoulder and was heading across the base toward the waiting Navy helicopter when a familiar voice stopped him in his tracks.

He froze for a second, then turned around and sure enough, Shelby was hurrying toward him. She was wearing a pair of faded jeans and a bright green T-shirt, and her wavy blonde hair was pretty much soaked from the rain.

He managed to hide his surprise as she walked toward him with quick strides. What was she doing here? After the way he'd left things back at her apartment, he hadn't expected to see her again this soon. If ever. Damn, he'd really fucked up, blowing up at her like that, but could anyone really blame him? He'd made it obvious how much he liked her, how badly he wanted to be with her, and in return she'd asked him if he was going to screw someone else when he was gone. Her distrust in him had been crushing. Maybe he shouldn't have yelled at her the way he had, but hell, how could she have so little faith in him?

"Do you have a minute?" she asked, pushing wet strands of hair out of her eyes.

It was possibly the most absurd question she could've asked. Not only was the sound of the helicopter blades whirring a clear sign that no, he didn't have a minute, but her polite tone made him want to kick something.

"Who let you out here?" he returned without answering her. His question made more sense, anyway, considering civilians weren't usually allowed in this part of the base.

"I did," came another voice.

Garrett glanced past Shelby's delicate shoulders and saw Carson striding toward them. Stopping only to give Shelby a quick side hug, Carson slung his bag over his shoulder and headed for the helicopter, where the rest of the team was waiting. "Don't fuck this up," Carson called without turning around, his words swallowed by the sound of the rotors.

Garrett glanced back at Shelby, wiping drops of rain from his face. "So...what's up?" Wonderful. Another stupid question to join the mix.

"I couldn't let you leave without..."

She hesitated and his brain quickly filled in the blank.

Breaking up with you.

Voicing my extreme dislike of you.

Kissing you.

"Apologizing," she finished.

"Apologizing," he repeated.

"Yeah." A shaky breath slipped out of her mouth. "I acted like an idiot. A jealous, insecure idiot. And you had every right to walk out on me the way you did."

He shook his head. "I should've stayed."

"Well, I shouldn't have asked you if you planned on sleeping with someone else when you're gone. And I definitely shouldn't have compared you to my ex."

"I shouldn't have said 'screw you'."

She laughed. "That was kind of harsh, but I think I deserved it." Her laughter faded quickly, and he could see the uncertainty floating in her gorgeous blue eyes. "Can you forgive me, Garrett?"

Jesus, he couldn't remember the last time a woman had stood before him and asked for his forgiveness. Usually he was the one doing the asking.

"I know you're probably still mad," she continued quickly, "but I really am sorry for the stuff I said, and I really do want to be with you when you get back. Whenever that is. I don't care if it's a day or a week or a month. I'll wait. I promise to be here when you come home."

Her words were so earnest that his heart expanded. His mouth went dry, and he couldn't seem to get any words out, which wasn't a good thing because Shelby's face fell as she obviously took his silence as a rejection.

"Yeah, that was probably dumb," she said with a self-deprecating smile. "The *I'll wait for you* part. A little too Jerry Maguire, huh?" Her gaze drifted to the helicopter roaring behind them. "You should go. I'll just get out of your way and—"

He kissed her. Just kissed her, right there in front of a helicopter full of SEALs a few of whom started whistling.

"It wasn't dumb," he murmured into her lips. "And I'm not mad, Shel. I was before, but God knows I can never stay mad at you." A drop of rain fell directly on her freckled nose and he leaned down to kiss it away. "I'm not going to screw around on you like your asshole boyfriend did, and now that I know you'll be waiting here for me when I get back, I'll work my ass off to make sure I come home as fast as I can, okay?"

"Is that a promise?"

"It's a guarantee."

"Good." She leaned up on her tiptoes and brushed her lips over his, then gently pushed him away. "You should go."

"Yeah, I really should." Yet he still couldn't stop himself from kissing her once more. This time he slipped her a little tongue.

"Go," she ordered, looking breathless and happy and so ridiculously hot he was almost tempted to face the wrath of his commander and simply not get on the chopper. But she gave him another shove and repeated, "Go."

"Fine," he grumbled.

"I'll see you when you get back."

"Good."

He'd only taken a few steps toward the waiting helicopter when he stopped and turned to shoot her a devilish look. "Hey, you know that ice thing you were doing last night?" he called. "When you were rubbing it all over yourself and pretty much driving me crazy?"

Laughing, she waited expectantly for him to continue.

"Well, when I come home, we're taking out the ice again. I don't care if there's a heat wave or not. I'm definitely rubbing a couple of ice cubes all over your very un-vanilla self, all right?"

"Is that a promise?" she called back.

"Nope." He grinned and repeated his earlier words. "It's a guarantee."

About the Author

To learn more about Elle, please visit www.ellekennedy.com. Send an email to Elle at elle@ellekennedy.com or visit her blog at http://sizzlingpens.blogspot.com/.

Look for these titles by
Elle Kennedy

Now Available:

Bad Moon Rising
Dance of Seduction
Midnight Encounters

Going For It

Out of Uniform Series
Heat of the Moment (Book 1)
Heat of Passion (Book 2)

Print Anthology
Midsummer Night's Steam: Hot Summer Nights

Lady Sings the Blues

Mallery Malone

Dedication

To Bailey, my own personal guitar hero, for being my cheerleader in so many ways. And to the other Bailey for crawling into my lap and licking my face when I needed it. I love you guys!

Chapter One

Hotlanta was earning its nickname tonight.

Alina Gabriel surveyed the crowd packing the lower level of her club, The Scarlet Lady. Ladies' night always brought out a good crowd of hot bodies wanting to see and be seen, and this June night was no exception. She'd made sure the beer tubs and bars were well stocked, knowing that scantily clad women would be rushing the nearest bartender to order shots, beers and fruity drinks.

The anticipated rush had nothing to do with the ninety-degree temperature outside. She had Joshua Hanover to thank for that.

Brilliant blue eyes, somewhere on the spectrum between turquoise and teal, mesmerized the crowd through luscious dark lashes. His hair called to mind a luxurious mink coat, sleek, rich, begging to be touched. Generous lips almost always caught in a secret smile softened the strength of his features, the determined chin and proud nose.

Still, Alina knew it wasn't just his looks that had women packing The Scarlet Lady three nights a week. No, she also had his guitar to thank.

For Joshua, his guitar was muse, lover, friend. It was bitch, goddess, mistress. He loved it as much as he needed it. He could make it cry and sing and moan. Every woman who flocked to his performances wanted to be his guitar.

Night after night Alina would watch as his fingers, long and strong and callused at the tips, danced over each string, stroking, pressing, plucking. Every woman in the audience felt an answering chord strum deep in the channel of her sex. If they didn't, they were dead.

Alina wished she could be immune to his charms, but she wasn't. After nearly three months of performances she still creamed her panties watching him make love with his guitar. Joshua had been very good for her bottom line, but he was hell on her hormones.

Not that Joshua noticed, she thought ruefully. He didn't notice his hordes of adoring fans either, no matter how desperately they jockeyed for position during his shows, knowing he was single. When Joshua performed, he was in a world by himself, just him and his guitar, with his band, Blue Highway, there almost as window dressing.

Even if he would glance up from molding his guitar to his will to whip the audience into sonic bliss, he wouldn't see the thinner, prettier and more desperate women clamoring for his attention. He wouldn't see Alina standing at the glass wall of her second-floor office or prowling the bar top.

Joshua was blind.

Sometimes he wore tinted shades over those magnificent eyes, sometimes he didn't. Having sat across from him in her office on more than one occasion, Alina was glad Joshua couldn't see. Otherwise he'd realize just how hot and bothered he made her.

She bit her lip in sexual frustration. The need had been building all night. Blues music always made her horny— Joshua's music intensified that desire until it went from a need for sex to a need to be well and truly fucked. Joshua's specialty:

singing sensual songs about softly sexing someone.

God, he made her wet.

"You going down, Miss Scarlet? He's playing your song."

Alina looked up, surprised to see Bobby, one of her bouncers, standing a step below her. She surveyed the crowd and found a large portion of the male contingent turned her way, rhythmically clapping. Over the applause, she could hear the bluesy opening riffs of what they'd all come to think of as her song, "Red-Letter Woman".

Alina smiled. As much as the women came to see Joshua, the men came to see her in her club persona as the Scarlet Lady. Miss Scarlet was known to dance atop the main bar with a riding crop in one hand and a bottle of Stoli in the other. Her alter ego was a throwback to her former life as an exotic dancer, a life that had financed her business degree and provided seed money to start the club. She'd made her money by looking good, and knew she had exercise to thank as much as the genes passed down from her black father and Latina mother.

Tonight she had a different sort of exercise in mind, thanks to Joshua and his damned guitar. Since she had a while to go before she could sneak away to her private office, she'd have to get her kicks by dancing instead. The bar top wasn't going to cut it, though. Joshua had gotten her hot. It was time to return the favor.

She extended her left arm, encased from fingertips to elbow in red silk gloves. "You know what, Bobby? Since this is the last set of the night, I think it's time to mix it up a little. I'm going to the stage."

Joshua hid a smile as the applause grew louder, accompanied by whistles and catcalls. Miss Scarlet had obviously taken the bait and agreed to grace the club with a dance.

He didn't need to see her. His band mates couldn't talk about anything or anyone else since they'd started this gig. They debated whether she was black, white, Latina, or a combination of all three. Not that it mattered. A hot woman was a hot woman, his sax man said, and everyone agreed Miss Scarlet was definitely that.

Alina Gabriel, aka Miss Scarlet, with the body of a fallen angel, wore a shade of red every day. Pete had gotten good at describing every outfit she wore and every move she made. Tonight, Miss Scarlet wore a pair of red leather boots with lacing up the back, a strip of black that would be a skirt on a first grader, a red corset and matching gloves up to her elbows.

Joshua hadn't seen colors or much of anything else since he was twelve, but he remembered red. It was his favorite color.

No, he didn't need to see her to know her. He knew the husky alto of her voice, the particular cadence of her words as they talked business and shows and receipts in her office. He knew her scent, a tantalizing combination of licorice and ginger and sometimes leather whenever she passed him or leaned close to make a point. He knew that most days in her heels her chin topped his shoulder, which probably put her at five-seven in her bare feet. He knew she had a soft laugh that made things tighten low in his gut.

He knew he wanted her. Hell, every man in the club wanted her—and some of the women too. He also knew he didn't have a chance. It wouldn't stop him from trying, though.

The heat around him receded some. Obviously they'd taken one of the spotlights off him. He leaned away from the mic, towards the left where Pete always stood. "Has she hit the bar yet?"

"No, man, she's coming to the stage!"

Well, well. Joshua leaned into his microphone. "Ladies and gentlemen, please welcome to the stage the one, the only, Miss Scarlet!"

The crowd screamed as Blue Highway launched into the first verse of "Red-Letter Woman". Joshua could feel the electricity of the audience focusing on the stage, ratcheting up in intensity. Normally that was all he needed, though most times he didn't even need that. For years he'd just played to the cobwebs. Tonight though, he wanted more.

Miss Scarlet's dances happened when she wanted them to and not a moment before. Joshua had composed the song to entice her to dance, even though he couldn't see her. The lyrics had come to him easily, whispered in his ear like a dirty little secret in the middle of the night. He'd put everything into the musical homage, every hungry, hot, horny need. Knowing his song could prod her to dance gave him a thrill of pleasure.

Come here. He sang out to her, plucking notes from the guitar to wrap around her, draw her closer.

"She's a red-letter woman/She'll make you lose control. When she's done having her way/She'll own you body and soul. She's a red-letter woman/Lord, what a way to go."

Then he felt her. Felt the heat of her body and the spotlight as she strutted across the front of the stage between him and the crowd. They screamed in response and Pete missed a note. What the hell did she do?

He caught the licorice scent beneath the sultry perfume she usually wore, knew she'd come closer to him. His concentration rose away from the music, the guitar, and focused on her.

She moved behind his stool, her hands lightly balanced on his shoulders. Somehow he kept going with the song even though all he could think about was the woman behind him.

Her breasts pressed against his back as her hands slid down his arms. Now it was his turn to miss a note, then another as she breathed into his ear, "Thanks for the song, darlin'."

Next thing he knew, she'd pushed him to his feet, moving the stool away. It was time for his solo anyway, and he poured all his frustration and need into his guitar, wringing his want from the strings.

Miss Scarlet only granted him a temporary reprieve, moving away for a four-count before pressing her back against him to slide slowly to the floor. He went as still as he could when he felt her slink between his legs. The crowd shrieked their approval, and he was very grateful for the wide-body Fender in his hands. The last thing he wanted to do was show the audience just how much he wanted Miss Scarlet.

She moved away from him at last, allowing him to clear his head enough to finish his solo and rope the rest of the band back into the song. Somehow they managed to finish the number, but with none of their usual tightness. Joshua couldn't hold it against them, though. He'd give his left nut to see her dance.

Thunderous applause rocked the stage, but Joshua knew only a portion of it was for Blue Highway. He adjusted his neck strap so that he could shift the guitar to his right hip, then grabbed the microphone. "Thank you—and a special thanks to Miss Scarlet. I'm surprised the fire alarms didn't go off after that!"

An arm slid around his waist from the left, bringing warmth, the hint of licorice. "Come on, people—let's hear it for Joshua Hanover and Blue Highway!" Miss Scarlet called out. "And while y'all are doing that, let me give Joshua a proper thank you for my song."

She leaned into him, put a gloved hand to his cheek, then kissed him.

It was a hot, open-mouthed kiss. He couldn't do anything but respond—except that he had a damned guitar in the way. Knowing there wouldn't be a better time, he snaked his left arm around her waist to haul her closer, taking over the kiss as the crowd went wild.

Damn, she felt good against him! His hand slid up her back, over the laces that held the satiny top closed, to brush the smooth bare skin just below her shoulder blades. She gasped against his mouth, a beautiful sound that made him want her more, want her writhing beneath him, singing his name.

Finally she pulled away. "Hot damn," she said into the microphone, her throaty voice breathless. "I think I need a drink after that! Which reminds me, it's last call."

A chorus of boos and groans answered her. "I know, I know, but the city rules. Besides, that's all the show you're getting tonight, pervies. Remember, you don't have to go home, but you can't stay here."

The heat of the spotlights left his face, but the heat of her body lingered. "Thanks again, Joshua," she said, and with a final stroke of his cheek, left him.

Oh, hell no. Joshua pulled his guitar off. She might consider that kiss just part of the show, but damned if he would. If she wanted a show, he'd give her a show—a show she'd never forget.

Chapter Two

Alina made it to her second floor office without incident. The last thing she needed was to have witnesses to her horniness, or be stopped by someone who could fit the bill of Mr. Right Now.

Damn Joshua and that song! She'd been able to resist the first two nights, but not tonight. Tonight he'd been on her mind, and he'd launched into the song—her song—as if he knew it would bring her to the stage. And it had.

She moved quickly through the reception area of her office, just a level above the VIP area of the club. Sitting behind soundproofed glass and offering a bird's-eye view of the club, it boasted the expected black leather couches and chairs, crimson neon and a fully stocked bar. A flick of a switch piped the club's sound system into the room, perfect for her rare private parties.

Impatience had her muttering a curse as she used her teeth to strip her gloves off before punching in the private access code to her office door. She had a desperate need to masturbate. She needed Joshua. Since she couldn't have him, her toys would have to do.

The door swung closed behind her as she stepped into her personal sanctuary. Here the industrial décor gave way to warm, rich wood tones in the desk furniture and muted reds in the carpet and the oversized couch sprawling beneath a Renoir print. The two-hundred-gallon fish tank served as an additional soothing barrier, but she didn't need soothing. She needed the collection she kept in the bottom left drawer of the massive maple banker's desk.

Reaching under her micro mini, she hooked her fingers into her G-string, pulling it down her thighs and over her boots. With a thrill of pleasure, she plopped into her leather chair, propped one booted foot on the desk, and prepared to vibrate herself silly.

A soft knock was the only warning she got before the door opened. She looked up, prepared to fire the intruder on the spot, but it wasn't Bobby or Salazar, her manager.

The red tip of the cane poked through the open door a moment before Joshua's foot, then the rest of him.

"Alina," Joshua called softly.

Flushing, she started to pull her fingers away, embarrassed at being caught. Then she stopped herself. There was no way Joshua could know what she'd been doing. "Joshua. What is it?"

"I think you know what." A soft smile bowed his lips as the door closed behind him. He looked too damn good for her peace of mind with the snug jeans, the dark brown shirt, sleeves rolled up to his forearms, those amazing eyes. He moved confidently through her office—she'd made sure not to move anything since he'd started playing in the club. "I could help you, if you want."

Alina took a cautious breath. She was pretty sure she hadn't made a sound. "Help me with what, balancing the books?"

His smile widened as he took the seat across from her. "Is that what you call it? A task you tick off so you can get back to your busy schedule? Somehow I don't think so."

Temper rose as arousal ebbed, but she didn't pull her hand away. "I don't know what you're talking about."

"I think you do." His turquoise eyes—it was so wrong for a man to have eyes like that—seemed to bore right into her as he sat forward. "Don't you want to come?"

Shit. Somehow he did know. Still, she played it. "Come where?"

His grin widened. Alina had an urgent need to lean across the desk and close her teeth gently on his lower lip. "On the desk, the floor, or your couch—doesn't really matter, does it? You're just about at the edge of it now. I can smell and hear how excited and wet you are."

"Really?" She tried to sound angry, but it came out breathy.

"Really." He sat back. "And unless I'm mistaken, you've got one leg up on your desk and two fingers working your pussy."

Busted. "I'm not getting myself off in front of you," she exclaimed, trying to sound outraged, angry. She failed.

"Not now you're not. Like I said, I could help you with that."

It was tempting. Way the hell too tempting. She'd been simmering for him for months.

"That little dance you did on the stage," he said, his voice low, compelling. "My band never misses a beat. Never. Bar fights, boob flashing, hot girls kissing each other—the guys have seen it all and tell me all about it. But they never lost it. Until you came to the stage."

He swept a hand lightly over the surface of her desk, stopping when his fingers brushed across her booted foot. "Pete told me exactly what you're wearing and every move you made before you came over to me. I didn't need the play-by-play for that. And then there was that kiss."

"That kiss," she repeated, her fingers brushing against her

pussy lips.

"Was that just part of the show?" His fingers plucked at her laces. "Your reaction when I kissed you back—was that just for the audience?"

She knew he couldn't see her, but his eyes, now a dark teal in the dimness of her office, seemed to bore straight through her, compelling the truth. "No."

"Good." His fingers stroked over the leather encasing her foot. "Then there's no reason why we can't have our own private show, now is there? Unless, you have a problem with this?" He tapped his index finger against his temple.

"I don't have a problem with your blindness," she exclaimed, heat creeping up her cheeks.

"Prove it," he shot back, his face set in implacable lines. "Come here."

Damn. He had to issue a challenge. She never backed down. Ever. It was her stubbornness as much as her business aptitude that made The Scarlet Lady a success. And her love life a mess.

The only other thing she couldn't seem to resist besides a challenge was Joshua's voice and the mesmerizing play of his fingers.

As if reading her thoughts, he stretched out a hand to her and gave her a smile as smooth as jazz. "Come here," he repeated. Only this time, his voice was soft, full of promise and seduction and sin. Just as it was when he sang.

She slid both feet to the floor and stood. Keeping her eyes on his face, she moved around the corner of her desk until she stood in front of him.

"Sit on the edge of your desk," he ordered.

She raised her eyebrow at the tone, not that he noticed,

then sat. "Well?"

He shifted his chair forward, pushing her thighs apart. "Put your feet here," he requested, patting the sloped armrests of his chair.

Alina complied, mesmerized by that voice, the promise of his fingers. The balls of her feet balanced on the edge of each armrest as her thighs fell open for him. She briefly wondered how long she could keep her balance like that, then decided she'd hold the position for as long as it took.

Pure challenge filled his grin. "Why don't you lean back? You'll still be able to see what you need to see."

She snorted in response and was rewarded with a low chuckle. "I promise, I won't let you miss any of the show."

She didn't know what she expected him to do next. Certainly not make her wait. She watched his hand, strong, long-fingered, sweep over her boot. From the pointed tip to the stiletto heel, back up over the laces to her knee.

"I've become very tactile," he told her as his hands skimmed up her knees. "This is the way I see."

She had to swallow before she could speak. "All right, you're free to look all you want."

His fingers stroked over her thighs. "Just look?"

Little electric pulses zinged through her, heightening her need for him. "God, I hope not."

"Good." His hands moved over her skirt. "Wow, that is a blink of a skirt, isn't it? No wonder those guys were screaming at the foot of the stage."

"You had your share of screaming fans," she felt compelled to remind him. "I think a few of them lost their panties."

His fingers dipped between her thighs. "So did you."

Alina's heart triple-beat as his thumb brushed over her

pussy. Desire ramped up another notch as she whispered his name. The whisper became a gasp of protest as he continued "looking" at her, rising from the chair as his palms skimmed up the front of her Chinese brocade corset.

"May I?" he asked, his fingers hovering over the hooks running down the front.

"Please."

He took his time unhooking the busk, working his way from top to bottom. She took a deep breath as he eased the corset away from her breasts, then lost it again as he lowered his head to brush his lips across her belly button.

She thrust her fingers into the lush thickness of his hair, closing her eyes as his lips roamed up her belly to her breastbone, leaving fire in his wake. So focused was she on his lips that she gasped with surprise when he cupped her breasts.

"Joshua." Her head lolled back as the string-roughened pads of his fingers stroked over her already hard nipples, tightening them further. His mouth warmed her skin as his lips traced her throat, her chin, her cheek.

Finally, oh God, finally his right hand slid down her belly to stroke her clit. "Kiss me, Alina," he demanded. "Kiss me like you did onstage."

She curved an arm around his neck and plastered her mouth to his, kissing him with everything she had. She'd been on a slow burn and he'd just thrown kerosene on the fire. His tongue slid against hers, imitating his fingers sliding into her pussy, thrusting boldly, retreating, thrusting again.

Then his thumb pressed against her clit. All at once she exploded, crying out against his lips as he strummed an orgasm out of her.

"Have you 'seen' everything you wanted to see?" she asked against his lips when she could form words again.

"God yes." He pulled away from her long enough to fumble free his belt and unzip his trousers.

"Good." She made quick work of the buttons on his shirt then pushed his trousers and boxers down his hips, freeing his cock to her gaze.

"Happy birthday to me." She stroked the hot, hard length of him. God, he was the perfect size for fucking, and not overly thick. What would it feel like to have him filling her ass? The thought made her breathless.

"Do you have condoms?" he asked her, his husky voice strained. "I wasn't planning for this. I'm clean—I get tested regularly—but I believe in being safe."

"So do I," she told him, relieved that there'd be no drama about dressing for the party. She twisted around, rummaging through the assorted condoms she kept for her various toys in her center desk drawer. Finding one, she quickly tore it open then turned back to reach for him.

She gripped him again, enjoying the feel of him in her hand. Joshua hummed his appreciation as she stroked him then rolled the condom down onto his erection.

His hands palmed her butt, impatiently dragging her to the edge of the desk. The head of his cock bumped against her before slowly breaching her pussy. They groaned in unison as he pushed into her, filling her.

"Damn," he breathed. "Hot, so hot. Hope the desk can take it."

"The desk can take it and so can I." Her teeth closed on his earlobe.

It apparently was all the permission he needed. His hands gripped her shoulders as he began to stroke in and out of her, his hips pistoning with the effort. Alina wrapped her legs around his hips, her arms curving around his shoulders.

Pleasure rippled through her, driving mewling sounds from deep in her throat.

Joshua laid her back against the desk, driving into her with dizzying intensity. She wrapped her legs higher around his waist, settling him even deeper, gasping as he repeatedly hit a perfect spot deep inside her. Her nails sank into his shoulders as she struggled to hold on, struggled to contain the pleasure that threatened to burn her up.

Her inner muscles spasmed, tightening around him again. Joshua's thrusts became wild, his breath harsh against her ear. All at once he stiffened against her, a long, low groan seeping from him as he came.

His hands bracketed her face as he levered his weight off her. "Now that was a show," he said, then gave her a slow, drugging kiss before pulling away. "Are you all right?"

She let him tug her upright, trying to get her bearings. "I think so, but I think the edge of my blotter is permanently imprinted on my ass."

"Let me see." His hand stroked over her buttocks, sending a delicious shiver through her. "I could massage that out for you, if you like."

She rolled her eyes at him. "Haven't you done enough already?"

His answering grin lit a new fire low in her belly. "If you think so, darlin', you need to learn more about me. What happened to the box of tissue you keep on your desk?"

"Uh, we must have knocked it off." She felt an irrational blush creeping up her cheeks as she retrieved the tissue box from the floor. "Here you go." She guided the box to his outstretched hand.

"Thanks." He disposed of his condom. "Don't you have a couch in this office?"

"Yeah. Why?"

"Showmanship 101, babe. There's always an encore." He quickly shed the rest of his clothing.

Laughter bubbled out of her. "Then I'll make sure to properly show my appreciation for your performance."

Grabbing a handful of condoms from her desk, she took his hand to guide him to her seating area, pushing him down onto the sofa. Humming, she shimmied out of her tiny skirt, leaving nothing but her boots on. It would take too long to take them off, and she had more interesting ways to spend her time.

Joshua smiled up at her. "I guess you like the song, huh?"

She blushed as she realized she'd been humming the melody to "Red-Letter Woman". "It does grow on you," she admitted.

"Grow on you?" he repeated. "And here I was, hoping it would get me laid."

Instead of answering, she knelt in front of him, fisted his cock in her hand. "Got anything else to say, funny man?"

"Yeah." He swallowed. "Keep doing that."

She obliged him, pumping his hardened flesh with long strokes. God, she really wanted to take him into her mouth, but lubricated condoms weren't made for taste. Besides, what would she look like throwing safe sex rules out the window the first night? Mama didn't raise no fools.

"You have a beautiful cock." She blew a bit of cool air across the tip.

"Gugh." Joshua's head thumped against the back of the couch. "I'll get a new test done tomorrow if it means I get a real blowjob."

"Compose another song for me, and you never know what can happen." She bent forward, nestling the hot length of his erection deep between her breasts.

"Alina." His cock jerked against her, hardening further as she stroked him with her tits. Fingers threaded through her hair. "God bless America."

She laughed, thrilled that she could make him feel as good as he made her. "You say the craziest things."

His hips rose from the couch, the movement pushing his dick up and down the path of her cleavage. "You keep that up, I'll be speaking in tongues next."

"I'll take that as a compliment." She eased back to tear open another foil packet, and he sighed in obvious disappointment. A pleased flush crawled up her cheeks. In all her fantasies featuring Joshua Hanover, she'd never imagined he'd be this appreciative of her skills.

After sheathing him in the condom, she straddled him, her hands resting on the back of the couch for leverage. He guided the head of his cock to her pussy as she slowly sank down. The slow impalement had her moaning in pure delight. "You feel so good."

"So do you," he whispered as she settled against his thighs. "So damn good."

Wrapping her arms around his neck, Alina brushed her lips across his as she rode him with slow, shifting movements. With that first frantic hunger sated, she could concentrate on the feel of his body moving inside hers, the play of his fingers on her nipples.

"Joshua." Her lips brushed against his mouth as the insistent song of desire rang through her body. His hips rocked in a sensual rhythm beneath her while his lips blazed a seductive trail to her throat. Pleasure spiraled through her as she leaned back to get even more of his cock inside her.

The movement thrust her breasts up against his chin, but

he didn't seem to mind. He followed the curve of her skin, unerringly finding the hardened tip. Another groan was pulled from her as the warmth of his mouth surrounded her nipple.

She bounced now, riding him harder, straining to reach that elusive peak of pleasure. His hands gripped her ass, helping her as his hips bucked wildly. When his teeth grazed her sensitized flesh she cried out, her body arching against his as the orgasm steamrolled into her. His breathing harsh and deep, Joshua slammed upwards once, twice, then again, his fingers almost painful on her buttocks as he came.

Alina collapsed against him, forehead pressed against his as she struggled to catch her breath. When she did, she said the first thing that came to mind.

"Now *that's* what I call an encore."

Chapter Three

After a week of pure sexual bliss, Alina was well and truly addicted to Joshua.

Not that they had sex every day. Just every day that he came to the club. They'd talk business, then hit the nearest horizontal surface. He'd go do a sound check while she met with her staff. He'd perform, she'd dance or not, then they'd retire to her office for more orgasmic duets.

Joshua was the most attentive lover she'd ever had, one who enjoyed every aspect of sex from foreplay to afterglow. Kissing him was the equivalent of doing premium tequila shots, smooth, powerful, intoxicating.

They'd gone for each other almost as soon as her office door had closed, somehow making it to the oversized couch tucked against the far wall. She straddled his lap, wanting more of those drugging kisses.

"What's this you're wearing?" he asked, his fingers running over her back. "And why are you still wearing it?"

"It's a mesh bodysuit."

"Do you really like it? It's kinda in the way, and I don't want to rip it trying to get it off you."

"You don't have to get it off me." She took his hands, brought them to her exposed breasts. "It's very convenient." She slid his hands down her belly to the open crotch.

"You're the gift that keeps on giving," he breathed in appreciation as his fingers played a sensual melody between her thighs.

"Actually," she began, lifting her hips to give him better access, "there's something you could give me, if you don't mind."

"Really? What do you want, Alina?"

"My ass." She gasped as he nibbled her collarbone. "I want you to fuck me up the ass."

"Damn, I love a straightforward woman. Do you think I'll fit?"

Alina loved anal sex. Some women walked around with Ben Wa balls in their pussies for private pleasure, but not her. She preferred a tapered four-inch butt plug and a slow drive down pothole-riddled roads. She had to admit though, what Joshua had to offer was so much better.

"I've got lube, and I know how to use it."

He grinned. "Excellent."

Alina gasped as Joshua dumped her off his lap. He slid to his knees on the floor, pushed her legs apart, then lowered his head.

The touch of his tongue to her clit was electric. She fell back against the pillows, breathless and boneless as he slowly slid from her clit, deep into her pussy, then down to the circle of her ass. By the time he reversed direction, her entire body quivered with need and want.

Joshua pressed even closer, spearing her vagina with his tongue repeatedly. Alina moaned as desire coiled deep within her, liquefying her insides. She opened her thighs as wide as she could, giving him complete access to her body.

"Baby, you're so wet," he murmured in appreciation, sinking two fingers inside her.

"And you're so good," she managed to say, her body burning for him. She thrust her fingers into his luxurious hair, lifting her pussy against his hungry mouth as he continued the duet of tongue and hand, driving her higher and higher. One thick finger slid from her pussy to her ass, pressing against the tight opening. She gasped in full sensory overload as he breached her, then screamed as he sucked on her clit, catapulting her into orgasm.

She slid off the couch and into his lap, wanting, needing his cock inside her. He shifted, sliding into her waiting pussy in one smooth, thick motion. Little purrs of satisfaction seeped from her as she began to ride him, fastening her mouth to his, taking her taste from his lips.

His hands clamped down on her shoulders, pushed her away. "Why?"

"Condom." The word rasped from his throat. "On the ottoman."

She found a foil packet, handed it to him, then bent over the ottoman, knees spread for support. Her entire body vibrated with anticipation. She heard the rip of foil, the soft sounds as he rolled the condom onto his cock. Finally she felt the rubber-wrapped head of his cock slide along her pussy lips to bump against the bottom of her clit. Knowing what he wanted, she reached between her thighs, helped him enter.

He growled in soft appreciation as he slowly slid in and out of her, the condom getting good and coated in her pussy juice. Her insides warmed, breasts aching as her need for him increased with each thrust. His hands slid up her waist, skimming around to cradle her breasts, the rough pads of his string-callused fingers teasing her nipples to bullet points. The sensation skittered over her nerves, stealing her breath and heating her blood.

He pulled out, then pressed the slick head of his dick against her ass. She held still, a little bit uncertain. Joshua had a nice-sized cock, and the reality of his dick, even in a lubed condom coated with her juices, was a whole lot different from her favorite vibrating butt plug.

"Alina?"

She licked her lips, then planted her forearms on the ottoman, shifting her hips to lift her ass. "Do it, please. Fuck me now."

Without another word, he slowly eased the head of his cock into her ass. She groaned, arching her back in an attempt to relax into the shock of pleasure-pain.

"That's it," he whispered, lightly raking his fingernails down her spine. She shivered in response and he pushed an inch deeper, then deeper still. Finally he bottomed out, his balls lightly pressed against her.

"Damn, you feel good," he growled, leaning over her. He withdrew slowly and just as slowly returned. She moaned and closed her eyes as sweat beaded on her skin, shifting against him as he shifted forward. Pleasure rippled through her, his name breaking on her lips as he began a steady pace.

Then he stopped.

Her eyes popped open. "Joshua?"

His breath brushed against her ear. "Go to dinner with me."

She looked over her shoulder at him. Dark hair fell into his brilliant eyes. Passion tightened his gorgeous features, or maybe it was determination. "What?"

"You heard me." He withdrew with a long stroke that made

her breath stutter. "Dinner. You and me. Tomorrow night, anywhere but here, and we actually go to bed when we go to bed."

"Can't we discuss this later?" She tried to impale herself onto his cock again, but his hands gripped her waist.

"Say yes." He took his sweet time filling her again, flattening her against the ottoman. "You go to dinner with me, Alina, and leave The Scarlet Lady at home."

How was she supposed to say yes? All she knew of relating to Joshua was within the club as Miss Scarlet. She wouldn't know the first thing to do or say with him outside of these walls. Alina knew he'd realize in the first five minutes how much of a fake she was, and then he'd be gone.

Still she tried. "You do know I'm black, don't you?"

"You do know I'm blind, don't you?"

Point taken. It was a stupid thing to bring up now considering how many times they'd had sex in the past week. Here it didn't matter at all. Outside though, was a different story.

At that moment, she didn't care. All she cared about was getting more of his cock inside her.

He leaned over her again, his chest pressing into her mesh-covered back, his hands once again cupping her breasts. Rolling her nipples between his thumbs and forefingers, Joshua quickly pumped her ass four, five times, then stopped again, the head of his cock barely lodged inside her.

"Joshua!" Caught between begging and anger, she pounded her fist against the leather beneath her. "Stop fucking around and fuck me already!"

His fingers tightened on her nipples, but his teeth nipping the back of her neck made her moan. "Dinner. Tomorrow."

"All right!" she wailed, ready to say anything, do anything, to get him to make her come. "Dinner tomorrow."

His tongue stroked between her shoulder blades before his teeth closed on her right earlobe. "Rub your clit," he breathed, moving inside her, plunging deep.

Alina thrust her hand between her thighs, her middle finger stroking her swollen, hungry flesh. His right hand slipped around her hip, his fingers framing her clit and squeezing gently.

Her knees almost buckled, but that thick cock kept her upright. Those blunt fingers, played a duet with her, squeezing and teasing her clit with deliciously increasing pressure as he steadily fucked her ass. One moment she was pushing up a hill of pleasure, the next she was over it, sobbing as her orgasm hit her.

Clamping his hands to her hips, Joshua began to thoroughly fuck her, driving into her ass with methodical intensity. The orgasm still held her, tingling her skin, creaming her thighs, ripples of sensation that had her reflexively squeezing his dick in a sexual massage as he slapped against her.

Joshua groaned in response, his hips bucking wildly as he slammed into her, making her breathless, making her cry out again. He rammed her once more, causing the ottoman to shift as he came deep inside her ass with a guttural moan.

"Holy fuck," he breathed, then collapsed onto her.

Alina had to agree.

Chapter Four

She was out of her mind.

It was the only explanation that made sense to Alina. Experiencing multiple orgasms with Joshua had obviously driven every rational thought out of her head. Why the hell else was she standing in the middle of her walk-in closet, wearing nothing but a bra and panties, trying to figure out what to wear on a date with a blind man?

Joshua had made it perfectly clear that he considered their outing a date. He'd picked the time and place for dinner, told her he'd pick her up and to wear something nice.

Something nice? She had leather corsets that cost several hundred dollars, but those wouldn't work in Atlanta in June. They certainly wouldn't fly at any of the upscale restaurants in the entertainment district near her club. Besides, he'd made her promise to leave Miss Scarlet at home. He wanted to take the real Alina out to dinner.

The real Alina was scared shitless.

She'd been Miss Scarlet for seven years, starting the summer before her junior year of college. The persona was an indelible part of her, more Alina than Alina herself. The only time she wasn't Miss Scarlet was during family visits, and that wasn't out of shame. Mom had been a Vegas showgirl, after all.

She could admit to herself that she wanted to look good for

Joshua. She wanted to believe that this was a real date, that they were two people at the start of a beautiful relationship. But the thought just flat-out terrified her. She didn't know what Joshua wanted beyond what she was already giving him, but it couldn't be to actually date her.

Nobody wanted to date Miss Scarlet. Fuck her silly, yeah. Photos with her, a lap dance, sure thing. But stroll down the street arm in arm on the way to church? Hell to the no.

That didn't mean that she couldn't pretend. She pulled on a lightweight strapless dress of deep cherry red that fell in a full skirt to just above her knees. After slipping into a pair of silver sandals, she added a silver beaded necklace and matching earrings to complete the simple silhouette.

She regarded herself critically in the cheval mirror. Elegant, yes, but with her bust defying gravity against the bodice, hardly demure.

Not that she cared. She was who she was, and if people couldn't handle it, it was their problem, not hers.

Maybe if she kept repeating that to herself, she'd actually start to believe it.

"May I ask you a personal question?" she blurted out.

Joshua pushed his plate back, then braced his elbows on the table. "As long as I get to return the favor."

He could almost hear her weighing the ramifications. Apparently she'd decided the risk was worth it because she continued. "All right. Were you born blind? Sometimes you say things that make me think you weren't."

"You're right. I lost my sight completely when I was twelve.

238

Since it was a gradual thing, my parents made sure I had as much visual stimulation as possible beforehand. Thanks to them, I got to see the Grand Canyon, Niagara Falls, the Great Pyramid. And my dad's Playboy collection. You can probably guess which one I thought was the best at the time."

"I can imagine," she said dryly.

"Despite all that, I became a rebellious teenager." He smiled. "Combine new hormones and teenage angst with losing my sight, and it's a wonder my parents didn't ship me off and wash their hands of me."

"What happened?"

"What didn't happen?" He gave a self-deprecating laugh. "There's the time I stole my mom's car and actually made it out of the driveway and four houses down the road before I took out a mailbox and a little Toyota."

"Oh my God!" Alina smothered a laugh.

"Go ahead and laugh. Dad beat my ass good over that one. Then I had some friends leave me at the mall so that I could try to find my way home on my own, all Kung Fu master-like. My mom tore me up over that one, which was really embarrassing considering I was already taller than her at the time."

"You were hell in high tops," she said in amazement.

"Damn right. I was mad and I had to get it out somehow. Finally Dad told me that if I was going to bitch and moan about my handicap, I might as well set it to music. Then he gave me my first guitar. I went to college on a musical scholarship. The rest is history."

"That's a terrific story." She fell silent, and he wondered about her expression. He'd been intent on giving her a memorable night on the town, not only for his benefit but because she deserved a break from spending every waking moment at the club. He couldn't do her job for her—and knew she wouldn't want him to anyway—but he could provide a respite. At least for starters.

"So what about you?" he wondered. "How did you end up being Miss Scarlet, proud and beautiful owner of The Scarlet Lady?"

"My boobs."

"Excuse me?"

"You heard what I said. I've got a killer body and I've put it to good use. Miss Scarlet was an exotic dancer for seven years. My breasts paid for college and the down payment on the club."

He digested that. "Your parents didn't have a problem with that?"

"Seeing as how they weren't paying for my higher education, no," she answered. "But then, my mom was a showgirl in Vegas, so she really couldn't say much. Besides, all I did was dance. I didn't do drugs or extracurricular activities on the side. I danced, got my money, got the hell out." He heard her draw in a careful breath. "Do you have a problem with that?"

"No," he answered, his voice firm. "But I gather some people have?"

"It's to be expected." She sighed. "Sometimes it's easier to avoid the drama and be single. Besides, I'm all but married to the club right now. Every waking moment is spent making sure The Scarlet Lady is a success."

A saxophone sounded the opening bars to a jazz version of "I Get So Lonely". Joshua tugged on her hand. "Let's dance."

She resisted. "We don't have to."

Why didn't she want to? "What?" he asked, his tone deliberately teasing. "You think this white boy can't dance?"

"No, I know you've got some moves."

He felt a stupid grin spread across his face as he gently pulled her to her feet. "Come on, Alina," he whispered in her ear, pulling her closer. "I've been giving you what you want for the last few days. Give me this. Be with me tonight."

"All right." She led him a few paces away from their table, then moved into his arms.

Joshua closed his eyes as she melted against him, her head resting against his shoulder. This was what he'd had in mind for their date: Alina letting go, daring to just be.

He took a deep breath, inhaling the sweet spice of her skin, the products that told him she'd gone to a hair salon. His hand brushed the bare skin of her shoulder blades before settling against the small of her back.

She snuggled closer, a bone-deep sigh easing out of her. Her fingers slid from his shoulder to his cheek.

"Are you tired?" he asked quietly. "Maybe it's time to go home."

"I'm not tired," she answered, her voice surprisingly shy. "But I wouldn't mind if we went home."

It began to rain as soon as they climbed into the taxi. By the time they reached the entrance to Alina's building, the drizzle had intensified to a thunderstorm, pounding mercilessly on the roof of the taxi.

"We could go around the block and see if it lets up," Joshua suggested. "Or maybe find the nearest Walgreens for an umbrella."

"A little rain never hurt anyone," she said gamely. "Of course, hail is a different story."

"What if I promise to kiss each and every bruise you get?" he asked, reaching for his wallet to pay the driver.

"You know exactly what to say to make a girl daring," she

241

said. "And hey, it's not like I don't have plenty of towels."

He pulled his jacket off. "Put this over your head, and you'll only get slightly drenched. I'll get out first since I won't mind the rain nearly as much, then take your arm. Is it okay if we walk quickly instead of run? I'm trying to impress this really hot chick and I'd hate to wind up on my ass on the sidewalk."

She laughed. "I think I can handle it."

He thrust open the door. A sheet of water greeted them. "Bonzai!" he yelled, then climbed out of the cab. She followed, getting instantly drenched.

Giggling like school kids, they locked arms and walked sedately up the sidewalk and into her building.

"Just for the record, 'slightly drenched' is an oxymoron," she informed him.

He grinned so hard his face hurt. "I just wanted to get you soaked so I could take my time rubbing you dry."

She linked her arm with his. "Darlin', when we rub together, neither one of us is dry for very long."

Chapter Five

"It's a pretty simple layout," she told him as she unlocked the door then guided him inside. "There's a hall table in the foyer on the left. Just beyond that is the door to a half bath. The tile continues on into the kitchen on the right, but the main room is hardwood."

His cane tapped out a soft rhythm as he navigated her furniture. "Let me guess. You bought it for the view?"

"Yeah. It has a great panorama of downtown, and it's not all that far from the club. There's a guest bedroom and bath just past the kitchen, and the master suite's on this side."

She swallowed nervously, acutely aware that she verged on babbling. "Why don't you get out of those wet clothes and I'll go grab a couple of towels for you?"

Without waiting for an answer, she darted out of the living room and into her master suite.

She sucked in a breath as she peeled off her wet dress and underwear, then pulled on a robe. Joshua Hanover was in her apartment, currently stripping off his clothes. Her stomach gave an agitated lurch. She couldn't explain why tonight felt so different from being with him at the club, it just did.

If it had only been dinner, she wouldn't have been so freaking clumsy about inviting him up. But it had been dinner and dancing and conversation and soft handholding, and she had no idea what the next steps were or how to do them.

Joshua was hell on more than her hormones. He made her nervous and excited and horny and sad and happy and satisfied, all at the same time. The simple act of being next to him overloaded her, scared her.

After tossing the dress over the shower door to dry, she grabbed a towel to dry the sopping mass that used to be sassy waves. "Eighty dollars down the drain," she murmured to herself, brushing the tangles out then securing her hair with a ponytail holder.

She looked up—then shrieked as she caught sight of Joshua's reflection in the mirror. "Joshua! I didn't hear you."

"Sorry about that, I thought I'd explore a bit. Hope you don't mind?"

A gorgeous man stood in her bathroom doorway wearing a smile and pale blue boxers. What was there to mind?

"Here." She unfolded a thick towel, draped his head, then pulled another one out of the basket to wrap around his hips. "I don't want you to get cold."

"No danger of that with you around," he told her, using one hand to run the towel over his hair.

Heat swept up her body from her toes to her cheeks. Thank God he couldn't see it. He had such a beautiful body. "Give me a sec while I scrub my makeup off," she managed to say, turning the brass tap to flood the basin. "My mascara's given me a beard."

"I think you look great."

She had to laugh at that, but it sounded thin to her ears. "I bet you say that to all the girls you want to bed."

"Seeing as how I only bed beautiful girls, I guess you're right."

She frowned. He burst out laughing. "What's so funny?"

"Hey, I may be blind, but even I know that pissed you off," he said with a chuckle. "Don't worry, I sleep with the ugly ones too."

She threw her towel at him. "You're impossible."

"And completely irresistible."

"And modest, I almost forgot modest."

"But you did forget sexy," he said with a fake pout. "If I had an ego, it would be bruised."

"Oh I think your ego is definitely alive and well." She brushed past him. "Healthy as a horse."

"Did you say hung like a horse? Madam, I'm flattered."

She turned to see him lounging in the doorway, looking as if he'd just stepped out of the shower. Looking as if he belonged. Her heart literally skipped a beat.

"Would you like something to drink?" She deliberately avoided looking at her bed as she moved towards the living room.

He spun like a human divining rod, tracking her movements. "I'm not thirsty."

"Uhm, okay. Do you want a snack? I think I've got some microwave popcorn and Froot Loops, but that's about it."

"Froot Loops?"

She hunched her shoulders defensively. "My favorite vice happens to be eating sugary cereal and watching Saturday morning cartoons. Some old ladies will wear purple, I'll be watching Bugs Bunny and eating Sugar Smacks."

He walked slowly towards her, navigating his way. "Why are you nervous, Alina?"

"I'm not," she denied hotly. A crack of thunder answered

her. "Not really."

Another crash of thunder, followed by the unmistakable sound of lightning scoring a direct hit on something nearby. Alina squeaked as her flat instantly plunged into darkness.

"What's wrong?" Joshua asked.

"I can't see!"

"Funny, neither can I."

"I didn't mean anything by that," she said, her voice wavering.

"Babe, it's all right. I didn't mean anything either," he soothed her. "I guess the power went out?"

"Yeah, and it's pitch black. I can't even see you, and you should be glowing in the dark."

"Hey—I'm not that pale. Am I?"

"Not really, but compared to me you are." She jumped again as something touched her, then realized it was Joshua. "Sorry."

"Don't be. There's no reason to be afraid of the dark." He caught her hand, lifted it to his lips for a kiss, then moved it to his shoulder. "Just follow me. I'll make sure you don't stub your toe."

Alina tried not to sink her nails into Joshua's shoulder as he led her back to the bedroom. She'd lived in the apartment for two years but had never tried to traverse it in the dark, always keeping a nightlight on in her bathroom and in the kitchen.

She tried to relax, knowing Joshua wouldn't let her bump into anything. "It's got to be difficult, letting other people guide you around like this."

"I usually guide myself just fine," he said. "I only let people I trust lead me."

He'd allowed her to lead him tonight, in the restaurant and

into her building. "You trust me?"

"Of course I do." He said it so matter-of-factly, she had no choice but to believe it.

A sudden lump clogged her throat, and it was all she could do to whisper her thanks.

He came to a halt. "Here's the bed. I don't suppose it's a four-poster, is it?"

"No, platform with a console headboard. Why?"

"Have you ever been tied down?"

"Nope, and I don't intend to be," she answered, her nervousness easing. In the dark, in her bedroom, it was easy to figure out what the next step was. "Besides, when you're done with me I can barely move as it is."

He gave a low laugh. "You sure know how to make a man feel good."

"I'm about to make him feel a whole lot better." She pulled loose the towel around his waist, letting it fall to the floor. His boxers followed.

She pushed him gently onto the bed. "I want to touch you the way you touch me," she whispered, shrugging out of her robe. "I want to see you the way you see me."

Kneeling at the foot of the bed, she let her hands find his feet in the darkness. Slowly, she stroked up his shins to his knees, her fingertips tracing the muscles beneath hair and skin. He murmured her name, a bare whisper of sound over the rain pouring outside.

It was a pleasure discovering him this way, using every other sense but sight. Feeling the different textures of his skin, the crisp hair at the base of his cock versus the soft feel of his balls. The heat of his shaft against her cheek as she stroked her jaw along the rigid length. Smelling the spiciness of his pre-come just before she tasted it. Feeling the warmth that suffused her as she heard his sharp intake of breath, then his groan of pleasure rumbling like the thunder outside.

As much as she wanted to linger, she continued moving up his body, using taste and touch to chart her course. He shivered as her body slid over his, her breasts brushing against his cock. Still her mouth moved over him, tongue dipping into his navel, gliding over the flat planes of his stomach, up the wide expanse of his chest. He had a swimmer's body, she knew, deep chest, developed shoulders, strong arms, all waiting to be tasted.

He hissed as her teeth closed over one nipple. "God, you're going to kill me."

She smiled, taking pleasure in pleasing him. "What a way to go though, right?" She moved to the other nipple, bit down gently.

His fingers wrapped around her ponytail. "Kiss me," he demanded, giving a gentle tug.

She deliberately misunderstood him, sliding back down his body to his cock. Gripping it by the base, she ran the flat of her tongue along the bottom ridge, enjoying the pleasured sounds he made in response. She licked down and then back up again, swirling around the head, flicking the tiny opening. He shuddered wordlessly, hands trembling in her hair.

She sucked him in, matching the pressure of her lips with her hand wrapped around the base of his cock. His moans encouraged her to fuck him with her mouth and her hand, to suck every drop of come out of his balls.

"Alina. Alina, baby, I need you to stop."

"I want to swallow you down." She sank her mouth onto him again to slowly suction her way back off.

"Argh." He groaned again. "I need you to ride me, baby.

248

Ride me wild like that storm outside."

Now that sounded like a good idea. "All right."

She quickly straddled him. "Are there condoms in the nightstand?" he asked.

"I don't want to use one."

He stilled beneath her. "Are you sure?"

"We're both clean," she reminded him. "I hadn't been with anyone else for a while before we hooked up. And I'm on the shots."

She bit her lip, suddenly unsure. "I want to feel you, really feel you, but it's okay if you don't think that's a good idea—"

"Alina." He pulled her down for a bruising kiss that burned away her doubts. "Ride me, sweetheart."

She straightened as he wrapped strong fingers around his cock. They moaned a duet as he slid the thick head along her slit, making them both wet. She shifted slightly, then guided him inside.

A bone-deep sigh left her as he filled her completely, pushing away everything but sensation. The storm seemed to mirror the desire raging inside her as their bodies crashed together repeatedly. Joshua's hands moved up her waist to her breasts, teasing the tips the way he teased notes from his guitar, with expert command.

She leaned forward enough to return the favor, flicking her thumbs over his nipples as she ground her clit against the root of his cock. Her name was a ragged groan of approval on his lips as his hips rocked her off the mattress.

Sweat slicked her body as she rode him, but she didn't care about the lack of air conditioning just then. All she cared about was the man fucking like a dream beneath her, giving her pleasure she turned back to him.

"Sing for me, baby," he crooned, his thumb pressing against her clit as he stroked deep. "Sing out for me."

Sing out she did, arching her back as the orgasm slammed into her like a lightning strike. Her inner muscles clamped down on his cock as wave after wave of pleasure rolled through her. Joshua gripped her waist as a mangled cry tore from him, hips thrusting off the bed as he jetted deep within her.

She collapsed against him, boneless and breathless and struggling to retake her senses from her clit. She could still feel Joshua's cock pulsing deep inside her, feel her hips rocking against him in tiny tremors.

"Fucking hot," she murmured against his chest.

"Yeah, it was." His arms wrapped around her to keep her in place.

"No, I mean the air conditioning's still out and it's really hot right now." She aimed a kiss for his mouth but caught his chin instead. "But yes, you're absolutely amazing."

He caught her chin. "We're amazing," he corrected, then kissed her properly.

Her pussy clenched in pure self-defense from the sensual onslaught, causing them both to groan. Joshua rolled them until her back hit the bed. Deepening the kiss, he began to move, a series of slow, deep slides that had her body thrumming.

Joshua didn't seem to be in any hurry and neither was she, letting her hands glide down his back to his buttocks, marking the way his body moved over hers. She traced the outline of his lips with the tip of her tongue, breathing in his moan of pleasure.

All too soon that familiar tension coiled inside her. Joshua shifted higher, his cock stroking her at a different angle. She clutched his shoulders, gripping him inside and out. "Come with me, baby," she urged. "Give it to me."

"Yeah, sweetness." His thrusts grew more shallow, more rapid. With a muffled curse he came, triggering her orgasm. It rolled through her as she held him close, pure and profound.

When she could move again, she felt her way to her bathroom, cleaned up, then brought out a warm, damp washcloth for him. The strange, tender mood she'd been in earlier hadn't dissipated with mind-blowing sex or the intimate step she hadn't known she'd planned to take, and it seemed the most natural thing in the world to slowly and thoroughly run the washcloth over him.

"What are you thinking?" he asked, his voice a soft rumble.

So many things, a confusing jumble of thoughts and emotions she couldn't begin to straighten out. She sighed, dropped the washcloth to the floor. "I'm wondering if taxis are still in service in this storm."

"Why? Are you planning to go somewhere?"

"You're not leaving?"

"No, I'm not," he told her. "You're going to wake up in the morning with my arms wrapped around you and my cock pressed against your gorgeous ass. Then we're going to have sleepy morning sex, then a shower, then breakfast. We might even get to have sex again before work calls both of us. You got a problem with that?"

"Uh, no, that sounds wonderful," she assured him, meaning it. She crawled back into bed beside him. "I—it's just that it's been a long time since I've actually slept with someone like this."

He was silent for a moment. "If I say I don't believe you, will you get offended? Because I wouldn't mean that you're lying, just that I can't believe you haven't had the opportunity to wake up with someone else."

She snuggled against him, enjoying the feel of his body next to hers, lack of central air be damned. "It's not that I haven't had the opportunity, I just didn't want to. I'm not big on bringing just anyone here."

He folded one arm beneath his head, the other wrapping around her shoulder. "So I guess that makes me pretty special, huh?"

She yawned again, her body heavy with sleep against his. "Of course you are, silly. You're so special, it's scary."

Chapter Six

"What are you doing for the Fourth of July?"

"The horizontal tango with you?"

"That's a given." His finger idly stroked her nipple. He could never seem to stop touching her. It was a fetish bordering on addiction, an addiction he didn't want to break. "Have you made any other plans?"

"My family's out of town and I can't take time off for a visit," she admitted. "I was hoping you'd want to do something."

Joshua kept the surge of elation to himself. Alina rarely initiated their time together almost as if she had an allergic reaction to the word "date". That she wanted to spend time with him—and had admitted it—made him want to crow with joy.

"Well, I do want to do something." He pulled his hand away from her breast, sliding it down her arm to gather her hand, tangling their fingers together. "My parents are having the extended family over for a cookout and pool party, and I sorta told them I was bringing someone."

"You did." She kept her voice even.

"I sure did. I want them to meet you."

"Why?"

He frowned. Was she holding her breath? "Why not? They're curious about the woman I've been spending all my free time with."

She stiffened beside him. "You told them about me?"

He shifted so that his chest pinned her to the bed. "I told them that I was dating the owner of The Scarlet Lady."

"What did they say about that?"

He touched her cheek with gentle fingers. "They said they'd be pleased to meet you."

She remained silent, obviously unconvinced. "They're good people, Alina," he assured her. "They had to be, to put up with me as a teen. They're not saints—and I've got a couple of cousins who are downright assholes—but they're all right. And yes, my parents know you're black, and no, they don't care. Just be yourself."

She sighed. "Which self is that?"

"How about the one who surprised me with a home-cooked meal last night after strutting across a bartop in four-inch heels, slinging vodka? I really like her."

"You would."

He stroked her cheek. "This isn't a big deal, sweetheart. Some of the band members will be there too, and tons of first and second cousins. There will be beer, barbecue and baseball. We'll get our eat on then come home and work it off."

She giggled. "You didn't just say, 'get our eat on', did you?"

Relief pushed the tension away. "Hey, I can be down."

"Oh, God." Laughter bubbled out of her. "Stop, just stop. I'll be me if you'll be you, okay?"

"And who might I be?"

Her fingers caressed his cheek, her skin soft against his morning beard. "A gorgeous man with the soul of a poet and the hands of a god."

Joshua's chest tightened. "I think you just became my muse."

"Really? Then how 'bout I give you some morning inspiration?" She slid down his body.

⚙

Fourth of July with the Hanovers consisted of beer, barbecue and baseball, just as Joshua said. It also contained blistering heat, curious glances and cousins that lived up to Joshua's description of them. His parents were as cool as he'd promised, and Alina found herself bonding with Jessica Hanover over several old photo albums and Southern-style potato salad.

Trouble didn't start until after the first round of burgers and brisket, when she went downstairs to get another bottle of water and look for Joshua.

"Hey, baby, how's it goin'?"

Alina looked up, then fought the urge to roll her eyes as a thick-shouldered man in a Braves Jersey with the sleeves ripped off and a UGA cap shuffled to a stop in front of her. She could smell the six-pack on his breath from three feet away. "Going good. The name's Alina, by the way."

"Really? You look like a stripper I used to go see. I'd know those hooters anywhere." He reached for the collar of her tank top.

She immediately shuffled backward, a move she'd done hundreds of times before. "Well, you obviously don't see her anymore, and my hooters are off limits."

"'Lina, baby," he said, putting one thick paw on her shoulder. "You the chick that showed up with Cousin Josh, right? You his nurse or escort or something?"

Alina fought the urge to gag. The guy was obviously more hammered than a home improvement store, and Joshua's cousin on top of that. That meant she had to play nice. No worries, she'd handled drunks before.

"I tell you what." She moved behind him and started shoving him towards the stairs. "I'm going back upstairs, and I think you should too. Let's say I help you up and we go get some fresh air, huh? You can always send someone else down for more beer."

"All right." He made it up three steps, then stopped. "Hey, shouldn't you be in front?"

Right. "I like to switch it up every once in a while," she said with a laugh, pushing against his sweaty, pudgy back. She was so going to need to wash her hands.

"What's going on here?" a woman's voice asked.

"Hey, babe," the drunk cousin said. "I was jus' talking to Joshie's sweet thing. She's got the nicest tits."

Oh God. Everyone at the cookout was in earshot of that. "I went to get some water and saw him down there," she explained. "I didn't think it was a good idea to leave him by himself. With all that beer."

The other woman glared at her before grabbing her drunk husband and dragging him away. Some of the other cousins smirked at her as they dispersed. This was not going to go down well. Where the hell was Joshua?

Standing in the kitchen, less than six feet away. And he didn't look all that happy.

Joshua's mood worsened on the drive back to his place. By the time they made it to his door, he wouldn't even speak to her.

She frowned as he threw his keys on the table. "Can we talk about this?"

"There's nothing to talk about," he told her. "I know you didn't flash Danny."

She blinked. "You do?"

"Of course. That's how Danny gets when he's drunk off his ass. Last year he chased Aunt Margaret around the pool."

"Oh." Her shoulders sagged in relief, then immediately tensed up again. "Then what are you mad at me about?"

"The way you introduced yourself."

"What?"

"You introduced yourself as my friend, or Alina, or as the owner of the club my band plays in."

"What's wrong with that? I didn't lie to anyone."

"My friend," he repeated, anger hardening his features. "We've fucked six ways to Sunday for the past month, and you describe yourself as just my friend?"

"That's what we are—"

"No! That is not what we are!"

Alina stepped back, trying to comprehend his anger and her part in it. "Dammit, Joshua, what do you want from me?"

"Everything!" His hand snaked out, unerringly found her wrist, snatched her hard against him. "I want you to give me everything!"

His mouth crushed hers, taking, demanding. Waves of pleasure rolled through her. Alina had few defenses against this man, this man who made her want to dare, to dream. The wanting was so strong, so overwhelming that it almost pushed out the fear. Almost.

She pulled away from him, needing the space, needing to breathe. "I can't," she managed to say. "I can't give you everything."

"You can't, or you won't?"

"I can't." She took another step back from him, shoving her hands through her hair in an effort to get her emotions under control.

"Why?"

"Because." She stopped, then started again. "Joshua. This wasn't supposed to be about anything other than sex, and you know it. Guys like you don't date girls like me."

"You're going to have to be a little more specific for this guy, since I'm apparently too dense to understand," he said, his voice bitter. "By guys like me, do you mean musicians? White guys? Blind guys? Or is it just blind white guys who happen to be musicians?"

"No." It was none of that, and all of that, and she didn't know how to tell him.

"What is it then?"

She just shook her head. If she said it wasn't him, it was her, would he even believe her?

"Do you think this was easy for me?" he asked, his features pinched. "All I kept hearing, every single night, was how hot you are, how men and some women follow you around like sick puppies everywhere you go in the club. I would sit in your office, listening to you speak with that whiskey-and-sin voice, smelling the licorice and ginger scent of your skin, and I knew there was no way someone that sexy and that smart would go for me. But I had to try. Just like every other guy, I had to try to for the Scarlet Lady."

"See?" She almost choked on the bitterness in her voice. He'd just proven her point, even if he didn't realize it. "It wasn't about dating me."

"And for you, it wasn't about dating at all. I get it now. I may be blind, but I'm not stupid."

"Joshua—"

"If that's the way you want it, fine. We're not dating. We're not anything. Feel free to leave now."

Blinking back tears, Alina gathered her things and left, absolutely certain that she'd just made the worst mistake of her life.

Chapter Seven

"So what do you think?"

Salazar closed the lid of his laptop with precise movements. "Having a contest to hire Scarlet Lady dancers is a great idea. It'll create a lot of buzz for the club, especially if we can get some radio tie-in."

Alina nodded. "I've got some contacts in that area. My plan is to roll this as soon as possible. I could use a break."

Her manager was nice enough to not point out that she hadn't danced across the bar in more than a week. Not that she was hiding or anything. Miss Scarlet didn't hide. Alina, on the other hand, was starting to get a little stir-crazy holed up in an office in which every flat surface reminded her of her time with Joshua.

Salazar's expression turned sympathetic. "Well, it has been a while since you've had a vacation. No one would blame you for being scarce right about now."

Except running away would be a punk-ass move to make, and she wasn't a punk. Okay, maybe she'd run out of Joshua's place on the holiday, but it wasn't like he'd been in the mood to listen to her half-assed explanations anyway.

She sighed, trying to ignore how shaky it sounded. "I made a mistake, didn't I?"

"Somehow I don't think you're talking about switching the brands of bottled water we carry."

"No." Alina settled her elbows on the blotter then rested her forehead in her palms. "I usually don't have regrets. I can make a decision and be done. This feels like a wrong decision."

Her manager leaned back in the club chair, the dark suit hanging elegantly on his wiry frame. He fit in with everyone from presidents to pimps, which was the main reason she'd stolen him from her former boss when she opened her club. "You want me to be real?"

Uh-oh. Alina shifted uneasily. Salazar and Bobby were the only people on her staff who'd known her before she'd bought the club, the only two people who automatically looked her in the eye. When Emilio Salazar broke out the accent, she usually ended up in trouble. "I'm not going to like what you have to say, am I?"

"Probably not," Salazar answered. "I wasn't gonna drop it on you at all because I thought you'd figure it out yourself before now."

"Figure what out?"

"It's your same M.O.—break up with the guy before he breaks up with you."

Alina opened her mouth in automatic denial, then closed it. "It's that obvious?"

The club manager nodded. "Let me break it down for you. You wear those corsets like a sexy stop sign, making sure you keep everyone out. You get all bent about people relating to you because of how you look. Hanover's the only one you've let in for a good long time. Maybe you decided to roll with him because he's blind?"

"That's ridiculous. I decided to date him because he's hot, he's creative, and he's damn good with his hands. He makes me

261

feel special and normal at the same time, and I love that about him. I love his smile, his wicked sense of humor and the fact that he doesn't give a rat's ass what other people think."

Salazar smiled. "Do you hear what you're saying?"

She mentally replayed their conversation. "Oh hell. Did I really say love?"

"Sounded like it to me. What did it sound like to you?"

"It sounds like I'm in love with Joshua Hanover."

The words hung in the air between them. Alina waited for a panic attack or a lightning bolt or some other sign, but nothing came. Instead, she felt a tiny smile tremble across her lips, an outward sign of the fledgling emotion fluttering in her chest.

She released a rueful laugh. "I think you're in the wrong line of work, my friend."

"You know a bartender's one part chemist and two parts psychiatrist," Salazar answered. "I haven't been behind a bar in a while, but I still got skills."

"Impressive skills. I think you just earned yourself a raise." She pushed away from her desk, then climbed to her feet. She loved Joshua, and she'd hurt them both by not realizing it sooner. Now all she had to do was tell him the truth. The rest would sort itself out. At least she hoped so.

She'd made it to the door before she realized it. Pausing, she turned back to Salazar, nervous and hopeful. "Wish me luck?"

"Like you need it. The man's just as head over heels as you are, know what I'm sayin'? Go get him."

Alina moved quickly through her office. A wall of sound hit her as soon as she opened the outer door, hard and angry.

Joshua Hanover was pissed, and everyone in The Scarlet Lady knew it.

The band was as tight as ever, but the bouncy, party songs had been expunged from their set. Joshua's solos deteriorated into angry, wailing diatribes. Even "Red-Letter Woman" had soured from a song of admiration to a tune of condemnation.

Ignoring the acid bubbling in her stomach, Alina squared her shoulders then moved down the stairs to the lower level with as much bravado as she could. It was time to end this, one way or another. Her club suffered, Joshua suffered. And, she could finally admit, she'd suffered too. It was time to put on the big girl panties and deal. She had to tell Joshua why she'd been so incredibly stupid. He'd probably be too angry to care, but she had to let him know how she felt about him.

She made her way to the stage after their last set, while they were breaking down and packing up. Besides the band, only a handful of her crew was left to witness her potential embarrassment.

Pete stepped in front of Joshua, blocking her view. "May I help you?"

She lifted her chin. "I'd like to talk to Joshua."

The mountain of a man folded his arms. "I think you've said all you need to say to him."

"Pete," Joshua called. "Let it go. I'll talk to her."

Dark sunglasses covered his eyes, she noted, and he unfolded his cane as soon as he packed his guitar away. He took his time leaving the stage, relying on the cane to guide his steps even though she made sure the tables were set precisely in the same spot every night after their show.

"What can I do for you, Miss Scarlet?" he asked, his voice remotely polite.

She bit her lip against sudden tears. "Okay, I deserved that. I'd like to talk to you privately, if you don't mind."

He gestured with his cane. "Lead the way."

She offered him her elbow, then led him towards the front of the club, just beneath the staircase leading up to the VIP level.

"Joshua, I need to apologize to you."

"Really?" His voice retained that cool, distant tone, but she could feel the tension in his hand. "For what?"

"For lying to you. You thought that I didn't want to be with you because of your blindness, but that isn't true."

"Could have fooled me. You didn't want to go to dinner with me, you didn't want to meet my family, but you sure as shit had no problem fucking me. Why the hell would the smoking hot Miss Scarlet stoop to date a blind man when she could have any guy in the city?"

She couldn't stop the gasp of pain his words caused. Just because she deserved it, didn't make it easier to take. "I'm sorry, truly deeply sorry for letting you think that. It's not true, I swear to God it isn't."

His jaw worked for a moment. "Then what's the truth?"

"The truth is, I've always known what type of girl I am." She had to force the words past a sudden hard lump in her throat. "I'm the kind that guys like to hang with, have sex with, the hot chick that everyone wants to have but no one wants to keep. They don't take me home to their parents, or to their office parties. Since I hit puberty, I've always inspired lust, not love, and I know it. That's why I became Miss Scarlet."

He laughed, but it was a bitter, empty laugh that hurt to hear. "That's what you thought this was? Lust? That's what you thought I felt?"

She heard the past tense. "I've never experienced anything else. People only wanted Miss Scarlet, not Alina. After a while, that was all that I knew how to give."

He moved away from her. "Did I ever call you Miss Scarlet before today?"

"No."

"Did I ever say all I wanted from you was sex?"

"No."

"Wasn't I the one who had to convince you to go out with me?"

She hung her head. "Yes."

"Wasn't I the one that took you to meet my family?"

"Yes, but—"

"So how the hell can you say that guys like me don't want to date women like you?" He threw his arms wide. "As far as I'm concerned, I've been dating you all this time! What does that tell you?"

She heard the present tense, and the ache in her heart eased. "It tells me that you're crazy."

His lips curved. "Yeah, I'm fucking certifiable. About you."

"Joshua—"

"Dammit, Alina, I can't see you! It was never about Miss Scarlet to me. You wanna know what made me pop a woody for you? Your voice. From the beginning, when we were sitting in your office hammering out the performance contract, your voice made me hard. Not your leather, or your tits, or your legs. Your voice. And that goddamn laugh. Holy shit, that low and sexy laugh drives me fucking nuts."

He spun away, then back. "And you know what's the best part about making love to you? Not your legs wrapped around my waist, not getting you out of those boots. Not cupping your breasts in my hands. The best part of making love with you is hearing that catch at the back of your throat just before you

265

come. It's feeling your body tighten around mine. It's tasting your sweetness on my tongue. And yes, it's even smelling our sex mixing together."

He held out a hand to her. "But the best part, the absolute best part about being with you, Alina, is that you see me. I'm just a man with you. Not a guitarist, not a blind guy, just Joshua. You see me. Even when you want me to think you don't."

"Joshua." She shook so hard she thought she'd fall apart, but she reached out for him, took his hand, and her world steadied.

"You see me, babe, and I see you," he said, his voice unsteady. "I see you in the way that matters, right here." He drew her closer, holding her hand to his heart.

His name cracked in her throat. She wrapped her arms around him and held on tight, unable to say anything else, do anything else.

"Goddammit, Alina." His arms engulfed her. "What the hell else can I say to let you know that I love you?"

"Say that." She buried her face against his chest, tears spilling from her eyes. "Just say that."

"That," he murmured against her hair, then gently cupped her face with his. "That, and that," he said again, then claimed her mouth.

Applause sounded around them. "All right!" she heard Bobby cheer. "Miss Scarlet and the blues man."

They sheepishly broke the kiss, but still held each other close. "You can be Miss Scarlet to them all you want, but you'll always be Alina to me," Joshua told her.

Her heart overflowed. "Miss Scarlet's going to retire. We're going to have a contest to find several Scarlet Ladies to take my place."

Then because she couldn't hold it in any longer, "I love you. It's been a miserable week of wallowing in my own stupidity, and I just want it to be over. Can we leave now? You asked me for everything, and I'd like to give it to you."

"Absolutely." Keeping his arms securely around her, Joshua turned back towards the stage. "Show's over folks. The encore's going to be just the two of us."

About the Author

Mallery Malone lives on the outskirts of the Little Five Points area of Atlanta, a community known for its funky, eclectic vibe. When not writing, she shovels down tater tots at the Vortex, drools over the shoes at Abbadabbas, and walks her mutt Bailey with her own personal guitar hero, also called Bailey.

To learn more about Mallery Malone, please visit her at www.mallerymalone.bravehost.com/index.html. Send an email to Mallery at mallerymalone@gmail.com.

One woman's campaign to win the hearts
of the two men she loves.

Brazen

Jasmine left the Sweetwater Ranch and the Morgan brothers, no longer able to bear the painful dilemma of loving them both. After a year away, in which she gains new perspective, she returns home with one goal. To make Seth and Zane Morgan hers.

Jaz may have left an innocent girl, but she's returned a beautiful, sensual woman. Seth and Zane aren't prepared for the full on assault she launches and each battle an attraction they've fought for years.

She wants them both, but Seth has no intention of sharing his woman. It's up to her to change his mind because she can't and won't choose between two men she loves with equal passion. For her, it's all or nothing.

Warning, this title contains the following: explicit sex, graphic language, ménage a trois, handcuffs, a committed ménage relationship.

Available now in ebook and print from Samhain Publishing.

Before she leaves town, she's going out with a bang...

Going For It
© *2008 Elle Kennedy*

Sam Taylor has lusted after ex-baseball-player Riley Scott for far too long. Now, her business bought out from under her, broke, and with nothing to lose, she refuses to leave town without getting the one thing she's always wanted. Riley. In her bed.

Riley had the reputation as a player on and off the baseball field. He's wanted Sam for years, but valued her friendship too much to let sex ruin it. Now, after a forced retirement, he's looking for a purpose in his life. Sam's bar, the Diamond, is just the thing to get his life back on track.

But before he can reveal that he's the new owner, he finds himself the willing victim of her full-on seduction. As he succumbs to her feminine charms, he begins to think maybe there's a way he can have it all—the Diamond, the woman, and the friend.

Until she finds out he's the one responsible for taking away her most treasured possession...

Warning: This title contains sex in the shower and on a pool table (a bed does make an appearance). Be prepared to stand in front of an air conditioner after reading.

Available now in ebook from Samhain Publishing.

GET IT NOW

MyBookStoreAndMore.com

GREAT EBOOKS, GREAT DEALS . . . AND MORE!

Don't wait to run to the bookstore down the street, or
waste time shopping online at one of the "big boys." Now,
all your favorite Samhain authors are all in one place—at
MyBookStoreAndMore.com. Stop by today and discover
great deals on Samhain—and a whole lot more!

WWW.SAMHAINPUBLISHING.COM

GREAT
CHEAP
FUN

Discover eBooks!

THE FASTEST WAY TO GET THE HOTTEST NAMES

Get your favorite authors on your favorite reader, long before they're out in print! Ebooks from Samhain go wherever you go, and work with whatever you carry—Palm, PDF, Mobi, and more.

Samhain Publishing Ltd

WWW.SAMHAINPUBLISHING.COM